HUNGER IN AMERICA

DAVID CATES

SIMON & SCHUSTER

NEW YORK   LONDON   TORONTO   SYDNEY   TOKYO   SINGAPORE

SIMON & SCHUSTER
Simon & Schuster Building
Rockefeller Center
1230 Avenue of the Americas
New York, New York 10020

This book is a work of fiction. With the exception of Pam Carter, the singer in the first chapter, all names, characters, places and incidents are either products of the author's imagination or are used fictitiously. Any resemblance to actual events or locales or persons, living or dead, is entirely coincidental.

SIMON & SCHUSTER and colophon are registered trademarks
of Simon & Schuster Inc.

Designed by Irving Perkins Associates
Manufactured in the United States of America

10 9 8 7 6 5 4 3 2 1

Library of Congress Cataloging in Publication Data

Cates, David.
　　Hunger in America : David Cates.
　　　　p.　cm.
　　I. Title
　　PS3553.A84H86　1992
　　813'.54—dc20　　　　　　　　　　　　　　　　　91-42715
　　　　　　　　　　　　　　　　　　　　　　　　　CIP

ISBN: 0-671-73817-8

Portions of this book have appeared in Cutbank *magazine.*

ACKNOWLEDGMENT IS MADE TO THE FOLLOWING FOR PERMISSION TO QUOTE:

"Love the One You're With"
Stephen Stills
© 1970 Gold Hill Music, Inc.

(Permissions continued on page 203)

For Rosalie—
her gift was hope

These Bataan Men—most in their late teens or early twenties when the war began—entered a wilderness that had no rules. What a prisoner did to stay alive one day might cause death the next. There were no maps to show a prisoner how to get from sunup to sundown alive. Every emotional and physical path had to be explored afresh each day.

—DONALD KNOX,
Death March

All that is solid melts into air, all that is holy is profaned, and man is at last compelled to face his real condition of life and his mutual relations with a sober eye.

—KARL MARX AND FRIEDRICH ENGELS,
The Communist Manifesto

HUNGER IN AMERICA

DUSK

The sand of the sea and the rain drops,
and the days of eternity, who can assess them?

—ECCLESIASTICUS 1:2

*Across the bay the mountains are sharp and covered with snow, but you
can't see them now for the fog. Pewter gray today. When it's overcast,
Kodiak is an island of ten thousand gray shades, and it's almost always
overcast. Beyond the parking lot and the cluster of fishing boats in the
harbor, past the faint outline of a Japanese freighter in the bay—its belly
full of new cars—out that way is the ocean, and the ocean goes on
forever. In back of us, over Pillar Mountain and into the heart of the
island, is the wilderness. Think of the glaciers cutting rock on the peaks,
of forests of Sitka spruce and clusters of alder on the scrub-grass hills.
Imagine thousand-pound mama bears and even bigger daddies—
nowhere on the face of the earth will you find a larger carnivore than the
male Kodiak grizzly—and imagine how the land extends forever too.*

*The island shoreline goes around and around and around again.
Kishuyak Bay, Cape Kuliak, Uyak Bay, Cape Karluk, Cape Ikolik,
Alitak, Aliulik Peninsula, Cape Kiavak, Ugak Bay, and back to Kodiak.
Danger Bay, Broken Point, Larsen Bay, Rocky Point, Olga Bay, Old
Harbor, Left Cape, Bull Point, Woman's Bay, but always back again to
Kodiak. Resting on shore pilings and little hills, town is a relative
megalopolis, a cluster of canneries, bars, shops, houses, boats—
humanity squeezed mercifully between the forevers. Built on a rock, of
course, a bit of solidity, the present tense. Seagulls and magpies feast on
yesterdays, gather on the rooftops and then swoop down squawking,
picking in the alley Dumpsters, gliding up again. Motionless on the wind,
the gulls' gray and white colors match the sky.*

1 JACK DEMPSEY CLIFF sits in cab sixteen outside the Beachcomber Bar, watching two teenage Filipino boys wander out the door carrying spaghetti on paper plates. It's May 30, Memorial Day, 1983, the evening of the day before Jack's thirtieth birthday, the evening of the day before his namesake dies. Tomorrow the man on the radio will announce that teeth rot, gums bleed, pipes rust, hair falls out, bones—and even rocks—crumble. His voice will tremble with the weight of such bottom-line simplicity, such ultimate fact: *Jack Dempsey, age 87, one of the greatest champions of all time, is dead today in New York City.* He'll be sure to lay it on thick because death is his big shtick and only truth, this man on the radio. He won't let an opportunity like this pass by.

Jack's mother called earlier this evening, while he was waiting for dinner before his shift. It's been a month since he left the farm, and Jack thought she might be calling to tell him some long-held secret about his father, or anything about Mary. Jack wishes she had said something to make it easy for him to decide to go home. But instead she told him she'd found a lump and was pretty sure she might have cancer this time. Then, before he could respond, she asked if he's happy. Just like that. All the way from Wisconsin. What a morose tone that puts on everything. Not the cancer—she was always claiming fatal illness—but the question *Are you happy?* Jack didn't know what to say. What does a guy say? He finally promised he'd write her a letter and that thought makes him mad.

One of the Filipinos dangles spaghetti from his fingers and yells something. A black dog runs over from behind Jack and the kid dangles the spaghetti in front of its nose. When the dog jumps, the kid pulls the spaghetti away. The dog doesn't like this and neither does Jack, but the other Filipino kid does a lot. He laughs and laughs and laughs, and then he tries it himself. The sky behind them is magic silver, a light gray-silver from a thinning in the clouds that colors everything as if with a sheet of translucent plastic, softens roof lines and power lines, cools the green of the trees and the yellow of the house across the street, turns the bay silver across the gravel parking lot.

13

The second Filipino kid wiggles a pinch of spaghetti. The dog is hesitant: it sits, stands, and makes a small circle, then sits again, waiting. The boy dips the spaghetti in sauce and redangles it. Jack is hoping the dog bites the kid's hand off. The dog laps the air with its tongue, lifts itself expectantly toward the noodle, each probe of the cautious tongue closer, lap-lap, front paws leave the ground, closer, lap-lap. . . . The boy smacks the dog square across the jaw with the heel of his hand, and the dog reels. It yelps and slinks off behind the first row of cars. The two boys are howling with laughter. Jack rolls down his window and yells to leave the dog alone, but this just makes the boys laugh harder. One of them licks the sauce off his middle finger and flips Jack off. Jack resolves that if they tease the dog again he is going to fight them both. He doesn't care about the finger. He can see himself jumping out of the cab and punching their damn faces until they bleed. He's thinking of how fast he'll move, when he decides to move, how they won't have a blessed chance.

HER FACE IS red from the light, small creases between her brows—that face needs kisses, sure it does. Jack Dempsey Cliff wants to hold it like a cat and be gentle. He's out of his cab and inside the Beachcomber Bar now, and he's wondering if petting a person is as good for the health as the man on the radio said petting a pet is. Not petting is certainly not good.

Jack counts at least two other men watching her from a distance; that's not counting the four young consumers at her table. The beers are two for one and the spaghetti is free for Happy Hour. Her legs are tan, her hair is blond, her skin shows good breeding. Jack skips the beers and gets in the too-long line for spaghetti. Are you happy is a useless question on an empty stomach. Blondie deserves a nice husband and a good, clean sex life, children and a neighbor boy to cut the grass, her very own bank account. But who doesn't? Now she is young and free and everybody tells her she should kick up her heels while she is still young and free, so she jets up to Alaska for the summer where the whole world is young and free and going bonkers.

14

Pam Carter sings between alternate sips of coffee and B-52 shots that freedom's just another name for nothing left to lose. She has a wonderful voice that at first makes Jack wish he weren't himself and then starts to make him forget that he is. Blondie gets up to leave with two of the four at her table, just stands up like any other mortal, flicks her hair back, pivots her hips and strolls out trailed by two handsome intellects. Jack wonders if they'll kiss smooth her brow. Maybe they'll try, but Jack doesn't think so. They're running on an abundance of testosterone—he can see that, all right. They're also doing their duty. Maybe one of them will marry her. The world is full of crimes against humanity, concessions to sanity. Pam Carter sings that if you can't be with the one you love, honey, love the one you're with—which puts Jack's heart down around his pant cuff again. There are times he misses Mary so much it almost makes him nauseous and this is one of them. Blondie looks as if she's from a trimmed and watered suburban city, Minneapolis maybe, so Jack tries to console himself with thoughts of what she will *become*: a rightly-smelling example of modern Minnesota womanhood. She will have a career, a family, and a *sensitive* hubby who is scared shitless of losing her. She will be in touch with her feelings. She will know her genitals. She will be in all things good. If she is lonely or unhappy, it won't be her fault but someone else's. It will be the fault of the Mythmakers, the Experts, Phil Donahue, the fault of those who sold her cosmetics and Pepsi-Cola when she thought she was buying fun. It will be the government's fault, or that of the people who told her rising in the ranks at Minnesota Life and Casualty is the ticket, all right, and especially for a woman. That's it: she will be a victim. She will have her girlhood snatched away by a big, dirty man. All she ever *needed* was someone to smooth her brow, to hold her head like a cat and be gentle. Someone to touch and to be touched by. But she didn't know that: they didn't tell her—or if they did they forgot to mention the tears. Sue the bastards. Once, in Alaska, when she was young and free, she walked past Jack Cliff and brushed his shoulder with hers and didn't even notice. Bummer.

But of course Jack is imagining things. Women are liberated now, and Blondie can do anything she wants. It's just that his mother's phone call kept him from eating dinner before work, so he's very hungry, and now when he gets to the food window the spaghetti's all gone. Hell. Perhaps Blondie's an ax murderer.

JACK SAID GOOD-BYE to Mary in the Madison airport (she even drove him to the airport), and he walked out to the plane without looking back except once. A big guy pressed up behind him at the top of the stairs and he thought what the hell, so he glanced back around the guy's shoulder, across the pavement to the gate and then along the building to the fenced-in viewing area, and he didn't see anybody anyway. He had only the vaguest idea of where he was going: *kodiakalaska,* the syllables rolling across his tongue like an old incantation, an impotent one he'd said to his pillow at night as a boy, trying to make his father come back. And he wasn't too sure anymore what he was leaving: a valley farm, a fold in the earth, a narrow strip of sky and pasture surrounded by steep wooded hills, a body-warm mother of a prairie, soil six feet deep clinging to his soles as he walked out across the airport tarmac, up the stairs and into the plane.

It was a survival tactic, going to Alaska, at least that's how he tried to explain it to Mary and to his mother, Lorraine. Jack knew the men in the Japanese prisoner-of-war camps had a lot of survival tactics and one of them was to stop waiting for things that weren't going to happen. Jack was tired of waiting for a dead father to come home. And he was so tired of being angry he didn't think he could feel anything else anymore.

As the plane took off and reached cruising altitude, Jack picked up the Northwest Orient magazine and read an article about the Brewers winning the pennant the previous fall.

Whenever Jack wants, he can close his eyes and imagine he's back in Wisconsin after a good night's sleep, a great dream of the West, and already the leaves are turning colors. It's as if the chilly wind were whispering airy obscenities, making the leaves show a hint of blush. Jack likes the breathable air of autumn; he likes hunting season and football, yellow and orange hills, October's blue sky and blue rivers, and best of all the Brewers chasing the pennant like a pack of hounds.

So somewhere over the Great Plains on a jet to Alaska, his insides suddenly lost their structure. In the article was a testimonial from a father who'd taken his son to see one of the exciting last games of the regular season. The man had written the Brewer president expressing his gratitude for the wonderful time they'd had. He wrote that he hadn't been able to talk to his son for a long time, but they'd been thrown together by the euphoria of the game, of the whole season, and afterward had driven around Milwaukee getting reacquainted, like old friends, until late into the night.

Jack couldn't finish the article. He traced with his finger the picture of the players, watched their features disappear behind his tears. He kept thinking how fantastic the pennant race had been, how happy it'd made everyone, what wonderful human beings must be Brewer players Gorman Thomas, Cecil Cooper, and Rollie Fingers.

2   THE OLD WOMAN sitting in the front seat of Jack's cab is dressed like a birthday cake: big white Easter bonnet, lavender scarf knotted on the side of her neck, lacy pink dress, and white anklets under her sandals.

"If my old man'd stayed home sober today," she says, "I'd have no reason to come down here but I get so darn disgusted"—she blows her nose twice into a red bandanna handkerchief—"mad at the world sometimes, you know?"

Jack's driving her into town. He's just left the unsatisfying Beachcomber spaghetti feed. He doesn't know what to say.

She folds the hankie in half, then quarters. She squeezes the folds between her thumb and forefinger.

"I checked the boat and Harry left it a perfect mess, so I worked my tail off cleaning up junk. If we could get someone who knew starters, we'd be okay."

She slips the hankie into a braided handbag, takes a deep breath through her nose. Staring through the cab window at the green slope of Pillar Mountain, she seems to relax a little.

"You ever feel like I feel?" she asks.

Jack doesn't answer. He doesn't have to. He drives and he doesn't know what she's talking about.

They are passing nice houses on each side of the street, and then to the right the yellow-and-blue high school. The old woman stares at the empty parking lot and then asks, as if the answer has just occurred to her, "You want to know why I like The Ships bar?"

"No," Jack says.

"For a few reasons, to be truthful," she says anyway. "One is I can't stand those places so dark you can't even see what you're drinking. With all the strangers in town! Heavens. They'll steal you blind when you're looking for your glass on the bar. And I have good friends at The Ships. I do all of my hiring there."

She pauses to catch her breath, pats her chest and closes her eyes. When she opens them again she says, "Do you know what restlessness is?"

Jack grunts. Then, because he thinks he knows, he says, "Sure."

"What, then?"

"Wanting to do something," Jack says. "Not wanting to do nothing. Thinking too much, maybe."

She lets out a sharp hoot and shakes her head, smiles as if he's way off, way way off.

"What?" Jack asks. He's amused now, and curious.

She's pointing to her chest. Then she covers her mouth, coughs, clears her throat. "Restlessness," she says finally, "is the devil calling."

They pass the high school dorms and head down the hill toward the center of town, squeezed against the harbor by the base of Pillar Mountain. They pass two walking yellow oilskins on the curb, hoods up. Are they listening to the voice of the devil? Jack wants to laugh but hasn't for a while. A low ceiling of clouds extends out across the bay to the coast guard base, where pinpricks of blue and yellow light break the fuzzy monotony of gray. Rainwater on the windshield picks up the color and bends it, blurs it.

"Listen," the woman says. "If Harry rides with you, make sure he tips."

"Who's Harry?"

"I think he went back to the boat, but he's in no condition to work. Not now, so please take him home."

"Who is he?"

"My husband."

"Oh." Jack still doesn't know who Harry is. He pulls into The Ships parking lot and the woman lays a five-dollar bill on the seat.

"Times are hard," she says, matter-of-factly, as though it's so true it hardly needs saying anymore. "Thank you for the ride. Thank you. I don't care if he's a veteran, and I don't care what day it is. Do you understand me? Of course not. But see?" She spreads her arms and looks directly at Jack for the first time, joy and sadness in her milky blue eyes.

"I wanted to go out," she says.

"You look very nice."

"Oh you're hardly more than a baby." She quickly touches the brim of her bonnet. "What do you know?"

Jack gets out and walks around the front of the cab to open her door.

"You look nice," he says again.

She smiles sweetly this time, with her whole face. Her hand is large and rough-feeling, but her touch is light. She lifts her dress and holds her hat and tiptoes past a puddle safely up onto the curb.

"This awful rain," she says, waving but hardly looking back. "What do you do with it?"

"Of course this is between you and me and the fence post," the fat man says, leaning across the front seat toward Jack Dempsey Cliff, and winking. "I was gonna . . . we was gonna . . . ."

His voice trails as he watches a group of young girls run from Kraft's supermarket across the street into the Dairy Queen parking lot.

"What?" Jack says.

"But then I got drunk and Rose got pissed and . . . You know something?"

"No."

"I was in the Battle of the Bulge."

"You were?"

"Yup." All his movements are slow. He sinks low in his seat, his face expressionless and heavy. "I was in the Battle of the Bulge and I was gonna put it to Rose today."

Jack doesn't know what to say. He's thinking about lucky Rose, whoever she is, about lucky Rose who got away.

"One of your injectors is bad," the fat man says. "Maybe two."

Jack grunts, turns out onto Marine Way. He tries to imagine the fat man in the Battle of the Bulge. He pictures him skinny, with a helmet too large, leading charges, hiding in the woods, leeching a cigarette from a buddy. Jack saw a movie once about the Battle of the Bulge and he remembers it was foggy and there were a lot of trees and tanks and snow, and these guys shot a dog and ate it.

"I'm all done with work now," the fat man says. "I'm gonna see my Rose."

"Who's Rose?" Jack asks, thinking it might give him a clue as to where to drive.

"Rose?" His mouth is an O, a pink wound in his fat face.

"Yeah."

"Yeah what?"

"Who's Rose?" Jack asks. "Where does she live?"

The fat man seems genuinely concerned. He leans toward Jack and furrows his wide brow. "You really don't know who Rose is?"

"Look," Jack says. "I don't know you. I don't know this place. How the hell should I know Rose?"

The fat man is dressed in a one-piece mechanic outfit, big bleary yellow eyes practically falling out of his head. He folds his hands on his lap like a good boy, intertwining fingers the size of bratwursts.

"Don't get mad at me, please," he says.

Jack slows the cab, begins to pull over. He asks the fat man where he wants to go.

The fat man points out the window at nothing in particular. "Here, around here. Just drive."

Jack squirms to show he's impatient, but the fat man doesn't notice. He drives on, past the movie theater and toward Kodiak Plaza. Small drops of rain hit the windshield without sliding down.

"I got shot in the ass in the Battle of the Bulge," the fat man says. "Had to crawl three miles before anybody noticed I wasn't dead."

Now Jack sees the skinny fat-man soldier lying facedown in the snow with a bloody ass. Crawling. Leaving a blood trail. No cigarettes, no buddies, just a very cold face and a bloody ass and an idea. What was the idea? To be free? To live? To put it to Rose?

The fat man pulls a lace doily out of his pocket, blows his nose. He clears his throat, making his neck shake.

"Lemme tell you something, mister." He pats the dash with his very large hand, pats the dash gently as if it were a dying dog. "It sounds to me like you got two bad injectors in this rig."

"I'll tell my boss," Jack says, beginning to believe he knows who Rose is.

"You're most definitely losing power, all right." Harry, it must be Harry, stuffs the doily into his chest pocket. "One thing I know for certain is diesels."

The one thing Jack knows for certain is that he hopes he never has as fat a head as Harry has. His mom doesn't have a fat head, and Jack has seen pictures of his dad, most recently on the wall of the Pier Pub here in Kodiak, and his dad didn't have a fat head either. If fat heads are a genetic kind of thing, Jack figures he's got it made.

"I think Rose is at The Ships," Jack says.

Harry clears his throat and looks away. Sits and breathes. "After the war I studied diesels," he says. "Everybody studied everything after the war."

Jack's dad tried to study something after the war. Jack doesn't know what, but he knows his dad went to college for a year, just as Jack did. Lorraine said his father had a hard time seeing much point in anything after the war. She said he'd been a hero, but peacetime was tough on him. Jack liked to believe it when he was a child. But once he entered adolescence, Jack began to have a nagging feeling—no, it was more than that. He began to be quite certain that his dad had been a coward.

Jack drives around the block a second time, a third. He wonders if this

Harry ever knew his dad, figures he probably did. He wonders what Harry could tell him and if it would suddenly make his life meaningful, if it would make the future hopeful and the past less lonely.

He looks over at Harry, giant Harry, who sits like a little boy with his hands folded, the flesh of his face almost too big to be real. Jack's about to ask him if he ever knew a guy named Kid Cliff, but suddenly Harry begins to laugh. Something in his body sends up bubbles of air that rise through the bulk of him, up through the wounded flesh of him, and come out . . . come out laughs. Maybe he's laughing at an old joke his diesel instructor once told. Maybe it's how fat and drunk and wet he is and how goofy Rose looks when she's dressed up. Maybe he can't (even on Memorial Day) remember why he crawled those three miles with a shot-up behind, and he's trying to imagine doing the same today. Maybe he knows he's going to die whether he crawls three miles or not—and for the life of him, for the lucky life of him, he thinks that's very funny!

Anyway, his neck shakes, his chest shakes, and the cab shakes.

"Listen," he says to Jack, "are you married?"

"No."

"Well, if you were . . . if you were . . . Oh what the hell."

Jack's thinking of Mary. He's trying to remember her face, the way she'd turn her head, let her eyes drop to her hands when she was puzzled, or hurt. Coming here was supposed to be for only a while, yet Jack hasn't called her, or written. Unable to tell her he's coming home, he simply has nothing to say.

"What?" Jack asks Harry. He's suddenly impatient. "If I were married, what?"

"Don't get mad at me," Harry says. "Please. I'm just asking is all, but if you were married, and your wife stepped out on you, what would you do?"

Enough of Kodiak already, Jack thinks. Maybe his dad needed to be here, needed to hide here forever, but Jack doesn't have to. He has a choice. He's been here a month, and he's looked around, and . . . what has he learned, really?

"Well?" Harry grunts.

"I don't know," Jack says. "I've never thought about it."

"Course not." Harry turns and leans his gigantic forehead against the window.

Jack's first night in town he saw the photograph behind the bar in the Pier Pub, hanging above the mirror among pictures of dead whales and sharks and bears, among photos of athletes and of destroyed buildings after the tsunami in '64: Kid Cliff, Kodiak Island Boxing Champion, July 4, 1953.

Jack pulls the cab to the curb and stops, smiles, but Harry's not looking. He's opened the door already, extending a foot, gently touching the pavement, as if he's testing the water in a pool. First one foot, then the other foot. Harry lifts his butt, his bloody butt off the seat, and the car dips and springs back again.

"Happy Memorial Day," Jack says.

Harry stands exactly where he stood when Jack picked him up, hanging on to the car door for balance. Behind him the tangle of masts and booms and lines in the harbor looks like a net holding the heavy sky. Rain splatters Harry's cheeks, making him squint a smile. He tosses some crumpled bills on the seat.

"Spend these simoleons and hope you never have to start thinking!" he says.

JACK'S PARKED IN the harbormaster's lot listening to a song about feeling good being good enough, listening to the drizzle on the cab roof. Seagulls stand in line on the dry sidewalk under the overhang of the Mecca Bar and Restaurant across the street. They look as though they're waiting for dinner.

Cars pass on Marine Way, trucks. The song changes, now the harp, now the guitar, now the sax—and now a woman with a sexy voice sings she's ready for love, oh baby, she's ready for love. Jack's thinking of Mary, and while just a few hours ago he could have sworn he was happy here without her, now he's . . . well, now he's confused again.

When the song ends, the man on the radio says Jack is one of a growing number of young adults who have made a conscientious opt for single-hood and childlessness. In light of his recent experience with Mary, this seems almost funny.

23

He's sucking on a fresh pinch of Copenhagen and he's got a cup of coffee between his thighs. He can feel the steam with his fingers, and he's thinking of that story about his father, the one his uncle used to tell, his mother's brother, about how Kid quit high school in 1937 to trap fox for bounty. Jack imagines his father as a young man, wearing overalls and a gray roadster cap. He pictures Kid hopping out of a Model A where the two-track road meets the rocks and ruts of the ridge trail. Kid pulls a sack out of the back; the sun's in his face so he squints. Young Kid Cliff's hair is genuine orange, matches the maple leaves on the hills. It is one of those damn yellow mornings—clear and sunny, so the dew sparkles yellow down the hollow. He looks strong and already a little mean, Kid does, striding up the hill the way a seventeen-year-old strides—long steps, arms swinging, head steady—when the seventeen-year-old thinks he's already a man. He's smelling the dampness in the leaves and grass along the shaded trail, and liking it. But he's also thinking about his traps, and how if he can smell what he can smell, just imagine what the fox can smell. And he's thinking about how much one fox'd buy, how much two fox'd buy, how much three fox'd buy. What he needs and how much he wants. He's seventeen and alone a lot, and if his stomach isn't empty, and if he has a little time and the day is blue or rainy or cold, and especially if it's clear like this morning, with a little breeze rustling the birch leaves on the ridge slope and the last of the morning mist still clinging to the creek bottom, especially on one of these damn yellow mornings in 1937 when the world prepares to kill itself and he strides up the hill into the shade of the woods, Kid Cliff is hungry for something he cannot name. Sure he is. Everybody is. Anybody would be.

Jack was fifteen when he learned that his dad had died at sea. Jack couldn't picture a fishing boat icing up, and he couldn't picture his father because he'd never seen him except in black-and-white photographs. He knew his father had red hair because everybody told Jack that he had his father's red hair. But Jack had never seen Kid Cliff as a middle-aged man, so Jack had no idea what his hair was like when he died. Jack thought he should be sad, but he wasn't. It was like the death of a stranger. He thought he'd forget all about it, just as he'd sometimes forgotten that he even had a father, but that didn't happen.

24

Instead Jack began to read about Bataan and about the Japanese prisoner-of-war camps. He hid the books in the barn among the hay bales because he knew his mother never went out there. Jack would read a little whenever he fed the cows, and the descriptions of what the prisoners had to endure while in the camps both horrified and fascinated him. He tried to make some sense of it, tried to make it correspond somehow with the world he knew of hunting and haying and big breakfasts and long gray afternoons in the spring when the valley farm melted from ice to mud in the rain. The random cruelty, the casual beatings and tropical disease, the rotting corpses: he couldn't bring them close.

Nor could Jack imagine his dad's death in a frozen sea. So he made something up. He read in the newspaper that an old man froze to a tree on a farm near Wonewoc. It was something he could picture, and it did the trick. It could make Jack both angry and sad to think about.

Sitting in his cab now, across the street from the Mecca Bar and Restaurant in *kodiakalaska,* of all places, Jack imagines it once again:

Nighttime, and snow blows across the hollow, billowing over itself and swirling up in the moonlight like a fountain of stars. There's music, rich lively music, a Vivaldi tape that somehow ended up on the farmhouse kitchen table. Kid Cliff the old farmer wears boots with new yellow laces, but he can't hear the sound of his own steps in the snow. He can't hear himself breathe, and he can't hear the pulse he feels in his neck. His nose is bulbous and red, ears like pretzels below scattered red baby hair. He wears a red hunting shirt, overalls, no gloves, nothing on his head but the plastic band of the stereo arching from ear to ear. He sits against a tree in the cleavage of two hills. The ridge trail winds up the draw behind him, soft and drifted. The slope lines show crisp beneath winter-black branches. The wind numbs Kid's scalp, races through his shirt to the skin of his chest. Tiny crystals sting his cheeks. In his mind, sunlight flashes from nowhere across a blue ocean, across fire-blackened trees, a bayonet, a boot, a yellow hand with blood between the fingers, the back of his friend's sunburned neck sliced open beneath the helmet. Kid Cliff closes his eyes and pushes a crooked thumb into his pocket and turns up the volume of the Sony Walkman. Vivaldi fills his head like a dream, maybe, or the memory of distant hunger. But after a while, even that's gone.

Jack opens his eyes and feels his empty stomach unwind. He doesn't remember when he added the Sony Walkman or the Vivaldi, but he likes them. They stick. He wonders if *his* kid might ever have imagined that right now, at this very moment . . . Jack wonders if Mary had gone through with it and the child had been born and had a chance to grow up, if his son or daughter ever would have known or imagined that on Memorial Day night, 1983, in *kodiakalaska,* when Jack squints just right, just right, the drops of rainwater clinging to the windshield look like slightly fuzzy crystals, like beautiful orange stars.

3 NEIL PASTERNAK SITS in a rusted white pickup truck with his friend Larry Laarson. They're parked along Kalsin Bay, looking into the Memorial Day evening fog. Neil's hoping to see some whales like he saw yesterday. He's hoping he doesn't see a mushroom cloud.

"Well, hell," Larry says, slapping the steering wheel, disgusted. Although he's just made a small fortune fishing herring in the Bering Sea, he can't tune his truck radio any better than Neil can, which is poorly.

"I'll tell you something," Larry says. "I had a dream last night, and I've got a new ambition in life."

"Yeah?" Neil has a full brown beard and curly hair that has thinned to baldness on top. He leans forward, presses his chest to his knees, stretching. He hurt his back last year, had to stop fishing, and now is an unemployed member of the builders' union. Only thirty-three, he often feels there's something vital he once knew but has forgotten.

Larry chuckles, rubs his big smooth face. "My lifelong goal as of last night is to get laid in a rock-and-roll Cadillac!" He shows a broad smile, nods his head for emphasis.

Neil sits up. He's been in Kodiak a long time—he knows that. He has a vague memory of the Beachcomber Bar when it was still in the grounded ship. He remembers not needing money because everyone had it and helped if you were short. He knows he fished with Kid Cliff on the *Dempsey II* from 1966 until 1968 and was off on a life raft the night Kid drowned. After that he left Kodiak for a while. He took a trip with his brother. He moved to New York City. He even became a soldier. Since Vietnam, and what he considers to be a blundering encounter with reality, Neil has read a lot of books.

"Beerski, please, Horatio," he says to Larry.

Larry reaches to the floor between his legs and hands a can to Neil. "Just imagine it, man. Tinted glass, love seat, music!"

Neil open the beer and takes a sip. He wishes he could remember other things as well as he can remember quotations.

"Know what Camus said?" he asks.

"Camus?" Larry cocks his head.

"He said a single sentence will suffice to describe modern man: He fornicated and read the papers."

Larry laughs and shakes his head slowly. "Well, what a fucking guy he must have been!"

Neil giggles. "And you know another thing?" He doesn't know what he's going to say, but he likes to put himself in spots like this because the surprise is fun.

"What's that?" Larry asks.

" 'Two-plus-two-makes-five is a delightful little item now and then.' "

"Who?"

"Dostoevsky."

"Damn Russians." Larry slaps his seat.

"Yup."

"I like 'My mother is a fish,' " Larry says. "That's the best. That's the one I remember."

"Yeah?"

" 'My mother is a fucking fish.' " Larry shakes his head, playfully amazed. "Faulkner. The guy was a genius, eh?"

"Yeah."

Larry lifts his arm. "See that, Neil?"

Neil is hoping it's a whale; he's not hoping it's a mushroom cloud, although in the fog that might be hard to see. No, it wouldn't. A mushroom cloud would instantly burn away the fog. Sure. He'd see it, and then he'd be blind. He looks up anyway. "What, a whale?"

"No, this." Larry's still holding his arm out straight.

"Your *arm*?"

"Yeah, my forearm." Larry's forearm is thick and crossed with blue veins.

"Strong boy, Ho," Neil says.

"My mother the fish made this." He squeezes his hand into a fist and the muscles bulge even more. "Damn right. For a fuller erotic and professional life!"

"Strong boy, Ho. You could make two plus two equal five if you wanted to."

Larry grins. He tosses an empty can out the window and into the back of the pickup, then reaches between his legs for another beer. "Now you're catching on!"

Neil wishes he made the kind of money in the past month that Larry made. He doesn't know what he'd do with it, but he knows that having it would make him feel better. And knowing that having it would make him feel better makes not having it feel even worse. Even though he hasn't the slightest idea what he would do with the money besides not work. And he's not working already.

"You know Nietzsche's formula for happiness, Ho?" Neil asks.

"Oh boy." Larry knocks his forehead with his knuckles. "I must have let that one slip."

"A yes, a no, a straight line, a goal."

"You don't say."

"Yup."

"That goddamn guy." Larry's grinning. He sips his beer.

"Yup."

"I bet I know what the straight line is." Larry runs a nostril along his forefinger, sniffs.

"Friedrich wasn't into drugs, Ho."

"Well, the goal is pussy, I can tell you that much. Where we come from, where we want to go. Home. Ya ya ya."

Neil laughs. "And the yes and no?"

Larry thinks for a moment, then snaps his fingers. "That's when to say no to the ugly ones!"

Neil smiles, but he's feeling distracted. He wishes the radio worked. He doesn't know if he has a headache or if he's just imagining the beginning of one. It depresses him that he lived in Great Falls, Montana, for the first sixteen years of his life and can barely remember it. And he's far from convinced that a straight line is even possible in a curved universe.

He says, "Where the hell are all the whales, Lar?"

"Too foggy to see 'em."

Now doom hits—*boom*—a why-do-anything doom, a Vietnam doom, in which only the officers and the very dumb could think of any reason at all for doing anything.

"Sorry, Ho," Neil says, "but I feel lousy all of a sudden."

"You look lousy." Larry begins to laugh, but quickly stops when Neil doesn't. He swigs his beer and pounds the empty can against his head, flips it out the window into the back of the truck. "A goddamn rock-and-roll Caddy, Neilipoo! What do you think?"

"Great."

There's a long pause.

Finally, Larry says, "Hey. What's wrong, man?"

"Nothing. I don't know. Reagan's a fuckhead is all."

"*Reagan?*" Larry laughs.

"He's gonna blow up the world and all the damn books and movies with it, so nobody will ever be able to guess why."

"Neil—"

"Somebody ought to shoot some old movies into orbit just to explain things, see? We're apes, Larry. We mimic. We feel bad but like to feel good, so we try try try."

Larry laughs, uncertain.

Neil continues: "He's such a jerk, but whenever I start to hate him I see the way he probably looks when he gets up in the morning. Can you believe that? The old bastard's breath stinks, and his chest is saggy and white, and his hair is messed up, and he's got these sheet-crease marks across his face. It always makes me feel sorry for him! That's the way he'll look if he ever makes the Last Phone Call, you know. Scum between his teeth and a plugged-up asshole, no suit, no makeup, just sitting naked on his bed, wishing Nancy'd come over and blow into his ear or something."

Larry is shaking his head, amused, concerned, and irritated all at once.

"See, he's just an old man trying to remember something about glory and guts because he doesn't want to be crazy," Neil says. "He's just like you and me and everybody else, but older."

"Huh?"

"So if we hate him, then we have to hate ourselves."

"Yeah?"

"And if we feel sorry for him, then we have to feel sorry for ourselves."

"Those are the options, huh?" Larry asks. "C'mon, get off it. Gimme another quote, buddy."

Neil reaches to the floor between Larry's feet for another beer. He opens it and feels better.

"C'mon, man," Larry says.

Neil is about to say he doesn't know any more quotes, but then he remembers one. " 'I don't know, Nick said,' " he says.

"Who?"

"Guess."

" 'I don't know, Nick said,' " Larry repeats. "Mmmm. Edgar Allan Poe?"

"Jesuscrist." Neil smiles. Larry's a kick.

"Jesus Christ?"

"No," Neil says. "Jesus Christ knew. Who didn't?"

"I don't know."

"Hemingway." Neil giggles. He's definitely feeling better. He likes Larry a lot.

"Hey!" Larry says. "Good one. Great! 'I don't know, Nick said.' All right, I'll tell you what." Larry starts the pickup. "Let's find the hell out what Betsy's up to tonight, then we'll know." He punches Neil lightly on the arm.

"Ow! Betsy?"

"Yeah, she digs you."

"She digs me?"

"Yeah. She doesn't hate you and she doesn't feel sorry for you. She digs you."

"Why do you suppose she digs me, Ho?"

"Oh, as Hemingway once said, 'I don't know, Nick said.' Maybe she heard you say something once that she thought was *powerful*."

"Jesus." Neil laughs.

"Sure! Her warrior! Her Studley Do-Right!"

"Jesuscrist, Ho."

"I'd lay her if I were you, Neil. In a goddamn rock-and-roll Cadillac, I would."

"Betsy knows I'm a jerk, Larry."

Larry starts the pickup, twists his neck to see behind him while he backs up. "Yeah. But does she care?"

No whales spotted, and doom having retreated gracefully, if only temporarily behind the fog, Larry and Neil share a laugh and at least one more beer apiece as they follow the road back to town.

4 JACK GOT A call from the dispatcher to go to the Hot Tubs, so he parks out front and waits for his fare to come down. He turns up the radio, puts in a fresh chew, and then grabs the empty coffee cup from beneath his seat. He uses his pant cuff to wipe the stray particles of tobacco off his fingers, then lifts the cup to his mouth and spits. The song on the radio tells of warm summer breezes, French wine and cheeses, which remind Jack of his empty stomach. Rainwater, french fries, peanut butter and jelly, fish, milk shakes, coffee, spaghetti, and an occasional beer are his staples. It's been two hours since he should have eaten. Before long he'll have to make another attempt at a meal.

A man descends backward down the Hot Tubs steps, waving to someone standing in the open doorway. He's wearing a red plaid hunting jacket, blue jeans, and laceless black rubber deck boots. In the gray light of the sky, he looks a little like Donald Sutherland: long head and nose, short blondish hair, and a rugged chin.

He climbs into the cab headfirst, and the first thing Jack notices is the smell of diesel oil. The guy's also got a book of matches in his hand.

Jack wonders if he's going to torch himself like some Asian fanatic. He tries to imagine what burned flesh smells like and then thinks about the many people in the world who not only know what burned flesh smells like but can't forget it. His father? The fat man, Harry, might have known something about Kid Cliff, but what could he have said that Jack didn't already know? *Yeah, your dad lived here. He died there.* (Pointing out to sea.) *Was a helluva boxer, damn right, and a prisoner of war too. So you're his son, huh?*

No, the fat man Harry couldn't have told Jack if his dad was a hero or a coward. He couldn't have told Jack if his dad knew what burned flesh smelled like. It wasn't the kind of thing people talk about, even old guys trading war stories.

"This is one hellacious town," Donald Sutherland says, slamming the door and settling himself. He lights a cigarette and pushes a quick hand back across the side of his head. "Wow. You been here long?" he asks, exhaling the smell of burned tobacco.

The radio song says four or five years slipped away, so Jack says four or five years. What the hell. He's already caught on that in Alaska, the longer you've been around, the cooler you are.

"No," Donald Sutherland says, laughing. "I mean waiting here."

"Oh," Jack says. "About two minutes is all."

Donald recovers from his laughter and says, "This is only my second night in this hellacious mother of a town. Wow. Beachwhatever. Let's go to that Beach place."

It's an easy ride, a decent payer, so Jack is glad. *Yeah, Mom, it's happy me! I'm going out to the Beachcomber Bar and am going to make some money and the guy lit a cigarette instead of . . . And hey, by the way, did Dad ever mention the smell of burned flesh?*

The cab groans as it climbs the hill, past houses and apartments, a couple of injectors short. The sky is charcoal now, and the rain light but steady. Donald Sutherland makes a funny whistle when he breathes.

"Yeah, my partner went up there with a couple of chicks already and I'm supposed to meet them, but then these guys in there"—pointing over his shoulder at the Hot Tubs—"I never met them before, and these guys are having a wild party and won't let me leave until I take four shots and four toots. Somebody turned forty-four! For crying out loud, I never met the bastards before!" He lets out a long breath.

The radio says all of the answers to all of the questions got locked in an attic one day.

"Hey, I like this man Buffett," Donald says, settling in again, this time unbuttoning his coat. "I've been down in Old Harbor. In the Bering before that." He makes a loud sucking sound. "Sucking herring."

"How did you do?"

"Lots and lots and lots. Pretty darn well. God, but Old Harbor's desolate compared to here. *Desolation, starvation,*" he sings, tunelessly. "Two frickin' bars is all. In one they throw you out for talking above a whisper. And the other . . ." He shakes his head and makes a face as though remembering the actual smell of boredom—a whiff of the dark side, and by gum, it ain't fresh-baked buns. But then he changes tack, flashes a smile.

"You been here four or five years, huh?"

"Yeah," Jack lies. "Four, almost five."

Steel guitar cries now: The war killed his baby, the bombs took his lady and left him with only one eye.

Donald chuckles, stares out the window. "Driving a cab must keep you busy."

"Yup."

"Wow," Donald says, exhilarated, not by Jack or by the thought of driving a cab, or even by Kodiak, but by the new cocaine awareness of who he is and where he is and all the innocent money in his pocket. It's the sudden whiff of possibilities is what it is. And it takes his breath away.

Donald rubs his face with his big hand, shakes his head disbelievingly. "Skipper wants me to take some salmon to Japan in a couple of weeks. Hundred and twenty-five bucks a day and all we have to do is cruise!" He uses his hand to show a boat cruising. "You ever been to Japan?"

Jack says yes. What the hell. Buffett on the radio sings hopped on a freighter, skidded the ocean . . .

"Just cruise. Frick." Then Donald seems to hear what Jack said. "You have? What's it like?"

"Super place."

"Like what's there? What did you see?"

"Oh, I saw a baseball game. Lots of stuff. Geisha girls. The works. I went to this place in Osaka where they kept some prisoners in the war. Went to Tokyo."

"Huh," Donald says. He takes a deep breath and tries to imagine the kingdom of Japan. But he soon gets frustrated because the only image he's got is Mount Fuji, and he knows, as only an American Westerner can know, that Japan has about a billion people crammed on those tiny islands and what mostly have to be there are endless cities.

"I forget where it is we're going," he says.

"It's all pretty neat," Jack assures him.

"Skipper says he bought two thousand bucks' worth of stereo equipment there last year," Donald says. "Stopped in Hawaii on the way back. He wants to run the same trip this year. Frick, I'm lucky to get the chance. I could stay here for a while, in this town, or I could go home. I got a sick chick at home."

Donald lets out a nervous laugh. "Actually, it's not too funny. She got in a bad wreck, to tell you the truth. She's not sick; she frickin' destroyed her legs. Beautiful girl, too. Tragedy is what it is. I don't know what to do. What do you do when something like that happens? I sent her one of those flowergrams this morning."

Donald rests his head back against the seat and gets quiet. Past the high school dorms on Rezanof, north by northeast, down the hill they glide. Low on the horizon, daylight lingers beneath the clouds.

Donald shifts uncomfortably in his seat and then explains again how it is: a hundred and twenty-five a day just to cruise to Japan and back to Hawaii and then San Fran; and hey, he's going to buy two motorcycles and stereo equipment, and the skipper knows what and where the deals are over there, and he's already got buyers for the cycles back in Cali, which is another reason he's kind of committed.

"On just those two cycles alone I can clear a grand and a half," he says.

Jack turns onto Fourteenth Street, a gravel road that forks and hooks past some houses and through the trees toward Mission Road. Thinking about Donald's girlfriend and her destroyed legs and flowergram, Jack asks, just for the hell of it, "By any chance do you know how the Brewers did yesterday?"

"The who?"

"The Milwaukee Brewers."

Donald shakes his head. "Don't hardly follow baseball," he says. "My mom gets all the Atlanta games, but I never know what's going on."

Jack stops at the stop sign, then turns left onto Mission. The cab bumps over a pothole.

"I don't know," Donald says, the enthusiasm gone. "The only guy from Dalsy, Wyoming, that ever went to Japan was Harry Snyder, and he bombed the frickin' place."

"Well, it sounds like you got a better deal to me," Jack says, trying to sound cheerful. "You don't have to drop any bombs and you get paid more."

Donald doesn't laugh. "Skipper says it's neater than anything to see the way all those people go around so damn busy," he says. "Real religious people, too. And clean as hell, you notice that? Clean. That's what skipper says, anyway. I say those frickers have to be clean, living on top of each other like they do. Ever think about that when you were there? How they have to live right on top of each other?"

"Yeah." As a teenager, when Jack would haul, split, and stack firewood next to the farmhouse, the phrase *the dead were stacked like cordwood* used to run through his mind, and now it does again. He'd read a book describing how prisoners traveled to Japan in the steel belly of Japanese freighters, Hell Ships. The holds turned into black holes of madness. No water and one hundred and twenty degrees of heat near the Philippines, no clothes and below freezing by the time they reached Japan, weeks later.

As they approach the crowded parking lot of the Beachcomber, Donald lets out a short, high laugh. His body lurches into action, buttoning his jacket, running his hands through his hair.

"What a place," he says.

Jack slows to avoid the two Filipino boys who clobbered the dog earlier. They give him the eye as he noses the cab up to the bar entrance, and Jack gives it back.

One of them slaps the hood with his hand.

"Fuckin' flips," Donald says.

The remark catches Jack off guard. It's the tone, the casual bile in the delivery. Donald's only been in town for a couple of days and he's already learned the local lyrics. Spics, niggers, wagon burners, kikes: Multiple choice, fill in the blank. In Kodiak, it's flips.

"They're not that bad," Jack says.

But Donald doesn't care. He's leaning forward now, smiling, doing his own drum roll on the dash with his fingers.

"This is one hellacious mother of a town, all right, ain't it?"

BACK IN THE center of town again, near the boat harbor, parked in the lot between The Ships and The Breakers bars, Jack's thinking about his mother and whether she's really going to sell the cows and move to her sister's in Milwaukee. Sometimes, just to avoid quiet moments, Lorraine will say something, anything. Whenever she begins a sentence with "Well, you know, I've been thinking . . . , " what she really means is "Well, you don't know, of course, because neither do I yet, because I haven't said it, but what I haven't even thought about is next to come out of my mouth, and we'll hear what it is, and then. . . ." But it was never anything about his father.

When Jack was a boy and old enough to ask questions, his mother answered only with lines like "People do unspeakable things to each other in wartime," introducing a mystery and horror beyond words that could creep from thousands of miles away and many years ago into any unsuspecting quiet moment. Sometimes after her last phone call at night, when the television was turned off and Jack could hear her slow steps on the stairs, and then the bed creak as she'd sit, sometimes into those quiet times broken only by a whippoorwill perhaps in the summer, or by the stove fire crackling in the winter, the seldom-heard voice of his father would boom out huge and living and plainly speaking the unspeakable: his horror, her loneliness.

Then the bed would creak again and the radio would turn on and the house would fall asleep to a long-distance talk show.

"People do unspeakable things to each other in wartime." His mother's explanation of why Kid left Wisconsin became Jack's explanation of all evil, all pain and disappointment and inequity: his failure to make the junior high baseball team, starvation in India, the casual meanness of friends, mass murders in Chicago, his mother's brutal and demoralizing loneliness, his own.

After he started reading about Bataan and the camps, the Hell Ships, and the mines and mills in Japan, after he learned how the Jap guards beat prisoners for diversion, how starvation and thirst and dysentery and beriberi made the living sometimes envy the dead, Jack began to see things differently. Maybe these "unspeakable things" were closer to human nature than anything he'd seen in Wisconsin. Maybe health and peace and love were the anomalies, and Lorraine knew it, which is why she suffered from one fatal illness after another. Maybe the late-summer morning fog and the sweet evening smells of grass and alfalfa and black earth were just an illusion of goodness, so she'd think she had leukemia. Sunrise after winter ice storms, and entire trees would light up like crystal chandeliers, the valley glittering under such a spell you could swear you were feeding cows in a fairyland. Sure, so his mother would feel as though she'd eaten something poisonous, maybe that apple, and she'd point to the brown and shriveled core on the bedside table.

Hate got a lot of Bataan prisoners through their tortures, not love. Jack read about a prisoner who was dying in a camp, dying slowly but smelling like death already because he'd started to pine, and this other guy, his friend, his buddy, picks up a canteen and starts beating the dying guy, beating him over and over on his shoulders and back, driving him closer and closer to death until, just when he's a hair away from giving up his ghost, he finally stops pining for his mother or his sweetie or maybe a cold beer, and he starts hating his friend for beating him, hating his sweetie for being sweet, hating his mother for giving him life in the first place, starts hating the Japs again. And that starts a fire burning—hate does, like gasoline when there's no patience for the tender manipulation of spark and twig—and the guy stops dying and starts living again, though never like he did, because the hate singed part of him, sacrificed it, burned it off.

What could men like that say when they came home to loved ones? What did they think?

Mary lost her patience with Jack. She said he was too angry. She said he wasn't a prisoner and his life wasn't that bad if he'd just stop being afraid to live it. She said, "Of course we're all going to die in the end. And maybe we'll be unfaithful at the last minute to everything we ever believed in; maybe we'll betray our mothers and fathers and gladly hand over our children for one last hour of comfortable life."

Then she turned away, leaned her head against the living room window, and looked across the hollow to the hillside thick with summer oak and hickory. Her neck was thin and white, her shoulders narrow.

"Maybe your dad was a brave man, Jack," she said. "He might have done the very best he could possibly do. But you . . . how would you even know?"

FROM BEHIND THE wheel of his cab, still parked between The Ships and The Breakers, Jack watches a couple of morons pile out of a rusty white pickup and shuffle drunkenly, or lazily, across the parking lot. He recognizes one of them as a fisherman named Larry something, who is not really a moron at all but has a reputation as a good fisherman with a darn good fishing boat. He's a skipper everybody wants to fish with. The other is a bar hanger-outer whom Jack has seen around. He has a reputation among the cabbies as a no-payer. Claire, in cab ten, drives him around on credit. She calls him The Philosopher.

A man shuffles out of The Ships, down the sidewalk toward the parking lot, holding something in front of him, to his chest, something Jack can't see because the man's walking backward. When he gets to the curb, though, he turns around and Jack can see he's paunchy and thin-faced, about thirty. And what he's got in his arms, in a blanket, is an infant. The man's face looks shell-shocked and dazed. He steps off the curb like a sleepwalker, his eyes aimed beyond the hood of Jack's cab.

Out of The Ships doorway slides a young native woman. Her feet stumble, legs like rubber, but she catches herself on the wall.

"Sto-o-op!" she screams. "Sto-o-o-opppah!"

The man opens the passenger door of Jack's cab, sticks his head in. In the baby's mouth is a sky-blue pacifier with a handle shaped like a pig.

"Where's my yellow Pinto?" the man asks.

"Your what?" Jack asks. Yellow Pinto, blue piggy.

The woman is making her way along the wall, face stupidly determined, closer.

"Sto-o-o-o-o-o-opppppa-a-ahhh!" she screams.

Still calm-faced, but with an edge to his voice, the man says, "My Pinto, dammit. My yellow Pinto."

Jack shakes his head, says, "I don't know what you're talking about," thinking, *Who the hell do you think I am?*

"All right. Forget it." The man withdraws his head and shuts the cab door.

Pulling her long black hair with one hand while holding herself away from the wall with the other, the woman screams again, this time no words, just a long, self-indulgent awfulness, a wail of shivers.

The man, crossing the lot in front of Jack, covers the baby's face with a corner of the blanket.

On the sidewalk by the video arcade, a crowd of kids giggle and whisper to one another. A few of them are looking at Jack. Jack doesn't know what to do—he feels stupid and frozen and inept just watching the man disappear around the corner of The Breakers and listening to the woman scream again, "My ba-a-a-aby!" One of the kids is pointing at him. Do something! Run, jump, lay the man out with a couple of strategically placed karate chops, rescue the baby for the grateful mother, who will then, of course, clean up her act entirely: love the baby, love Jack, become a nurse. Or maybe he should chase the man, tap him on the shoulder and say, *Sir, I believe you have that woman's baby. You must have picked it up by mistake. Here, I'll return it. Good luck with the yellow Pinto, though. Hope it turns up for you.*

Be a hero, Jack thinks. Go home to Mary. Live a good life. Make somebody happy.

Another scream, wordless, then *babybabybabybabybaby!* She's sitting on the sidewalk now, her hair in both hands.

The kids look from the man to the woman to Jack.

Jack puts his thumbs into his ears and waves with both hands, wagging the full length of his tongue at the kids. Of course this makes them laugh.

5 EDNA MACDONALD, THE Aleut woman with turquoise eyes, crashes out of The Ships bar, lopes across the parking lot, and climbs into the front seat of a cab. She looks long and hard at the driver, a young man with white skin and red hair, and decides she doesn't recognize him after all. She was thinking something beautiful but can't remember if it really happened or if it was only a dream—and now, looking at this guy's face, she's suddenly forgotten what it is she was thinking.

Edna used to know all the cabbies. She's lived in Kodiak her entire life but lately often feels like a stranger. The cabbie asks where to, and Edna mumbles something unrelated to anything visible. Although Edna is well-known in town, no one knows that she is magic and can turn herself into animals. Right now she's a gnu. Look at her, black hair pulled back in a ponytail, round face pouting, breasts sagging beneath a University of Alabama sweatshirt, being a gnu!

The cabbie again asks where to, and Edna snorts, gets out of the cab. She trots, tail in the air, across the parking lot to The Breakers bar, where she expects to share a drink with her sister-in-law, Pretty Gertie Saratov MacDonald, who is cheating on Edna's brother Herman because he can't get her pregnant, and whom you can bet Edna has contemplated strangling.

Inside now, Edna waits by the bar, sits slowly, properly on a barstool, tail to the side, front hooves on her lap. She stares at Pretty Gertie, sitting at a table near the door with Jerry Rostov, Jerry's wife, Nora, and Jerry and Nora's two-year-old daughter, Pam.

Jerry is drunk, leaning back in his chair, looking past heavy eyelids and the peak of a greasy engineer's cap at Pretty Gertie. Pretty Gertie is watching Nora put a potato chip on the table in front of little Pam.

When Pam reaches for the chip, Nora slaps her hand.

"What's the idea?" Pretty Gertie asks. She has a rough, sore-sounding voice, and Edna is amazed by the size of her head, the sheer breadth of her forehead and cheeks, and then all of that black hair, frosted silver on top.

"I got a cousin," Nora says, pushing a strand of blond hair back behind her ear. "And she don't go for the chip."

Nora is a skinny white woman with bony fingers and red lipstick. Her sweatshirt drapes her shoulders, making them look like a wire coat hanger under the cotton. She puts another chip on the edge of the table and waits, her brow furrowed as she looks at her daughter, her brown eyes dutiful.

"If Pam were raised in New York like Sally," Nora explains, "she wouldn't go for the chip."

"That's ridiculous," Pretty Gertie says.

Edna feels herself transforming from a gnu to a pretty yellow bird now, up high in a tree, listening, watching. Pam reaches hesitantly for the potato chip. Nora again slaps her hand.

"Jesus!" Pretty Gertie cringes. Her purple-rimmed glasses slip forward on her nose.

"It ain't hurting her, honey," Nora says. "Sally's about this one's age, and she's been taught not to go for the chip. In New York food don't just swim by like it does here. And besides, she's disciplined, smart as a whip. She ain't dumb like Pam. But that's my fault. And Jerry's. I admit it. We've been slack."

"Poor girl," Pretty Gertie says. "Poor baby."

"It ain't hurting her, honey," Nora says. "See?" She holds up Pam's hand. "Look. Couldn't be hurting her, or she wouldn't keep reaching. Just a little pink is all."

"It ain't her hand I'm worried about."

Pretty Gertie is a lovely person, Edna thinks from her perch, a laurel tree twig shaped like a barstool, a lovely person sometimes.

"You ain't got no discipline yourself, that's your problem," Nora says to Pretty Gertie. "And neither does my husband here."

Jerry sits up suddenly, tugs on his engineer's cap. He smirks at Pretty Gertie, winks, then says to Nora, "I take what the hell I want."

"Not for long, Jer." Nora has a habit of blinking a lot and holding her eyes closed for too long when she does, so sometimes she's sitting there talking to you, but her eyes are closed as though she's not really there at all. Then she opens them, and she looks so surprised to see you that she has to blink again, and there you go.

"Things are changing," she says to Jerry. She's warning him now, or seems to be, eyes wide open.

"Whatever the hell I want," Jerry says.

Nora ignores him and sets another chip on the green Formica table edge. She points to it, smiles at Pam. Pam looks at her mother's face, not daring to look at Pretty Gertie, who is frowning, or Jerry, who is drunk and bobbing. Pam's fingers reach the edge of the table and slide over to the chip. She grabs it, pulls it off, and—slap! The chip drops and Nora's boot crushes it on the floor. Pam starts to cry.

Any murderous thoughts swirling in Edna's pretty yellow bird head begin to enlarge and refocus on Nora. Edna feels her little bird feet grow to paws, the feathers change to fur, her neck swell. She's a lioness, sleek and beautiful and deadly. She crouches on a rock, prepares to strike.

Jerry cocks his head. "You shoulda been a goddamn Nazi Party member, Nora."

"Lots of people are ready to start slapping hands, honey. Just wait. Pam'll be ahead. She'll thank me for teaching her this."

"I take what I need, same as always," Jerry says, eyes on Pretty Gertie, affirming it.

Nora answers, "You ain't got no discipline, you crazy half-breed."

"You can stick discipline where the sun don't shine!" Jerry raises his beer.

Pam is crying loudly.

"Where the sun don't shine!" Jerry smiles. He likes this line.

"You're the real reason she's crying," Nora says, pointing at Jerry. "Not her hand and not . . ." Nora shakes her head disgustedly, sadly too. She gives a handful of chips to Pam, whose cry begins to taper. "Take, take, take. Never give. That's you, Jer. Always has been."

"Take a hike."

"She'll thank me for this. You just wait."

Edna springs toward the table, lights on a chair next to Nora. She's about to bite through Nora's neck but stops when she sees Pam's sweet face, shiny with tears, the plastic red butterfly barrette moving up and down on her temple as she chews. She can't kill Nora in front of her daughter.

"Nope," Edna says. "Pam won't thank nobody, I bet."

"Edna!" Pretty Gertie smiles broadly, glad to see her.

Nora wrinkles her nose as though smelling something unpleasant. "What do *you* know?"

"I know," Edna says, "what God wants me to know."

"I'm so glad you're here," Pretty Gertie says.

Nora stands up, lifts Pam by the shoulders, and tries to cover her ears but manages to cover only one of them. "You're a slut," she says to Pretty Gertie. She fumbles getting her purse strap over her shoulder and then begins to cry.

"Hey!" Jerry yells.

But Nora's marching toward the door, Pam on her hip. She pivots just before stepping out, and shouts back, "Shut up, you drunk!"

Then she's gone, and Jerry, whose face has turned bright pink, picks up his beer can and smiles vacantly. "I like my beer."

"You dog," Edna snaps.

Jerry snarls like a dog, curls his lip.

"Do you pray?" Edna asks Jerry.

"When I can think of something to pray about."

"Well think," Edna commands. Maybe she should kill Jerry. She imagines her big hind paws digging into his soft belly flesh.

"Okay." Jerry looks up at the ceiling, sniffs. There's a long pause, then he says, "I got something to ask God. We can ask Him anything, right? How about I ask Him whatever happened to old Joey Dougel after his wife bit off his prick?"

Edna sinks down in her chair, her beautiful lion coat gone. Oh boy. Her turquoise eyes are dulling fast. Scales replace yellow fur, a shell grows. She's a turtle. Good move.

"Everybody says they don't know, figure he went Outside," Jerry says. He slaps the table. "I'd like to know the truth!"

It's quiet for a moment, then Pretty Gertie says, "Only Dougel I ever knew got his toes froze, so shut up."

"That was his brother," Jerry explains quickly. "Wife snapped Joey's twig. That's what they say."

Edna reaches for Nora's half-glass of beer; dazed, blinking, she pulls it back into her shell. She closes her eyes and finishes it, drains it, aaaahhh, she's paling, sweet Edna, she likes her mud.

Pretty Gertie signals the bartender for three more.

"Vanished out of shame." Jerry is picking at a hole in his blue jeans. "Pheeew! Like that! Wife's still up in Afognak trapping. Now there's a legend. What they say about what she eats."

Edna sits with her eyes closed, praying for a truth and goodness with shape, and wondering how murder, specifically strangulation, would fit into the shape, and why oh why a person has to feel so many things when one or two feelings would do nicely, thank you. For instance, why, on top of all the colors, must she have to sit here and be nagged by this awful thirst? and what does that have to do with anything? and is it more or less important than murder or love, loyalty, friendship, honor, or her maidenhood? Well?

Oh, the questions! For instance, why did the only two men she ever loved have to die? First Jimmy. And then— Of course she was just a girl with Jimmy, so it was only one, really, one man, one real man, and she never even got the chance to do with him what Pretty Gertie does with Jerry here. Wow. The thought of Jerry naked makes her feel like puking. Anyway, where was she? Oh yes, God. The things she could ask God, seeing as how He's supposed to know so much.

Jerry's slumped, head fallen to his shoulder, thinking about who knows what, about something filthy with Pretty Gertie or Nora, probably, about how much fun it is to make women cry.

Edna leans toward Pretty Gertie and says, "I *do* believe in God, so I'll pray for you."

"Oh, Eddie!" Pretty Gertie says, folding her hands on her lap and looking down.

"Hey, hey!" yells a voice at the bar. "Hey, hey!" A young man with a black Mongolian mustache and a panama hat stands with his thumbs hooked through canvas belt loops, his back against the bar.

"Stan the Man!" Jerry shouts back.

Stan dips his head, begins a smile. He pushes off the bar and drifts toward the table, big wide toothy grin first.

"And I'll pray for Herman, of course," Edna says. "Your husband. My brother."

"Here," Pretty Gertie says. "Have the rest of my beer."

Stan strikes a boxer's pose, does a few shadow punches at Jerry, almost falls, sits down in Nora's chair, groans.

"My brother is a nice man." Edna holds the glass with two hands and sips. "A decent man."

"You're a beautiful person," Pretty Gertie says.

"Get a beer for this dumb shit!" Jerry yells to the bartender. "And don't forget the girls and me!"

"A fine human being," Edna says.

"I know that," Pretty Gertie says.

Stan, eyes wide open, looks at Edna and Pretty Gertie as though they were ghosts that have just appeared in front of his eyes. He laughs and slaps Jerry's thigh.

"I'm a red-killer, a sockeye-slaughterer."

"You're a bleeding a-hole," Jerry says.

"Got a set net site up on the Peninsula this year. Gold mine. The old lady's old man's old place." Stan grins broadly, slaps his chest. "Fuck 'em if they can't take a joke!"

"Oh, you're a good boy, Stanny," Jerry says. "You'd be home free if anybody gave a good goddamn."

"To hell with you bastard seiners. I'm a gill-netter now!"

Jerry claps. "Lovin' it, lovin' it!"

"I know what to pray for," Pretty Gertie says to Edna.

"What's that?"

"I'd pray . . . I'm praying . . ." She pauses, drops her eyes and begins to pick at lint on her orange Spandex pants.

Edna puts her wing around Pretty Gertie. She's a swan now, a beautiful, long-necked swan. "It's okay. Don't be sad. I was angry, but now I'm not."

"Nora's bad," Pretty Gertie says.

"Well, we're not. We're friends." Edna knows now that she won't kill Pretty Gertie tonight, or ever, probably, for that matter. What she wants badly now is to go to the Pier Pub and see the photograph of his face, his face, his handsome, beautiful face. It's the beer, and before that the vodka. Booze breaks down Iron Will and Independent Spirit. She'll end up back at the Pier Pub, staring at his picture above the bar, watery-eyed, probably. But it's all she's got and—dammit—sometimes a woman needs a little reassurance.

Pretty Gertie takes off her glasses and wipes her tears with her sleeve, then smiles. "I'm praying right now for the filthy bartender to bring us a beer."

Edna touches Pretty Gertie's cheek with long, feathered fingers.

Next to them, Stan has somehow used the heels of his hands to fold his eyelids inside out, pink side out.

"Watch out," Jerry says. "Good times!"

Edna leans toward Pretty Gertie's massive head, puts her nose into the frosted hair, her lips.

"Let's us tiptoe over to the Pier Pub," she whispers.

6 THE NEW WOMAN cabdriver, who is always writing things in a pocket notebook, pulls up next to Jack by Solly's Office Bar, rolls down her window the way she always does when she parks next to Jack, and says, "Listen to this. Believe it or not I copied this off a bathroom wall at APS."

"What?" Jack asks.

"APS?" She knits her brow, tilts her head to the side. "Alaska Pacific Seafood? The big cannery out on Shelikof?"

"I know *that,*" Jack says.

"Oh." Fourteen reaches for the notebook on her dashboard, shrugs. "Anyway, I think whoever wrote it has a point. Just listen."

Jack closes his eyes. She bothers him for some reason. She's got straight blond hair, stylish pink-rimmed glasses, and an intense look in her eyes. No, not intense; kind of busy. She's friendly, but she talks a little too much. The first time Jack saw her she was a passenger in his cab. She told him she'd been trying to get drunk but didn't think she was. He dropped her off in front of a house up on Larch, and when she paid him she leaned forward and he could see her left breast past the neck of her loose blouse, the tip of the nipple looking like a raisin. It made him feel sorry for her and wish he hadn't seen it. That and the glossy pink lipstick she had on. It made her look lonely.

Jack opens his eyes and sees her looking at him.

"You have a headache or something?" she asks.

"No, I'm okay. Just sleepy."

"I've got an aspirin."

"No, thanks." Jack isn't sleepy, and he doesn't have a headache either. He's hungry, but that's not why he closed his eyes. He doesn't know why he closed his eyes, but he did, then she asked him why, so he had to lie. Maybe that's why she bothers him. He can't remember her name, even though they must have been introduced five times since she came on the job last week. Her cab is fourteen. He thinks of her as Fourteen. With the red bandanna on her head she looks like a television farm girl. With the glasses, she looks like a contemporary thinker of sorts.

"Well," she begins, paging through her notebook. "You know how everyone is always talking about the Real Alaska this and the Real Alaska that? Everybody tells me I ought to get out of the cab and see the Real Alaska. Well, somebody wrote this poem and called it 'The Real Alaska.' I think it's perfect."

She laughs, and Jack tries to smile. But his stomach is turning and he wishes for the hundredth time that he'd eaten some spaghetti. Fourteen is the kind of person who makes you feel as though you *should* smile. She's nice, really. Jack wishes he liked her better.

" 'The Real Alaska,' " she begins reading:

> Have you learned yet
> about the Real Alaska?
> I'll give you a hint or two.
> It's behind your eyes, between your ears;
> it's in your mouth and up your nose,
> above your neck, below your toes,
> down your pants, up your skirt,
> in your hands;
> it's in any mirror
> anywhere
> in the goddamn state!

Fourteen closes the notebook and slides it back onto the dash. She seems a little troubled.

"I think it says something," she says.

Jack looks in his rearview mirror and sees the gray parking lot, the sidewalk, and a girlish-looking woman with blond curly hair. She's got her purse over her shoulder and she's walking briskly toward Solly's Office, where she works as a barmaid. Three Aleut men sit on the curb and watch her pass.

"Where are you from?" Fourteen asks.

"Florida," Jack says. Wisconsin sounds boring, and besides, he's not in the mood for life stories. One of the Aleuts playfully pushes the guy next to him. If Jack said Wisconsin Fourteen'd say something about cows, and then he'd have to laugh or moo or something. It's not that Jack doesn't want to laugh or moo or something; he just doesn't want to *have to*. Anyway, nobody ever wrote a song about Wisconsin, at least no song he can think of that's any good, and that thought depresses him. He was in a fine mood before Fourteen pulled up, and now, for some reason, he's grouchy. It's the not eating that makes him feel this way.

Jack was awakened that afternoon by the sound of rain on his tent roof and the feral dog Shit for Brains scratching through Jack's clothing on the other side of the mosquito netting. Jack likes Shit for Brains, but she

48

picked up one of his shoes in her mouth and ran figure eights across the candy-green moss, dodging spruce trees. Jack had to use the last of his peanut butter and bread to tempt her close, grabbing the shoe away when she went for the food. Later, just before his shift, Jack ordered ravioli and salad at the Kodiak Café, downstairs from the cab office. But before the food came, Gary, the day dispatcher, knocked on the café window and pantomimed a phone conversation, pointed upstairs to the office. It was the call from his mother, and it kept Jack from what would have been his big meal of the day.

Then, of course, the Beachcomber Happy Hour Spaghetti Feed ran out of spaghetti just as Jack got to the window. The Filipino boys teasing the dog delayed him. Sure. It was all preordained.

"All the way from Florida, huh?" Fourteen says, looking amazed.

"Yeah," Jack says. Once he heard a passenger say that Florida was nothing but Cubans, queers, in-laws, and humidities. So he adds, "Humid as hell."

Fourteen smiles.

Jesus, she can turn him in circles. Jack finds it hard to look at her. He tries to imagine making a clean breast of it:

Okay, you caught me, I'm not from Florida! Good joke, though, huh? Actually I'm just a guy named Jack from Wisconsin who had a girl named Mary, who looks a little like you. I suppose we were informally engaged, but after four years of raising cattle together and living with my mother, well, engagement is something you begin to suppose. We met in Missoula, Montana, where I was visiting an old friend and she was in college. Mary's from Chicago. Maybe she thought meeting a guy with cattle was what should happen to a girl in Montana. I was crazy about her so I stayed out there and even went to school for a year. The first time we made love was in the back of a pickup crossing Homestake Pass. We were hitching back from Bozeman and we had only one sleeping bag. A red moon rose over the mountain, and we took turns floating up to take bites. From then on we were a regular couple, Thing One and Thing Two. We moved back to Wisconsin, to the farm. Mom and Mary hit it off well enough, and I worked hard trying to make the pasture more productive, the herd bigger. I baled a lot of hay. We did all right on the farm. Mary worked as a receptionist for Dr. Sand, the same guy Mom's always worked for. We weren't exactly cattle baron and baroness, but I thought I loved her and she thought she loved me, and maybe we did for a while. Then Mary got pregnant. From then on things got weird. One day last fall Mary came home and said she was no longer a girl, that she felt like a woman. I said okay, babe, that's fine, but why this day and not the day before or the day after? Then I saw her face and remembered our talk the night before and realized that she'd been dead serious about her intentions. Her fingers on the back of my hand confirmed it. She said she felt *fine,* and we'd both decided it would be better this way, *remember?* and I listened and didn't argue but didn't feel very good either. I thought, Okay, Jack, it's your job to figure out how to be a man, and that's probably when I came to Alaska, although the plane didn't leave for another five months.

Here are two things I remember of those last months: being uncomfortable looking at Mary's face, and how I enjoyed the cruelty of ignoring her woman-tears.

Fourteen is taking a deep breath. She looks as if she's about to make a confession herself. "I'm from Oregon," she says. "A little fishing town. Not much different from this, except you can drive away at least."

Jack nods. He'd skip the bit about his father.

"I've lived up here for a couple years already," Fourteen says.

Jack nods again, watches through his rearview as the woman with curly blond hair walks past his and Fourteen's cab, neatly pivots on the corner, and then enters Solly's Office Bar in front of them.

Fourteen rests her chin on the car door, raises her eyebrows, looks cute.

"Did you see the finish of the Chiniak race?" she asks.

"Nope."

"Some people are crazy." She's squinting. Her chin is soft and her eyes little and tight. Tiny red earrings, at least a couple, sparkle in each ear. "All those people!" She sighs, blows the hair off her forehead. "I couldn't believe it."

"Must like the pain or something." Jack's smiling.

"Don't fool yourself," she says. "Nobody likes pain. They get a buzz off running like that. What, fifty miles? It *must* get them off!" She laughs a laugh that sounds like a hiccup, shrugs, asks forgiveness with her face. No makeup, which is different from the other women cabbies. That glossy pink lipstick must have been a bad day. Jack has to admit she's pretty. He likes the softness around her mouth, the pliability, the way she sticks out her lower lip to blow hair off her forehead. It's a miracle, her skin, the way it stretches and shrinks and looks so soft and covers all her face muscles. They both laugh.

Jack figures he should go up to the office and get Fourteen's name from Gil, the night dispatcher. It might make him feel more relaxed around her. Maybe they'd end up eloping to Mexico. She could make him laugh at the way her face changes expression all the time. She'd kick her feet up on the coffee table in the living room of their cliffside home on the Baja—red polish on the toes of one foot and white on the others—and she'd tell him how her life was a shambles when she spoke to him that evening in Kodiak, cab to cab, but now she's happier than she ever thought possible, happier than she ever thought possible, yes indeed. He'd smile at that and stroke her pretty neck, think of it arched and full of passion. The wood of the coffee table would be heavy and dark and polished. He could write his mother a beautiful letter describing life with Fourteen, how happy they were now that she was pregnant with twins.

Just then a man wearing a leather jacket steps off the sidewalk and up to Fourteen's window. He rocks from foot to foot, hands in his pockets. Fourteen looks up at him and they talk in harsh whispers. The man is broad-shouldered and handsome. Hanging down into the V made by his open jacket and shirt is a fine gold chain. In second grade he probably stuck a pussy willow in his ear, Jack thinks. And the teacher couldn't get it out, nor could the school nurse, so he was sent home, where his mother finally picked it out with a pair of German silver eyebrow pluckers. But you'd never know it by the way he stands, legs apart, shoulders slumped, rubbing a hand through thick black hair.

Fourteen is whining something. The man makes a gesture with his hand, like a karate chop, and spins on the heels of his boots. Jack hears him say, "I can't believe this," as he turns away. He walks back up the steps to the sidewalk, and then disappears around the corner between Solly's Office and Tony's Bar.

Fourteen looks over at Jack, her face red from anger. "The only time he sees me anymore is before he gets his check or after he's already spent it," she says. "He comes over when he's broke and needs a shower and a meal, but when he's got money I see him out strolling other women every time."

She pauses, gestures in the direction he went. "I suppose you didn't notice the sharkskin jacket he was wearing."

Jack shrugs. He wishes he hadn't told her he was from Florida.

"Well, anyway," she says. "I bought it for him. We came up here together from Oregon. He's heap big fisherman now. Ever hear of *La Cruz*? A first-rate highliner. He's got bucks, so don't ever let him fool you."

Jack doesn't know what to say. He feels bad for her. Maybe he should offer to beat the crap out of Mr. Sharkskin La Cruz. But what if she said, "Yes, sure, would you do that for me?"

Fourteen laughs a laugh that sounds like a hiccup, shakes her head. "You know something? You've got pretty far-out eyes."

She's staring, so Jack looks away.

"Not the color so much as just the way they are," she says. "I can tell you're not too full of shit."

Now, Jack thinks, feeling his insides begin to melt. Now tell her the truth. Tell her you don't know who you are or why you're here, that after a month on this island your father is still a stranger. Tell her you have no idea what you expected to learn by coming, that the facts of your father's life—where he lived, where he drank, what fishing was like—seem less and less significant. Tell her about the guy who walked out of The Ships bar with the baby and about Rose and Harry and Donald Sutherland, and about the only thing you've figured out so far is that these unending gray dusks and dawns are something more significant than just borders between day and night. Tell her that perhaps you're not as angry as you were, but you're still so lonely sometimes you feel like a sap. No. Don't. Just listen to the Scottish bagpipe music now playing on the radio. When all else fails, think of what you loved about the farm: walking out the driveway to the bridge over the creek on summer nights, the moon bathing the valley in silver, the black hills and the phantom cattle across the pasture, deer snorting in the alfalfa, you and Mary, a beer apiece, the creek echoing loudly under the bridge, the smell of damp grass and hard apples and sweet manure. Think of feeding cows in the winter, the feel of cold air in your lungs, the red cattle and green hay the only colors in a black-and-white world. Think of the cows' steamy breath mingling with yours in the barn and how the smell of cud makes you feel safe. Think of the smell of summer sun on your skin, the clean look of a well-stacked hay wagon, the dirty water swirling by your feet in the shower after a day of work. Yes, and dancing to the rhythm of the baling machine while your mother, suffering from some new and unpronounceable disease she heard about at Dr. Sand's, sits straight in her seat and drives the tractor along the windrow. Think of how finding marbles buried in loose hay, marbles you shot at pigeons fifteen years ago, makes you know where you're from. Could you go back? Sure. Why not? Actual possibilities can make the prettiest fantasies.

A young man wearing a green baseball cap with silver wings sewn to the sides gets into the front seat of Fourteen's cab. Fourteen waves quickly. She starts her engine and sits up in her seat, lips pursed like an old woman's. Through the rearview now, Jack sees them back away, Silverwings talking and laughing and leaning toward Fourteen with a sickeningly happy predator smile.

7   JULIE JORDAN, FROM Moscow, Idaho, walks into Solly's Office for the start of her shift. She throws her purse on the bar, shakes her curly blond hair off her forehead, and says to the bartender, "What's wrong with him? I've given him great tips on good boats. He ought to have one of those jobs by now. I tell you, something is definitely wrong with Dodge."

The bartender, Betty Jo Jorgeson, sits on a stool behind the bar, smoking a cigarette. She crosses her legs, bounces her foot a few times, knowing just what Julie means. Betty Jo's boyfriend tried to pull that not-working stuff once, said he wasn't going fishing again because he couldn't keep a girlfriend when he was at sea. So she said she'd go fishing with him! Crabbing in the winter and . . . Ugh. It was awful. She can barely stand to think about it. Nobody did very well. She gets so sick of winter anyway, and then to not make any money . . .

"Dodge just lays around all day long," Julie explains, coat off now. She's twenty-five years old and has been married to Dodge for five years. She's petite and has a little-girl face.

"That's where I draw the line," Betty Jo says, exhaling cigarette smoke toward the ceiling. "I won't support a man who won't support himself."

"Lloyd's great," Julie says. "I mean, he loves it here. Fishing, all that. But Dodge barely leaves the apartment anymore. Mopes." Julie is doing trunk rotations. "Wow! Did you hear that?"

Betty Jo giggles, cringes at the cracking sound from Julie's back. "You've got to make love on top," she says.

"Huh?" Julie begins to bend backward, arms outstretched above her head.

"You've got to make love on top." Betty Jo laughs, her eyes bright with the thought. "It's good for your back, and his stomach!"

"I used to be in gymnastics but my back was always bad," Julie says. "It used to crack in the middle of my routines." She has lowered her hands gracefully to the floor and now speaks from a backbend position, her feet firm and her hands firm and her body an inverted U. She's thinking of Lloyd, her husband's friend Lloyd, who came to Kodiak with them from Idaho last fall. Sometimes it seems as though she's always thinking of Lloyd. Of his face, his voice, the way he stands like a cowboy on the heels of his fisherman boots.

"I don't know what it is," she says, easing back up. "I mean, I still love him and all." She means her husband Dodge.

"That's good," Betty Jo says, shifting on the stool, her eyes wandering along the ceiling to the restaurant in back, knowing just what Julie means and what she doesn't mean. "There's Lloydo himself," she says.

"Huh? Where?"

"There."

Julie looks but doesn't see. She says, "Oh," pretends a wave, feels her face get hot. She tries to continue where she left off. "I mean, I really don't care what Dodge does, as long as he does something. I just won't stand a man who doesn't do anything!"

Recoiling, reconsidering, Julie adds, "I mean, why should I? Would you?"

Betty Jo is examining the thumbnail on her right hand. She turns it this way and that, bringing it closer to her face, looking from her thumbnail, to Julie, to Lloyd (who has approached and now stands right behind the unwitting Julie with his arms above his head, eyebrows raised, like a playfully outraged bear) and then back to her thumbnail.

"No way, José," Betty Jo says, biting it.

8 AFTER FOURTEEN PULLS away with Silverwings drooling at her neck, Jack puts in a fresh chew of Copenhagen and turns up the radio until the Scottish bagpipe music rattles the speakers. He watches the sky across the harbor turn from gray to kind of purple just beneath the clouds. There's something intriguing about the color, the change, but Jack doesn't get to think about it because an old guy who looks like Moses sticks his head in the back door, hears the loud music, and says, "What the hell are you, some kind of religious fanatic?"

Jack says no and quickly turns down the radio.

Moses has a long white beard down to the middle of his chest, of course, and a pair of wild blue eyes. He giggles when he sits down, slaps his palms on the back of the front seat, and says, "What's your name, anyway? I like to know my drivers."

Jack tells him.

"Well, take me to the Beachcomber drinking establishment, Mr. Cliff." Moses sits back and spreads his skinny arms. "Hey, you don't happen to have any relatives in Wisconsin, do you?"

Jack radios his fare to Gil, the dispatcher, and turns left onto Marine Way, crossing past the Mecca, and then takes another left up Mission.

"Yes," he says.

"Ever know a guy named Kid Cliff, an old fisherman, dead now, the bastard?"

Jack waits for a few seconds before answering. He feels he's on the verge of a great truth but has no idea what to ask to learn it, and he's scared. It's the damn questions that are hard. The answer could be sitting in the back seat, but Jack doesn't know what to say.

Finally he says, "No."

"Too bad," Moses says. Then he tells a story about how thirty years ago he, Moses, sailed down to Mexico and Colón, Panama, with a New Jersey girl named Laura, and how he tried to whore her but she was plain no good at it. So he married her! This quiets him, the memory of the marriage, maybe, but he stops talking and begins tracing the outline of the window with his finger, around and around and around. Then he begins to hum; it's a hymn, something Jack's mother used to sing. Jack can't remember the name, or if he ever knew the name. Now Moses is singing:

> I liked her in satin
> I liked her in lace
> But I liked her best
> When she sat on my face.

Different lyrics than Lorraine sang. Jack drives north up the hill, over the rain-wet pavement, past the curbless curves, alder and cottonwood thickening in the too small gaps between houses. The road climbs and curves and then starts descending. To the east, and below them, is the channel separating Kodiak from Near Island. Mill Bay spreads out to the northeast, the light-gray waves near shore darkening almost to black along the horizon.

Moses stops his song and snaps his fingers. "Like that—I lost her. The

Lord's work. Apparently she weren't no good at having children, neither. Maybe that's why she was such a sorry-eyed, uncooperative bitch."

Jack has been waiting for the right moment to tell Moses that Kid Cliff was his dad, but now he feels he should say he's sorry the old man's wife died. He's just about to, but then he's worried about seeming *sorry-eyed*.

Finally, he says, "Huh."

"I've had my ins and outs with religion," the man says, matter-of-factly, "and that was one of my ins. I came to Kodiak a Pentecostal preacher. First year I was here it rained forty days and forty nights and didn't raise the sea level one hairy inch. Right then and there I lost it. I surrendered myself to relativity and doubt, and then promptly forgot about both of them! Chucked the Good Book in the bay here and went gill-netting. I became an honored member of the fisher-of-fish profession!"

The man raises his forefinger and announces, mockingly, laughingly, "Here's a truth for you: *The salmon wait for no man!*"

Moses gives Jack the creeps with his wild eyes and belly-length beard. Jack doesn't know what to say. He pulls into the Beachcomber parking lot.

"Four-fifty," he says. And then, while Moses digs for his wallet, Jack says, "Kid Cliff was my dad."

Moses looks at him, eyes clear and blue under a smooth forehead. "Your dad?"

"Yup."

"Your old man?" Moses is studying him.

"Yeah." Jack squirms in his seat.

"I thought you said you didn't know him."

"I didn't."

Moses pulls a five-dollar bill from his shirt pocket, fingers it, rolls it, smiles ironically. "So you're on a pilgrimage, eh?" He laughs, he-he, like a donkey. "A pilgrimage is pretending you're chasing something in order to make yourself think you're not running away from something else!" He laughs again. "Yeah, I've been on those before."

"You knew him?" Jack asks.

Moses looks Jack in the eye. "Fishing'll make a man out of you," he says. "Don't doubt it."

"Huh?"

"Get a job on a boat. Wrestle hundred-pound halibut all day and night for a week without sleep, and you won't be afraid of nothing."

Jack looks away. He doesn't know why he's afraid, or even what he's afraid of, and so it irritates him all the more that this guy knows he's scared.

"Your old man and I used to drink together," Moses says, his voice suddenly kind. "I can't tell you much besides that. But take my word for it, nobody can tell you much. We talked about fish and boats and women. You want a story? How's this: One time I saw your dad climb up a rigging and hang from the boom of a deck winch for an hour because somebody told him he couldn't. He hung there, by his hands, thirty feet above the deck!"

The memory makes Moses laugh, shake his head. "Does that tell you anything about your own soul?"

Moses opens the cab door, but before he steps out he says, "What would you say if I told you I kidnapped the Lindbergh baby?"

"I'd say big deal," Jack says. He's trying to act uninterested, tired, bored—anything not to look scared.

"Well, I did," Moses says. "I did kidnap the Lindbergh baby!"

"Big deal." Jack wants to grab this old guy and hold him. He doesn't want him to get away. He's not the first person Jack's met who knew Kid Cliff, but he's the first who seems to understand the vanity of Jack's search, something Jack has begun to suspect himself, something he read in the stupidly sincere faces he saw those first days in town when he was asking everybody he met about his father. Jack saw where Kid lived. He saw where his boat, *Dempsey II,* had been docked. Jack drank where his dad drank and spent his first night in Kodiak passed out drunk on the sidewalk. Maybe his dad did that. Probably. The old bartender at the Pier Pub had been very nice. But so what? Jack was learning stories, but they were his father's stories. Not his. And they made things more complicated instead of simpler. It occurs to Jack, sitting in his cab outside the Beachcomber Bar at 9:00 P.M., Memorial Day, 1983, Moses himself with one foot in and one foot out the back door, that the story he's searching for is his own. Go home. Go back to the farm. Get a ride back to your camp after work in the morning, roll up your bag and your tent, hitchhike out to the airport, and catch the first plane to Seattle. Then home from there.

Could he? Sure he could. Before he left Wisconsin, he'd thought about getting a herd of Guernseys together. Dairy could make the farm pay. He'd walk into the house and say hello to Mary, sit down at the kitchen table, and take whatever came. He'd live slowly, day by day. Build the story of his life. He'd be brave; he'd be patient and kind. He'd be a good man.

Moses winks, tosses the curled-up five-dollar bill onto the front seat.

"Doubts," he says. "Demons. Little niggling bastards, aren't they? You have to take what you do know and make up the rest, Mr. Jack Cliff. It's a delightful game! Learn to do that, and you won't give a shit about me or what I say!"

Jack looks at his bare hands on the steering wheel. Although there's no escape from the past, there's no catching it either. Is that what the old man is saying? Is what's important whatever Jack Dempsey Cliff decides to make important?

"Listen," Moses says, nodding toward the bar, lifting his nose like a dog and sniffing the wet night air. "Any ladies in there?"

"A few," Jack says.

The old man's nostrils flare, his blue eyes sparkle as he takes another deep breath. "Ooooooh," he says, letting it all out at once. "Ever notice? A good woman smells a lot like kelp."

JACK DRIVES AROUND the block and then takes a call from the dispatcher to pick up a fare at 1818 Mission. He drops down the steep cutoff road, turns south along the lake where a mist rises when the mornings are clear and cool, and passes the Russian Orthodox seminary along the levee, a log building in a cluster of spruce where during the day Hereford cows graze the new green grass. He rounds the bay where last Monday he pulled four beautiful pink and blue Dolly Vardens out of the leaden water in time for dinner, and he slows down where the congested Beachcomber parking lot melds with the road. He drives another half block and turns into the short driveway of the little house squeezed between a liquor store and another little house, between the road and the ocean. He's been here before on calls, a couple of times every night. Jack knocks quickly on the front door, then gets back into his cab to wait out of the rain.

Jack doesn't recognize him at first, but as the man steps down and walks around the front of the cab, and Jack sees the red-and-black plaid coat, he knows it's Donald Sutherland again. Before opening the door, Donald depresses a nostril with his finger and sprays the gravel driveway. Leaving his scent, Jack thinks.

Donald gets into the back seat. He looks as if he's just left the doctor's office with bad news. His brow is furrowed and his lips pout. He looks like a disappointed little boy, but he's not little.

"Oh, criminy," Donald says.

Jack doesn't say anything. He expects that the next thing he will hear is Donald crying. Donald squints at Jack for a second and doesn't cry, but says, "You the same guy?"

"Yeah."

"Frick-shit, wouldn't you know it."

Jack sniffs and feels his shirt pocket for a handkerchief. He blows his nose and waits.

"In case you're wondering," Donald says, "I just spent the worst two hundred bucks I ever spent."

Jack lets that sit. Donald is fidgeting around in the back seat, then he settles, staring out the window, his elbow on the armrest, chin in his hand.

"You want to go to town?"

"Huh? Yeah. Take me down there somewhere. I don't give a gadzoo."

Jack turns on the wipers and backs up. The cab groans as it climbs on Mission. Jack thinks about the bad injectors Harry told him about, and the fear Moses told him about, and how a guy could learn the king's secrets driving a cab. Or if he didn't learn the secrets, he could learn enough to make them up. He stays well to the right on the narrow, winding road. The night is dark gray now and the rain suddenly heavy. Jack is very far from Wisconsin, and even farther from Florida, where he's never been. There's a guy sitting the back seat who's in from the sea with a lot of bucks, doing what men in from the sea with a lot of bucks have always done, or at least have always thought of doing. That's okay, that's fine. But the thing is, when you're young and rich and high-flying, everything is supposed to be so great.

In the rearview, Jack can see Donald unwrap some tinfoil, then take a rolled-up ten-dollar bill from behind his ear, stick one end in his nose and the other in the tinfoil.

Donald chuckles when he sees Jack watching. "Alaska State Vegetable," he says. "Who the frick needs lines?" His eyes blink when he sniffs the coke. Then his fingers close around the foil, and the bill goes from his nose to behind his ear again.

Emmylou Harris is whining sweet crying notes on the radio.

"You got good taste in tapes," Donald says. "She's my honey."

"This is the radio."

"Whatever. Emmylou, I love you!"

Jack says yeah. Her voice makes everything seem okay.

"Hey!" Donald says. "I gotta get drunk again."

"Yeah?"

"Whoofrickingpee!"

"What?"

"Whoofrickingpee! How's Tony's?"

Jack's driving down the hill past the Russian Orthodox church. "Pretty good."

"What the hell, take me to Tony's."

"You bet."

"Does Tony's have a country-western band, or is that Solly's."

"Solly's."

Jack turns the corner and heads past the Mecca, pulls into the mall parking lot and crosses over in front of Solly's and Tony's. Donald drops the ten-dollar bill over the seat. "Keep it, partner. You're all right. How's Solly's?"

"Pretty decent." Emmylou's voice soars and takes Jack with it. He imagines Kodiak shrinking through the plane window as he speeds toward the bounty of a Wisconsin summer. He can see a white house and a red barn, cows speckling the valley, their soft noses buried in the thick green grass of the front pasture. He can see a woman in the yard, Mary. This is his life. He can invent it. He can make it happen.

Donald gets out but lingers by the open door. He looks as if he's going to cry again, so Jack tells him a joke he heard from a man stiff with the pain of a fresh Chinese-warlord tattoo on his back. The guy said he thought of this joke whenever he needed a laugh: A married man goes to a banquet, meets a young lady, and spends the night with her. Next morning he walks into his house, and his wife asks where he's been. "Well," the man says, "I was coming in last night and I spotted the hammock in the backyard, and since it was such a nice night I slept out there." His wife looks at him long and hard and reminds him that they took that hammock down four months ago. "I don't care," the man says, stepping briskly past her. "That's my story and I'm sticking to it."

This cracks Donald up, and he laughs looking upward so the rain hits his face. "That's great," he says, "that's great. You know any more?"

Jack says not really any jokes, but he just heard something funny.

"What's that?"

"This old guy who looks like Moses just told me he kidnapped the Lindbergh baby."

"Really? Huh." Donald looks confused. "Didn't baby Moses float down the river in a basket?"

Jack had forgotten about that, but he nods.

Donald furrows his brow. "I don't get it. Then who the frick is the Lindbergh baby?"

"Nothing," Jack says. "Nobody. This famous guy's baby is all."

Donald throws his arms up and tilts his head back and lets the drizzle hit his face again. He shakes his head. "Jeez, man. I gotta get rowdy, don't I? I gotta wake up."

9 LONDA EVENS, FORMERLY Linda Evens, from Little Rock, Arkansas, is leaving her house after dinner with a musician named Johnny Stone, formerly Johnny Johnstone, from Billings, Montana. They are getting into the back of a cab.

Johnny is saying, "I like Joplin because she's the ultimate burnout.

She's a standard, you know, something I can always compare myself to and think, Well, I'm still okay."

"Yeah," Londa says, distracted. She tries to roll the window down but finds that it's stuck. She could use a cigarette. She's a barmaid at the Mecca Bar and Restaurant. Her hair is thick and black, and her face is pretty but made up too heavily. She's hoping the baby-sitter doesn't leave the burner on under the new fry pan, and there isn't a fire, and her four-year-old daughter, Esther, doesn't burn to death.

"The coke made me want to go so much longer," Johnny says. His band is on world tour. It's booked at the Mecca in Kodiak for two months, then South Korea for three weeks, Australia for a month, and India for two more.

"I mean, I think I was fine," he says. "I felt fine. I thought I was okay, you know?"

"You were as good as anyone." Londa smiles at him for the first time, and then looks out the window at the passing houses, irregularly shaped, yardless, surrounded by makeshift fences and clusters of brush and trees along Mission Road. She wishes she could get the window down because she really wants to smoke. She wishes she didn't have to go to work. She wishes Johnny would quit stopping by in the evening and riding in with her every night. She thinks she might get drunk if she didn't have to go to work. She thinks she might fall in love again. There would be no end to the possibilities if she didn't have to work, and if Johnny would get lost.

"I didn't want to stop when they were ready," Johnny says. "I wanted to keep playing. I felt damn good."

They are driving south down the hill into town. To the left, and below them, are the big canneries along the Near Island channel. Soon they are passing the ferry dock. Londa remembers how excited she'd been when she and Esther came in on the ferry. Sometimes she wants to leave the island just so she can come back again. Once, in Arkansas, she left Esther with her mother and skipped work to drive all night down to the Gulf, to Biloxi. She just *had* to see the ocean.

"You were fine," she says to Johnny. "You really were."

"You thought so? I'm glad, because I was pretty loaded. I felt great. I thought I was okay."

They are going slow now, through town. Only a block and a half until they arrive, but Londa can't stand it anymore. She searches her purse for cigarettes. When she returned to Little Rock from the Gulf, her husband, Paul, was still on his binge. Two weeks later she came to Alaska with Esther. It was all on a whim. And Esther! Talk about excited.

"That's super," Johnny says, squeezing her knee. "Because I felt damn good."

Londa has the cigarette between her lips. Thank God the hand on her knee is as far as he's been, she thinks. It's certainly as far as he's going to get.

Johnny reaches over to light her cigarette. He's smiling, showing the dimples on his cheeks. Her eyes moving this way and that, her foot tap-tapping the floor of the cab, Londa takes a deep drag and exhales toward the window. She watches the smoke hit the glass and make a cloud around the driver's head just as he pulls to the curb in front of the Mecca.

10 THE NIGHT IS busy, one call after another. Jack's cab smells of Londa's cigarette smoke, and his pockets are tight with money. A roll of bills in one, a pound of change in the other. He orders fish and french fries at the Beachcomber but gets dispatched to 1818 Mission again while waiting for the food. He picks up Evey and Marie and begins to drive them across town to Alder for a house call. Both wear stylish dresses, a lot of jewelry, and high, thick-heeled shoes. They look very nice, Evey and Marie. A little tired but kind of sophisticated, like chesty models. Their conversation covers a wide range of topics, such as:

How Marie cut her bottom on the spring sticking out of the seat padding in the last cab she rode in.

How she should be able to sue the cab company for a lot of money, but the legal system is fucked so she probably wouldn't get a penny.

How Evey's getting too skinny.

How Marie's a smoker, so even though she's in good shape she doesn't jog well.

How Evey has given up gin because of her stomach, but when someone offers to buy, well, what's she supposed to say?

How Marie is glad she doesn't have that problem.

How they all ought to jog together, get matching sweatsuits that say Eighteen Eighteen Camp for Girls and jog early in the morning along the bay.

How they could make up hilarious songs to sing while they ran.

How Marie wishes she could get a nice tan.

How Evey doesn't think Marie needs a tan, being Mexican, or whatever.

How the pizza they had for dinner wasn't sitting well with Evey.

How pepperoni will do that sometimes, but Evey should maybe go to a doctor for her stomach if it stays bad.

Then Marie says to Jack, "Haven't I seen you someplace before?"

"I ate a cheeseburger next to you at Solly's yesterday." It's true, but it's also true that he threw himself on the floor to look up her dress at the Pier Pub, his first night in town. He doesn't mention that.

"A what?" Marie asks Evey. "What did he say?"

"He said a cheeseburger."

"At Solly's," Jack says. Just thinking about it makes his mouth water again. "I was sitting behind you guys yesterday. That's the last thing I've eaten."

"What are you, fasting?" Marie asks.

"No," Jack says. "Just working and sleeping, I guess. You were eating clams."

"Oh," Marie says.

"Were they good?"

"What?" Marie asks Evey. "What's he saying?"

"He wants to know if the clams were good."

"Yeah," Marie says. "They were fine. You know, something's wrong with your car. Noisy!"

"Bad injectors," Jack says.

"Bad what?"

"Bad injectors."

"Injectors?" She giggles. "That's awful!"

There's a short pause. Jack's got food on the brain. "The clams sound great but I always get the cheeseburger. Best deal in town."

"You mean when you're not sleeping or going around with a bad injector!" Marie laughs. "You really ought to eat something besides cheeseburgers, you know."

"I do."

"What?"

"He eats something besides cheeseburgers," Evey says to Marie.

"Yeah, I heard him," Marie says. "That's very nice to know, but—"

"I like spaghetti too," Jack says.

"Clams are best," Marie says. "I really think you should try the clams."

"Clams are expensive."

"Damn right they are," Marie says. Then, "Oh, *now* I know where I've seen you!"

After he'd thrown himself on the floor between her legs that first night at the Pier Pub, Jack traced with his finger the inside of her calf and thigh up toward her black underwear. She could have stepped on his face but she didn't. Instead she said, *That's an expensive touch,* and he said, *No problem, I'll do it for free,* and she stepped away, over him, smiled nicely but said, *You're broke, right? Well, I work for a living.*

Then Jack stood up and walked back to the bar, stared again at the wall above the mirror, at the photograph of the Kodiak Island Boxing Champion, July 4, 1953. It was a close-up of Kid Cliff's face, so everything but his immediate features was slightly out of focus. The light gray of his cheeks melded with the lighter gray behind, until in some places Jack couldn't tell where the man began and the background ended. His head tilted forward so his dark-gray eyes looked up almost seductively from under bushy eyebrows, shiny hair combed neatly back and plastered close to his head. A suppressed smile curled the corners of his pale lips.

Jack stood at the bar and looked at the picture and imagined his father hearing laughter. The irony galled him. There he was, Kid Cliff, just three weeks after he'd left his wife and infant son in Wisconsin. A soldier, a farmer, a fisherman, dirty tattoos plastered the length of his body, and hands—the bartender told Jack—he had hands like chunks of raw meat. Sure he did.

Yet in his photograph for posterity they had him looking like John Barrymore.

In the cab, Jack can see Marie's dark eyes staring at him in the rearview mirror. Last time he was lucky to get away unhurt. This time he's got money to lose.

"Boy," he says, "I'm hungry."

She smiles. "That's your problem, mister."

"You know," Evey says, "if I drink just one glass of OJ when I get up, then I don't have to eat again until evening, sometimes never."

"Listen to her," Marie says to Jack. "She's worse than you with your cheeseburgers. She's going to starve herself."

Jack says that he heard on the radio that a person can be overweight and still starve to death without the right vitamins and stuff.

Evey says that hunger can be gotten over with your brain—there's a point where you don't care anymore—and besides, her stomach hurts even more when she eats.

Marie says she's heard about that brain stuff, but doesn't see much point in it or think anybody should push it.

Evey's sister had cancer and meditated her way out of it.

Marie can't even imagine that shit.

Evey says that a person never knows what he or she can do until faced with one of those big things.

Marie says that's true but still.

Evey doesn't have time to see a doctor anyway, at least not a stomach doctor.

Marie says she's feeling good tonight, feeling invincible.

That reminds Evey of the time someone laid a line of coke along the entire length of the Pier Pub bar.

Jack says he heard that too.

Evey says, "I could use a good bump right now, that's for sure."

At Alder, Jack drops them off and watches as they hustle up to the house. Under the porch light by the front door, Evey sags, puts a hand on her bony hip. Jack wonders if she's dying—and then he can see in the dark hollow under her eyes that she probably is. Marie lights a cigarette.

She lets it dangle from her mouth while she giggles and straightens Evey's pale lavender dress.

GIL, THE DISPATCHER, has radioed Jack that the Beachcomber called and his fish and fries are ready to be picked up. His stomach hurts. He drives toward town, fast because he thinks he might start drooling. He thinks about the guy he met with the Chinese-warlord tattoo on his back and wonders if anybody ever gets a hamburger-and-french-fry tattoo. He wonders if Evey's stomach feels like this all the time. He takes a left on Mill Bay and is starting up the hill when he sees three people on the side of the road raise their hands to flag him down. Jesus. He wants to drive by, but it's raining and he can't.

They're Filipinos. Filipinos never tip and some of the cabbies won't pick them up, but Jack likes them, generally. These three smell funny. The old man wiggles his nose like a rabbit and can't even get into the cab. He keeps stepping up onto the seat, so the women, maybe his daughters, show him where to step so he can sit down. Foot on the floor, now lowering his hips, twisting slightly—that's it—ducking the rest of his body through the door, yes, and sitting. Poor guy must be sick or something. Only three fingers and a thumb on one hand, two and a thumb on the other. Maybe he's never been in a car, but that's ridiculous. What is it they smell like? Some kind of greasy vegetable or spaghetti-fed dog meat. Eating dogs is the one thing he doesn't like about Filipinos. But it's possible the old guy was at the Death March and saved Kid Cliff's life and was crippled by a Jap bayonet. Tortured. It could be Jack owes his life to this old man. It could be, and yet there's no way of knowing. Only doubting, of course. Millions of things could have happened to keep Jack from being born, to keep him from living as long as he's lived (thirty years in some cultures is old age), yet here he is anyway! When he thinks about the odds against any specific person being born . . . against himself . . . well, he's either a miracle or a fluke. But if certainly Jack is (and he is), when the odds were so stacked against his even being born, then this old man who probably didn't save Kid Cliff's life certainly could have saved Kid Cliff's life. And therefore he saved Jack.

For if this old Filipino's great-great-grandmother had died of some disease along with the rest of her family when she was ten, then she would never have become the mother of X, who became the mother of Y, who became the mother of Z, who became the mother of this old guy, who saved Kid Cliff's life by giving him water during the Death March, sure, an act that cost him three fingers, which allowed Kid Cliff to make the sperm that he would eventually deposit in Lorraine one autumn evening when nothing else in the world mattered except the sweaty union of two mortals in an upstairs bedroom of a Wisconsin farmhouse. And now here is Jack, sitting in his cab *not* not-being. A possible fluke, but he just can't chuck the possibility of a miracle either. Like the ideas of falling in love and being happy, the idea of a miracle is tenacious as hell.

Mary could still be in Wisconsin. Mary could be waiting for him. . . . Maybe Jack came to Alaska to realize only this: there's no such thing as an answer, only hope.

But there's more, he thinks. Of course. Kodiak is his father. He came here to put his face against his father's strong chest, feel his father's arms wrap around his back and shoulders. And more too, which perhaps is the problem. His father is dead. Jack came to Kodiak to dig a grave and bury him.

But how? he thinks. And where? And how will he even know when he has?

All three passengers are dressed in their go-to-cannery clothes— rubber boots, colorful scarves, sweatshirts, cloth gloves on their laps. Maybe the old man is farting and that's what the smell is. He's wiggling his nose like a rabbit, so perhaps he smells it too. His daughter has to pronounce the name of the cannery three times before Jack can understand. Jack's very polite—*What's that, ma'am? What's that, ma'am? Oh yes, ma'am*—imagining the sound of a bayonet slicing off a finger, another finger, another finger. The sound a man makes. Is enduring pain in itself an act of bravery? Is dying? Or is bravery *risking* pain, *risking* death for what you love or believe in? And where does Kid Cliff stand in all this? Did he sacrifice Lorraine and Jack, long before he came home from the prison camps, in order to survive? Or did he sacrifice himself by leaving one sunny day in June 1953 so that *they* could survive? Was it painful for him? Or easy? Was he lonely? Or simply forgetful?

The questions. They go on and on. After the Death March, Kid Cliff had three and a half more years of starvation and capricious torture to endure. Would the fingers of the heroic old Filipino man have been wasted if Kid Cliff had died on the Hell Ship to Japan, throat slit by a thirsty comrade? Those things happened. There are lots of people who weren't born because their fathers died on those ships in 1944, regardless of any heroism or providence that might have kept them alive until then. Does Jack's existence validate the old man's sacrifice? *Don't think of it!* They can ride for free, sure, and Jack himself is going to help the old man out of the cab.

In a book Jack read about the Death March, a veteran told about a thirty-year reunion of survivors back in the Philippines. Hanging on the side of their bus was a banner that said, *Defenders of Bataan*. When the Filipinos read that, even the children, they held up their fingers in a V. "What do those kids know about us?" one of the veterans asked the bus driver, who answered, "Joe, they may not know English, or how to read and write, but they know about Bataan."

No matter how strange this old guy is, Jack thinks, if it weren't for him I wouldn't be alive. Sentimentality can be as seductive as pornography, so thinking this is irresistible, and by now Jack's almost convinced of its truth. Oh boy. It pleases him no end to feel goose bumps rising on the back of his neck. Sitting in the back seat between a couple of Asian princesses is a veritable king, a mortal god, a nose-twitching rabbit of a seven-fingered man in whose common-suffering corpse-reek lies the naked seeds of miracles. Yessir.

When they arrive at the cannery, Jack hops out and runs around to open the door. He lends a hand to one of the princesses, but she's already standing, so he bends to help the king. Standing next to him now, on the gravel, Jack leans over and whispers "Bataan" into the royal ear. The king cocks his head, straining to hear. One of the princesses points to her own ear, then to the king's.

Jack whispers it again, *Bataan,* louder; then, thumb to his chest, Jack points at himself.

Wrinkling his nose, sniffing, shuffling uncomfortably, finally the king breaks into a grin. Jack feels flushed. King extends his three-fingered hand, and Jack shakes it, thinking of miracles and torn flesh, falling in love with dog meat.

"José," the old man says. "Vedy, vedy fine, thank you."

11

JACK PARKS NEXT to the Beachcomber door and has to step through a puddle to get out of the cab, but he hardly thinks about it. He dashes in for his food and in a moment he's back out with a paper plate loaded with chunks of steamy halibut and french fries. He steps through the puddle again and again doesn't think about it. The deep-fried fish looks fresh and moist, and Jack sits behind the wheel with the plate on his lap. He's so excited to eat he can hardly stand it. He's got a little plastic cup of tartar sauce on one side of the plate and another of ketchup balanced on the other side. He rubs his hands together, leans over his meal, feels the steam, the warmth on his face. He picks up a piece of halibut with his thumb and forefinger. He dips it into the tartar sauce to the perfect depth, so that when he pulls it out just the right amount of sauce forms a white nipple on the golden-brown chunk of fish. It's beautiful, really, this food, this halibut. He'd never eaten it before he came to Kodiak. It looks beautiful and smells beautiful. What a wonderful, lovely place, Kodiak. He measures his movements, aware of the weight of his body, the feel of his face, his mouth, his tongue. He lifts the halibut and takes a bite, holds it before swallowing, savors the warmth, the taste, the rush of saliva. This, he thinks, is happiness.

Is anyone at the Beach? says the radio voice.

Jack picks up his microphone and says, with his mouth full, "Sixteen is, A-One."

Check inside for a fare, Sixteen. Somebody called without bothering to look outside.

"Roger, A-One." Jack takes one more bite of fish, then he sets the plate on the seat.

He gets out, steps in the puddle again (this time it irritates him), and checks out the bar. Nobody seems to be looking for him, and the music is very loud. The band, headed by a blond woman wearing a silver-spangled unitard, plays one of the same crashing songs it plays every night, a song about fantasy, about this being a fantasy life.

Jack asks the bartender if anyone called a cab. The bartender says yes, two guys, but he doesn't know where they went. Jack stands at the bar and lets his eyes adjust to the dark room. He notices the rough wood furniture, the lines and seines and other accoutrements of fishing that hang from the ceiling. Just when he's about to leave, he sees Fourteen sitting by herself at a table; a couple of yellow oilskin raincoats drape the other chairs. She must have seen him right away, because she's smiling, waving, looking impatient. She's taken the bandanna off her head, and her hair hangs straight down to her shoulders.

Jack walks up to her and says hello, asks where her cab is; he hadn't seen it outside.

"I quit," she says.

"You what?" Jack isn't sure he hears her because the music is so loud.

"I quit!" She's grinning, showing all her teeth, but Jack can see she's not happy.

Jack gives her a curious look, trying to avoid yelling another question. Why did she quit? Because she was tired of predators like Silverwings? Did Mr. Sharkskin La Cruz have a role in this? Or did she quit because guys like Jack never bothered to learn her name?

Fourteen shrugs.

Jack looks past her at the band, where the blond singer kneels on the stage in front of her no- and semi-shirted musical brethren. Clutching the microphone passionately, she appears to be quivering, just milliseconds away from orgasm. Should he tell Fourteen that this might be his last shift? Should he tell her he wants to go home? No. How can he do that? She thinks his home is Florida.

"I'm looking for a couple of fares," Jack yells, suddenly feeling awkward.

Fourteen waves him away, still smiling bravely. "Well, go look, then!"

Outside, two men stand at the driver's-side door of Jack's cab, the same two guys Jack saw climb out of a pickup and shuffle across the parking lot to The Ships bar earlier in the evening. One is Larry Laarson, the skipper everyone wants to fish with. The other is thick-necked, bearded, slightly bald on top. Jack recognizes him as the bar hanger-outer whom Claire calls The Philosopher. It's Neil Pasternak.

The two of them are hunched over a paper plate full of fish and fries. Neil holds the plate between them. He's chewing madly, cheeks bulging. He smiles when he sees Jack, and uses the back of his wrist to wipe his mouth. Larry snorts laughter through his nose.

"You the guys who need a cab?" Jack asks, not noticing the puddle now because he's looking ahead to the car and the car window and the car seat, the empty car seat where he put his food.

"Yeah." Neil sees where Jack is looking. He shrugs his shoulders and half turns. Then he hands the plate to Jack. "We're snarfing your food, man. Sorry."

Jack takes the plate. The ketchup and tartar sauce have been poured out of their plastic cups and smeared all over. The fries and fish are half gone. Larry and Neil crowd together like sheepish dogs, Larry still snickering.

"Oh hell," Jack says, sitting down.

Neil and Larry linger near the open car door.

"Sorry, man," Neil says.

"I can't believe it," Jack says.

"We were wrong, weren't we, Ho?" Neil says, a french fry sticking in his beard. "We're sorry, man."

Larry giggles. He's the drunker of the two by far. Tartar sauce makes a stripe on his cheek. He's tugging on Neil's sleeve, trying to pull him away.

Neil says to Jack, "Can we catch a ride out to Naughton's anyway, partner?"

Jack stares into the messy plate on his lap. He can't see anything but the already eaten food and the smeared-together ketchup and tartar sauce. He wants to cry.

"Hey, cabbie," Neil says, head daring to come closer. "Can we catch a ride out to Naughton's trailers? Huh? What say, man?"

"Here." Jack shows him the plate. "You can have the rest."

"Oh, no, man." Neil waves his hand in front of his face. "No. We just wanted a few bites. Thanks. You eat it. We just want a ride."

"No, you take it." Jack is sitting behind the steering wheel, but the door is open and his feet are on the ground. "Here."

Neil looks over his shoulder at Larry. "Goddamn, Ho. You want the rest?" Larry shrugs. Neil shrugs, then smiles a *much obliged* smile at Jack.

Jack looks at Neil's face and sees in the wide brow, in the eager smile, all his own phony hopes and expectations for Kodiak, for everything he asked Kodiak to give him, to forgive him for. A little taste, a quick dip, and . . .

Neil is leaning closer, expecting the remnants, expecting a ride, expecting forgiveness. Jack's holding the plate out for him.

Neil steps forward.

Did Jack really think he'd learn something by coming to Kodiak? Did he fool himself into thinking he could embrace the ghost of his father, and finally, finally be a happy little boy? When he was thirteen he bought an album called *Great Moments in Sports*. On it was a recording of a radio announcer describing Dempsey's seventh-round assault on Tunney, vicious and swift, during their famous "long count" fight. On the album cover was a black-and-white photo of Dempsey with his arms at his sides, standing over the fallen Tunney. Jack knew the knock-down sequence by heart. *Tunney jabs, jabs again, and Dempsey . . . Dempsey moves in with a right. Dempsey connects with a right! Oh my! And then another right to the head. And Tunney is hurt! He's against the ropes. Tunney is down. He's down! Dempsey hit him with two solid rights, and Tunney is down. And the count is . . . the count is . . . Oh my! Dempsey is standing there and the count is . . . He won't go back to the corner! I don't believe it! Oh my!*

Jack shadowboxed until he sweat, following the choreography, yelling *Oh my!* with the announcer's gravel voice, yelling *Oh my!* and trying to stand with his arms at his sides like Dempsey. He couldn't get enough. He listened to the record over and over again. Dempsey stood there, just stood there, refusing to go back to the neutral corner, so the count started late and Tunney got up just before the count of ten—even though he'd been down for at least fifteen seconds. And then Tunney went on to win the fight! Why had Dempsey delayed? Why? Jack's head swirled, drugged by exertion and the promise of self-discovery. This is what his father loved, he told himself, this eager, vicious man. This was Kid's dream of survival. This is my name, this is my name.

Neil steps closer now, just past the edge of the open car door. He reaches for the plate of fish Jack holds out for him, his face like a dog's.

Jack looks from Neil to the plate to the picked-over food. He doesn't want it. His wonderful, lovely idea of Kodiak, his hope of learning something true from a place so far from home, his dream of magically feeling happy, is suddenly stupid. It's a lie. It's a mess.

Now, Jack thinks.

He explodes like a coiled spring, a rocket, a bursting blasting bomb—*Jack Dempsey Cliff, Kodiak Island Boxing Champion, 1983!* He throws the plate and lunges out of his seat toward Neil's moving face, Neil's backpedaling body. He lunges until he's fully extended and his elbows lock and the corner of the open car door jabs him sharply between the ribs.

"Aaahh!" He recoils, doubled over against the spearing pain in his side.

Neil and Larry tiptoe quickly past a puddle to get to another cab, just now pulling into the lot.

Sixteen, A-One says, over the cab radio.

Jack's wrist hurts. It scraped against who knows what. He's still doubled over, trying to crab walk the step or two back to his car seat.

Sixteen, A-One says again.

Jack sits. He reaches for the mike. "This is Sixteen. Go ahead."

Sixteen, did you find the guys who called?

"Roger, A-One. I gave them to Claire."

Thank you, Sixteen, Claire says over the radio. She's smiling at Jack, waving through her windshield, as Larry and Neil climb into the back of her cab.

Sixteen, are you okay? A-One asks.
"Roger, A-One."
Because you don't sound very good.

JACK TAKES THE stairs three at a time, then strides down the long hallway to the office. The room is well-lighted and cluttered with jackets, books, magazines, boots, and food. Food. Jack pours himself a cup of coffee, gets somebody's Oreos out of the refrigerator, and sits down hard in the chair next to Gil's desk. The blood on his wrist has made his sleeve red. His father is a dead man. Jack is going home. The hell with it. There's nothing to bury, there's nothing to love, nothing to cry for. There's nothing.

Gil's on the phone; he smiles, big frontiersman mustache covering all but his bottom teeth. He pulls a joint out of his shirt pocket, twists the ends, and—lowering the phone and raising his eyebrows—he mouths the word "Medicine?"

Jack nods. He places a whole Oreo in his mouth and lets his saliva melt it, doesn't even chew. He grabs a piece of paper towel and presses down on his wrist. The towel turns red. Jack grabs about a yard of paper towel, balls it up, and presses.

Gil hangs up, makes a note on a piece of scrap paper, and then says, "What you got there, a cut?"

"Scrape."

"How'd you do that?"

"Tried to kill a guy."

Gil laughs, swivels, and leans back in his chair. He lights the joint.

Jack sucks on another Oreo. His wrist hurts, but he feels better. Mary told him before he left that it would be painful to go to Kodiak. She said there'd be nothing to it, and that's what would hurt so much. Jack wonders if she knew what she was talking about or if it was just a lucky guess. He wants to call her right now. He wants to tell her he loves her and he's sorry and . . . and he's coming home tomorrow.

Gil exhales, then smiles and passes the joint to Jack. "I don't know," he says, meaninglessly, spinning a pencil between his palms. "Some nights I can just feel how it is."

Jack takes a toke and passes the joint back. He dips a third Oreo into his coffee and eats it soggy. Gil has a smooth voice, an intimate way about him that puts Jack at ease.

Claire has come into the office and is rummaging through a box on the floor. "Anybody seen my apples?"

"Not me."

"How's that arm?"

"Fine. I was trying to murder your friend The Philosopher-Thief."

"I saw." Claire smiles and pinches Jack's cheek. "But you're such a sweetie you cut yourself instead."

"It's nothing. Look." Jack removes the wad of paper and lifts his wrist. The bleeding has stopped but Claire's already in the other room, the locker room.

"Hey, what happened to Fourteen?" Jack asks Gil. "Why did she quit?"

"All I know," Gil says, "is that she walked in here about an hour ago and dropped off her keys."

"Did she say anything?" Claire stands in the doorway now, shining an apple on her pant thigh.

"Who am I to ask questions?" Gil says.

"You're such a brave, bold man," Claire says, pushing a stray curl behind her ear with the back of her wrist. "I hope she's okay."

"Hey," Gil says to Claire. "You ever get the feeling you're just this small speck, and the universe is big, huge . . . out there somewhere?" He winks at Jack and takes another toke.

"Not lately," she answers.

"I saw her at the Beach," Jack says. "She seemed okay." He sips his coffee and shakes his head to the offered joint. He eats another cookie. Fourteen quit and he'll never see her again, so what difference does it make if he knows her name? He won't ask. He feels bad that she quit because the truth is she didn't seem okay.

"I'll take some of that." Claire reaches for the joint.

"You know, Claire," Gil says, eyes twinkling, "when I'm high, or I mean, when I'm not high, there's nothing. Going to bed, there's nothing. Waking up, there's nothing. Working on my truck, there's nothing! Doing sex there's something, but how long does that last?" Gil coughs and laughs at the same time. He takes the joint back from Claire and squeezes the lighted end closed with saliva-wet fingers, slides it back into his shirt pocket. "You know what I'm saying?"

Claire exhales, takes a bite of her apple. "You're depressing, Gil."

The weight of the cookies feels good in Jack's stomach. He gets up to refill his coffee cup.

Leaning back in his chair, lifting his palms, Gil squints at the fluorescent light on the ceiling. "Hey, but when I'm high, there *is* something. Even though it may only be my imagination, there most definitely is *something*! And it's huge. And it's not me!"

Claire rolls her eyes, says to Jack, "You think he likes pot, or what?"

Jack laughs, throws the paper towel across the room into the wastebasket. "Bango!" It's what the radio announcer used to say when a player on the Milwaukee Bucks hit a jump shot.

Claire gives him a thumbs-up.

The phone rings, and Gil leans forward to get it. He dispatches a cab over the radio, records the trip with his pencil. Claire takes another bite of apple and waves good-bye to Jack.

Gil points after her with the pencil, says to Jack, "Seriously, what she doesn't realize, what none of you realize . . . Hey, I was in finance, Jack. I was making forty-five grand, and that's Outside money, not Alaska money. I went to fucking London once on a business trip. Me! I was a fairly big shot, and I chucked it all. I don't know about you—you had a farm, didn't you?—but most of these people didn't have crap when they came up here. They might have crap plus change when they leave. I don't know. Do I regret it? Hey, I'm just trying to figure it out! My first year up here it took me a while to understand that people don't show up or do things when they say they will. Or they quit and are never heard of again. I mean, I understood, and I thought it was cool and all . . . but I really didn't *understand*."

Jack nods, watching Gil's face. He doesn't understand what Gil is talking about, but that's okay. Gil is from California, and Jack wants to ask something about California, but he can't think of anything to ask. Then, for some reason, Jack pictures a bullet striking that high forehead, where too much skin is exposed just below the cowlick. He remembers how when JFK was shot the brains splattered across the trunk of the car and the front of Jackie's pink dress. The thought frightens him, the way he can casually think it and not need to gag or anything.

"But hey," Gil continues innocently, "here's an example for you: This afternoon I was at the Mecca with Sharon. Remember Sharon? Well, she left and told me I should meet her at the K.I. Well, it starts to rain so I buy a drink and start talking to this guy. Suddenly I realize there's another place I'm supposed to be. I'm at one place, and yet I'm supposed to be at another. Ever feel that way?"

Jack nods again, and keeps eating, but smiles. He doesn't remember ever not feeling that way. Even now, he's thinking of packing up his clothing, rolling his bag and tent, lifting his home onto his shoulders and following the shaded path back out of the forest to the highway, then hitching to the airport. He's thinking of being in one place and going to another.

"Well, it's a dilemma of Time and Space, that's all," Gil says. "A physical impossibility that precludes and nullifies ethics. So do I worry about it? No! I think, By the time I get to the K.I. she'll be gone. So I stay where I am, and then I'm buying another drink and talking to this real interesting guy who's studying the bears. A scientist. Very into empirical-type stuff, interesting as hell. Oh, I'll run into Sharon later; tomorrow, maybe. But it's possible she'll go home to Saint Louis and I'll never see her again! Either way, we'll probably never mention what happened."

Jack likes the bright white light of the office, the cluttered desk and the walls tacked with announcements. He wants to remember it always. He likes Gil, and he likes the cookies. They've calmed him. Can a cookie make you happy? *Yeah, Mom, the bleeding has stopped and I ate a whole bag of Oreos, so now I'm happy as hell. Yes, fine, fine—except a little while ago I imagined I was the Kodiak Island Boxing Champion, and then Gil got shot in the head but not really.* . . . Jack refills his coffee cup and decides to drink it in the office, instead of in the cab where anything can happen. He wishes he could drive to the airport and get on a plane right now. He wants to tell Gil about the man with the baby and the screaming woman, but he's not sure what there is to tell. Put that baby in a basket of reeds and let it float away! He suddenly feels sorry he never learned Fourteen's name, because it's all over now and he'll never see her again. They might have become good friends. He wonders why anybody would shoot somebody else in the head. He remembers hearing on the radio not long ago that in one year Great Britain recorded eight deaths by handgun, Japan forty-eight, Canada fifty-something, and the United States of America ten thousand seven hundred and twenty-eight.

"What the hey," Jack says, collapsing back into his chair. "I'm going to stay here for just a sec. No walk-in fares, but ask me if I give a fart, Gil."

Gil smiles at Jack, making his big mustache rise and stretch. "You're a piece of work, Jack. You know that, don't you? You're connected and yet . . . Unreal! I mean, I know people who'd pay big money to know what you know. Guys work their tails off on fishing boats so they can earn enough money to buy a farm. You had a farm, and you're up here driving a cab!"

Gil laughs, and his green eyes sparkle. "I'd bet even *you* can't figure that one out, huh? Oh jeez! I almost forgot." Gil scrambles through the papers on the desk. "These letters." Gil hands Jack a couple of envelopes addressed to Jack Cliff, in care of the cab company. "They came today. Gary should have given them to you but I suppose he spaced it out."

12 G. CLARENCE ROBSON from Coos Bay, Oregon, coasts down Mission on his ten-speed bicycle. He's called Skin Man by most. His long hair streams behind like a horse tail. He's on his way to work the graveyard shift in the Kodiak Canning Company. It's fifty-one degrees outside and raining, but G. Clarence wears nothing but gym shorts and tennies.

Maybe G. Clarence was the victim of child abuse. Maybe he was an all-state tennis player whose glory peaked when he was eighteen. Perhaps his brother is running for governor of the state of Oregon. Nobody in Kodiak knows anything about G. Clarence Robson, but everybody guesses. They say his father died when he was born. They say he is his sister's son. They say he eats an apple a day and last winter he put on a T-shirt. When he dies, they won't know where to bury him.

NIGHT

On the stiff twig up there
Hunches a wet black rook
Arranging and rearranging its feathers in the rain.
I do not expect miracle
Or an accident

—SYLVIA PLATH,
"Black Rook in Rainy Weather"

13 MARY WROTE ABOUT the wet spring back in Wisconsin and the way Lorraine's cows looked sad and muddy in the pasture, and how some of the calves were dying because of the damp weather. She wrote that she'd had to start a fire in the wood stove even though it was late May already. She wrote that the daffodils were bright yellow, the way Jack likes them, and the tulips red, yellow, and mixed. Jack's roses must have died, she said, because none had leaves or even buds yet; her job was going okay but bored her, and she was getting along surprisingly well with Lorraine, although Lorraine seemed to be taking the cold spring pretty hard, what with the calves and then suddenly thinking she had cancer when Jenny Gerke told her the Russians were playing around with the weather. Mary mentioned that the neighbor's dog just ran past the window with a calf's head in its mouth, from the dead one she'd wheelbarrowed up the hill behind the house, and the cat slept curled in a ball by the stove with her tail over her nose. She wrote about the art fair coming up and the asinine little furor in town over the switch from angled to parallel parking on Jefferson Street. She wrote that the rain made it difficult for people to get their corn planted on time, and the mosquitoes were predicted to be bad, and that despite the unusual wetness in the hills, the sand prairie was blowing like crazy.

But then she got to the point. She wrote that she was moving back to Chicago. She said it wasn't as if she was totally enthusiastic about it, but she knew she wasn't enthusiastic about Spring Green or her job or living on the farm, with or without Jack. She wrote:

I know I should say something final—because I won't be writing you (or seeing you) again. But everything seems so long ago that saying something seems melodramatic, or anticlimactic. I'm sorry. I feel like I'm in the part of my life story they'd cut from the film version. Everybody would get up and leave, say it dragged on too long. Jesus, Jack, sometimes I'm angry. But then I just look at other people, a stranger, anybody, and I wonder what major event, what life-changing thing did or didn't happen to him or her.

Everybody's got a sad story. Lorraine probably isn't so far off when she says it all goes back to God and the beginning of time. I don't know. When you can't remember last month, even last year seems an eternity ago. Enough—I don't want this to get ridiculous. The abortion made me sad, but I'm not sorry. I hope you're doing okay. You deserve a lot of good things. I prefer to forget the craziness and think of our better times. You taught me something about tenderness.

Good-bye.

Quickly, Jack pulls the other letter from his pocket and thumbs it open. It's from his friend Tom Geary. Jack's parked under a streetlight in the harbormaster's lot. Before he reads, he pours the rest of his coffee out the window and watches it splash on the blacktop. He dips a pinch of snuff. Sweat breaks out on his forehead. He's remembering some radio fragment, a play or the review of a play. The horror of lost hopes, the announcer kept saying, the horror of lost hopes. Jack feels himself rush inside, his temples swell—is this what they call an inspiration? To do what? He's tottering, he's falling. What now? Reading Mary's letter is like hearing her voice, and he's struck by the absurdity of his being here, in Alaska, four thousand miles from the people and place that he loves, looking for traces of a father who, as he discovers him, means less and less.

Maybe the most necessary use of all fathers is as something to reject, and finally, a few minutes from his thirtieth birthday, Jack is finally coming to that. But now what? He was unhappy in Spring Green because he never felt that he chose it. His birth and life were something that happened by chance, and his loves seemed not to matter because they proceeded out of that original chance. Even Montana happened by chance. He went out there to visit his old high school friend Tom Geary, met Mary Fitzgerald at a bar, and stayed because of her, because she made him feel things that he liked feeling.

He'd been a dog! A happy one, sure, but still a dog. Jack feels embarrassed. Only a moment ago he allowed himself to believe they could be happy together. He was all set to go back and ask her to marry him, for crissake! What a fool! What an idiot! He can feel the shame burn his cheeks. He thinks of how decent Mary was to write such a kind letter when all he had a right to expect might be bitterness.

Tom's letter is dated April 30, with a Missoula postmark. It was sent to Wisconsin and then forwarded to Kodiak. Tom doesn't know where Jack is. So what. Jack is trying very hard to notice something, to think about something besides the swelling in his chest.

Dear Gunther—

Dont get the wrong idea (that news still crosses the Rockies via mule train) but I just heard your sex-kitten almost became a mother! I was depositing a shit after eating a cheeseburger and fries at the Copper Commons but before I started studying (syn: goofing off) on level 2 of the Mike (and Maureen, bless her heart) Mansfield Library, when I read your letter. See, I changed box numbers to escape responsibility i.e. bills, forgot to tell you, and this is why your Christmas letter arrives in April.

Jack stops reading. He lets his eyes move quickly over the rest of the letter, the description of Tom's most recent romance, his admission that for a time he was "pretty vulnerable to the old relationship bit— you know, all those good parts about having a main squeeze: caringsharingunderstandingyoure-the-best-Im-the-best-weretogether butseparatetoola-la-la (layman term for Suckie-Fuckie, Sailor?)—all the good stuff," to the last paragraph:

Be nice to Mary. Ive read about these things. I believe theyre called (il)legal operations on daytime tv. I know she, your wife/partner/sig-other/chick doesnt like me, but you know the feelings not mutual. Anyway, I think the right decision was made about the abortment et al. My mom says they are taking the humanness out the humanness (just like a mom, huh?) but can you imagine how weird it would be if a baby dropped out? Sorry. You probably can. Think of this: they say that if every woman who ever had an abortion suddenly turned purple we would all be very surprised.

Love and Fishes,
Ghee

A faint wash of silver shows over Pillar Mountain and then disappears, dusk's final face. Onward into darkness and short night. There's a flurry of activity over the cab radio, and Jack has been moved to number two.

He crosses Marine Way to the mall parking lot, cruising slowly past the front of the Mecca and The Ships on his way to the number two spot, in front of Solly's. Wafting through the crack in the window is the scent of something familiar. Leather and syrup? Beer? Cottonwood pitch, maybe.

Jack thinks of Missoula and Greenough Park in the fall, yellow leaves on the ground. Greenough Park, where the movie could have ended: wood chips lie new on the path, tangle Mary's hair, stick like burrs in her crumpled sweater, press marks in bare skin. (Let's get makeup over here and clean that girl up!) Rattlesnake Creek runs shallow and silver and very fast. (Mix music here. Something classical. It's gotta go with gold leaves and blue sky.) Cottonwood buds bleed red when you pop them with your fingers. *We could have ended it in Missoula, Mary.* (Begin to fade. Okay, looks good, looks good . . .) *But we were just starting, weren't we?* (Sweet, very sweet. This is a movie about being so close that you can't stand it anymore and you dive in without looking, which is the only honest way to do it when you are . . .) Let the fast water carry you. *How old were we?* (This is about converging pinpricks, got that? It's about a thousand emotions, just one of which is the nudge of nubile affection.) *Oh, Mary, Mary!* (Trust me. End it here. Cut. It'll be very nice.) But gratis. Real love you pay for.

Thinking of the stupid face with a smile, the circle with two eyes next to where Mary signed her name on the letter, Jack sucks air into his lungs, fills them up until they hurt, and then blows it out. But there's no inspiration, only puff and sweat. He feels empty.

He parks the car and stares up at the sidewalk, where a cowboy smiles cockily, rocking back and forth on his boot heels. His nose is crooked, and one ear is lower than the other. An American Indian woman in an orange dress slit up the side from knee to hip pinches the cowboy's cheek. The cowboy laughs and leans back on one foot, pushes her hand away with a casual swipe. He looks like a younger version of the phony who used to do the noontime television stock reports back in Wisconsin. He reaches under his shirt and pulls out a small pistol and hands it to the woman, who promptly slips it into her purse. The cowboy walks off; the woman leans back against the wall and hugs the purse with both arms.

She's good-looking, Jack thinks, long sturdy limbs, pretty face and hair. And now she's got a gun in her purse. A gun? Hell, probably just an early Christmas gift for her favorite sportsman. If every woman who had a gun in her purse turned purple, we would all be very surprised. Sure. Jack likes the way she pinched that cowboy's cheek as if she owned him. If she were Jack's girlfriend, they'd drink coffee together late at night like on the coffee ads—and she'd pinch *his* cheek. They'd talk about everything and laugh like hell and forget it all the next day. They'd hold hands in the grocery store, and it would be easy, like being in love ought to be, laughing a lot. Sometimes they'd fight, of course, but afterward they'd ball on the floor like bunnies. She wouldn't flinch or tighten up when he kissed her, make that heavy-heavy-something-needs-to-be-talked-about face, or ask him if he was laughing at her or with her. Why the hell should she? They'd be so damn happy it would be ridiculous, and if they weren't, there'd always be the gun in her purse. Why not?

Sometimes Jack feels as if his entire life has been lived without incident, without anything ever happening when he was conscious. When he was a baby his mother took him to the barn in a basket and set him in the manger while she spread hay. She told him the cows sniffed him and then ignored him, ate around him. But they imprinted on him the smell of their cud—a smell he would always, forever probably, associate with his mother. When he was old enough to help, Jack remembers walking down the manger breaking bales or using a coffee can to pour ground corn. His mom would be across the barn in the other manger, doing the same thing, singing. Jack remembers the tunes to some of the hymns but it bothers him that he can't remember the words. It's as though his brain's stuck, minus an injector or two. Mary had an abortion and it happened early one morning while he overslept. They talked about it one night and they figured it was for the best . . . or figured they ought to do it . . . or figured something Jack doesn't remember anymore! They agreed that they'd prefer she not be pregnant just yet—he remembers that—but he doesn't remember why. They wished the pregnancy hadn't happened so soon. They agreed. Yes. Jack doesn't feel at all tricked by Mary, never did. It's just that somehow, for some reason, he must not have been paying attention. Because when he woke that morning he thought for sure she'd gone out to run or something. She was gone and hadn't waked him and then didn't come back for breakfast, so she must have gone to work early.

Jack never asked where she got it done, although he knew it was Madison. He imagined a clean and carpeted clinic with white lights and walls, a lot of windows and plants, and colored geometric art behind glass. He knew it was performed by a competent *health care provider,* as doctors were called on the radio. He knew she'd talk to a specialist interested in her (the *health care consumer*'s) mental health, a billing clerk, and probably another *health care provider* or two, as nurses also were called on the radio. The nurse would have a friendly smile and ask a lot of questions about Spring Green and Chicago, and how Mary ended up in Spring Green from Chicago, and then Jack's name might come up, but probably not. They'd chat as if they just met each other at Rick and Pat's Café, but a little more carefully.

Mary told Jack that having the abortion was the first real womanly thing she'd done. It may or may not have been, Jack thought, but if so, then something was definitely odd. If not having a baby is womanly, then what is having a baby? And if it is cowardly to abandon a baby, as his father had done, is it brave to abandon a not-baby? What about leaving the woman who has just not had one? Abortion perhaps is not murder, and maybe not even a very big deal, but it confused the hell out of Jack, and the confusion made him cruel. He never asked Mary a thing except did it hurt, and she said, over her shoulder as if referring to a tetanus shot, not too much.

In the months that followed, everything about their life together bored him. When he watched Mary sleep or imagined her death, he felt nothing. He didn't think he loved her anymore. For a while it had been Mary and Jack and a question mark the size of a pea, a serendipitous future, a *mistake* he felt exceedingly capable of loving—although (who knows? some parents hate their kids) he might have been imagining things. Now, in his cab outside Solly's Office Bar, it is only him, and if the truth be known, he barely remembers anything else. In fact—the strangest thing—if he tries too hard he can't quite remember Mary's face.

The Indian woman in the orange dress with the pistol in her purse has pushed off the wall and stepped across the sidewalk to the stairs in front of Solly's. She seems distracted and nervous all of a sudden. She pauses at the trash can, leans back to rest, her face drawn and tired.

Country music spills out of Solly's. It picks and cries and picks and soothes, and it makes Jack want to die. It makes him feel as though he's not yet lived. All those songs of wandering road men! The wild and free path of the failed is so well traveled, so well worn, it couldn't possibly be wild and free anymore, could it? Jack had written Tom Geary a letter a few years ago saying *we've got to believe in something, don't we? We've got to believe in a cure and it doesn't even matter what the cure is as long as we believe in it.* But Tom wrote back with lyrics from a Jimmy Cliff song, saying he believed in freedom, in staying out of shackles, in freedom, quoted lyrics that said the same thing over and over again.

Mary said Tom had "Montana disease," the indulgent belief in the I'm-a-ramblin'-kinda-guy myth, in a false and irresponsible freedom. She said everybody talks about being independent, but most of the state is owned by corporations. Everybody from the governor to the holy cowboy is a company man.

Tom is getting his MBA so he can work in Denver or Chicago for five years (Ghee's Five-Year Plan), save a thousand a month and invest it, gather sixty to ninety thousand and buy a boat, quit working, sail around on Flathead Lake, be free, sail around some more, stay free, yeah, free. The song-lyric letter was followed by an odd postcard:

Gunther: Cruising through Hellgate Canyon on the way to swim under the cliffs in the Big Blue of the Blackfoot, truck bouncing, sun shining, wind blowing through the broken back window, I reach to the tape player and turn it down only long enough to tell you my Formula For Happiness: a truck, a Buffett tape, cash in my pocket, Montana USA and a day like today. I wish it were all in my hands but it's not. I'm moving inside, though. Thought you might like to know. Somebody must have dealt me a good set of cards. —Ghee

Then there was the time Jack and Mary had been visiting Tom, and Tom—high and free / free and high—got talking about the gold miners in Brazil.

"Nuggets the size of footballs, Gunther boy. Look at this!" He showed Jack and Mary a picture in a magazine; his pointing finger shook. "Check it out."

"In Brazil?" Mary asked.

"The Amazon. Anybody can go. Check this out." Another picture, many many men climbing out of a muddy pit, Tom's finger still shaking. "I already called the Brazilian consulate about a visa. Anybody can go."

"You what?" Mary asked.

"A visa!" Tom's eyes focused on nothing and everything, past the overflowing spittoon, stacks of *Detective* magazine and *American Dog,* a barbell and scattered weights, a yellow backpack—but not quite on Jack's or Mary's face. "It's like the Old West. I mean, some of these mud monkeys are millionaires!" His hands flew toward the ceiling. "Goddamn!"

"Really?" Jack was interested.

"Yeah! No gold left in the Rocky Mountains. Nothing Ghee can just pick up and carry away. Not anymore." Tom imitated a halfback running with a football. "Gotta go south, young man. Amazon country. Ghee can sink his teeth into that shit." Then he stood at the dresser, pulled a pistol out of the top drawer. The long blue barrel did what gun barrels do, and have always done: it gleamed. He spun the cylinder, spun it again.

Insane grin, Tom shook his head and turned. "Only piece of hardware you need, by golly."

Mary was clenching Jack's sleeve.

"Tom," Jack said.

"Remember that show *The Wild, Wild West*? Huh, Gunth? Like this." Aiming, Tom shoots six shots through the screen door: ping ping ping ping ping ping.

"Tom," Jack said, Mary tugging on his arm now.

"Yee-fucking-ha!"

Jack followed Mary, and the bullets, through the door—posthaste.

The woman in the orange dress with the gun in her purse slides into Jack's cab.

"Naughton's," she says.

Her strong fingers work on the string handle of her purse, twisting it, moving around it like a rosary. Jack shifts to reverse and backs up. He feels as though he's under water. If he can't go home, then what's next? He's thinking about long, boring life. He's thinking about how *the problem* (holding the opportunity to choose, the capacity for hope) may simply be a matter of staying conscious from moment to moment for one, three, fifteen, forty more years—not dying or being born . . . and certainly not dying early.

14 WHEN EDNA MACDONALD, the Aleut woman with turquoise eyes, was a little girl, she fell in love with Jimmy Rubenof. But she was just a little girl and Jimmy was a soldier, and he went to Korea and never came back.

She didn't think she'd ever forget him. She often does though, unless of course she's sitting here at the Pier Pub bar with Jimmy's father, Frank Rubenof, as she is now. But there's something else that's even more vivid when she's here in the yellow light, the smoky, beery air of the Pier Pub. She thinks of it as her almost-affair with Kid Cliff. It was something that was going to happen, something both of them knew was going to happen the same way you know it's going to rain, by the feel of things, by the look of things. He took her elbow, held it gently between thick fingers and lowered his head, whispered in her ear, called her Eddie, looked at her with light-gray eyes, and she knew—the way only a woman who's never done it before can know—that it was going to happen, and soon.

She walked him down to the boat. He squeezed her fingers. She can still feel them. Sure. Still. He kissed her, lightly, briefly, a grazing of the lips. She was twenty-five years old, and she wanted to absorb this man.

But he hopped over the rail and climbed up onto the bridge, waved through the window as the *Dempsey II* pulled out of the harbor that November day in 1968, never to return.

It was the last time she saw him, the last time she'd ever see that face except sitting here at this bar, drinking, staring at the photograph of his head—he had a nice head. He was a handsome man—the beauty of his lips and brow, of his face.

When Edna lost Kid Cliff she was still a virgin, so she made a vow to stay that way, to keep her virginity as a reminder of her love for him. And she'd been rewarded. God had taken her lovers, her sacrifice, and rewarded her with magic. Who could complain?

She's sitting on a red-speckled throne between Frank Rubenof, Jimmy's dad, and Corky Miles. She picked this spot at the bar for three reasons. First, because Kid Cliff's picture hangs directly in front of her above the mirror, his hair combed straight back, his eyes dreamy, chin strong.

Second, because she's got to keep Pretty Gertie out of harm's way. Pretty Gertie would fall, sure as anything, if Frank ever asked her to go pick berries.

And third, when Edna sits between these two, Frank and Corky, she never buys a drink.

Pretty Gertie is over by the yellow-and-blue jukebox, plunking quarters into the slot, and soon a Jerry Jeff Walker song drawls and drools across the barroom.

Corky is discussing the proposed bridge connecting Anchorage to the other side of the sound and how the people in Anchorage want the bridge so they can live like real Alaskans and how the folks on the Peninsula don't want the bridge so they can live like real Alaskans, and how nobody, including him, Corky Miles, knows how a real Alaskan lives; and if anybody would know, he would, seeing as how he really is one, and not some transplanted weed come up squeezed in the studded sole of somebody's Akron-built rubber mukluk.

> Dangling earrings for your fingers
> Big sparkling rocks for your nose

Edna feels the men squeeze her from both sides. She smiles, knowing her magic is strong, her forty-year-old maidenhood secure.

Frank, age seventy-three, who can't hear well in the first place and isn't listening to Corky anyway, having given up that avocation years ago along with booze, says, "That's something, huh, about the Illich family down in Old Harbor?"

Pretty Gertie is sitting on the other side of Frank now. She's yelling at the bartender, a substitute hired for the summer, who looks too young to be serving drinks, too smooth, too hairless, like a baby mouse.

"Hey baby!" she yells, giggling. "Bay-beee!"

The bartender turns, wrinkles his forehead. Huh?

Frank is explaining how the Illich boy—Reuben's his name—just this past winter shot and killed his father. "A seventeen-year-old kid, mind you, shot his father in the chest; jesus, just imagine that once, without even considering what they say he did to his mother, and try to say what's what in the world and what ain't, huh?"

Oh I love you, yeah, oh I love you
Someday we're gonna travel far away

"Hey baby!" Pretty Gertie yells again. The bartender looks over, wrinkles his forehead, blushes. Blushes! Which makes Edna embarrassed even to see! His pink face as soft as a baby's bottom.

"And then on top of shooting the old man . . . his mother is about like this." Frank uses his hands to show Edna. "Take a guess what everybody is suspecting. No, don't. Don't even imagine that one. That one'll do you in. Turn you to stone, it will. A pillar of salt."

We're gonna roll all the way to la-Louisiana
Maybe we'll just roll around in bed all day

"He's such a baby!" Pretty Gertie is still staring at the bartender, who's busying himself with dirty glasses, new drinks, bites of a Slim Jim, anything not to look at his tormentor, the large-headed, broad-faced, gravel-voiced sweetheart, Pretty Gertie Saratov MacDonald.

"Yessir, babies!" Frank is saying. "Babies making babies with mommies. That'll turn you to stone, that one will."

Edna feels Frank leaning closer, his shoulder touching hers. He hands her a red crepe poppy, which she slips behind her ear. She can see herself in the mirror and she looks pretty, so pretty she's glad she knows magic and can still change shapes and become a man or a dog or a frog—or a tree, even? Now there's an idea! Frank lifts her hand, holds it between his like a treasure.

"Hey, Cork," Frank says.

Corky's eyebrows rise.

"Whatever happened to Alex Odensky's wife?"

Corky keeps his mouth closed, drops his jaw, shakes his head.

The bartender's clean blue jeans grip his hips and butt as if there's something in there sucking. "The guy's a jerk, I can see," Pretty Gertie is saying from way over there on the other side of Frank. "He's a grown-up baby. A tall one."

Edna feels Frank put her bejeweled hand on his thigh, plop. She doesn't blink, doesn't do anything except sip her beer and grow leaves. Hey, wha'd'y'know? She's a tree! This Odensky story is for her, Edna knows. It's Frank's little concoction, but it's okay, she's ready, she's prepared. She's got branches and roots. She's a fine tree.

"Penny," Frank says. "Remember Penny?" Then he goes on to tell Edna's left ear about how Penny Odensky was the most beautiful woman on Kodiak, a regular princess, but she wouldn't let no one touch her, never, since nobody ever found her husband's body over in Vietnam, old Alex, even though he left back in nineteen hundred and sixty-five and still hasn't come back, and this was ten, fifteen, well, by now it's been eighteen years, can you believe that nonsense? And she's still thinking he might come back, the old prude, as if anybody'd want her now anyway. Talk about a waste and a half. And then when that rancher come over from Kalsin Bay and knifed Jon Jonsrud over who was gonna talk with her in the checkout line of Kraft's supermarket—mind you, the supermarket! Talk with her! And then there's Jon Jonsrud dying on the floor, bleeding like mad, and when the police come they find her sitting down by the front window with her knitting on her lap, working away, not wanting to waste any time. While Jonsrud is dying in front of her, she's knitting old dead Alex a sweater! Of course it was only a matter of time before somebody got killed waiting for her to make up her mind, the silly woman. Talk about a double waste. Yes ma'am, talk about it. They say Alex was a hero in Vietnam, too, say if they ever find him he'll either get a chestful of medals or a hero's burial, or both. But they always say that kind of thing when you're dead, so who knows. I tell you, I don't. I know Alex was a hell of a skiff man, that's what I know. Talk about a triple waste.

> Getting out of bed just ruins my whole day
> 'Sides that's the way I heard babies are made

Frank's nose is shriveling as he talks, or so it seems to Edna, the creases deepening, his lips paling, his tongue drying. He talks and talks, and as he talks, he ages, dies of an invisible bleeding, poor soul. Pretty Gertie, on the far side of Frank, has put her broad face down on the bar to nap. Corky, on Edna's right, is half listening, nodding occasionally, grunting *Ai* or *Yaai* or a very guttural *Mmmm* on cue. Frank's stories run into one another, the sound of his high, smooth voice giving musical accent to certain words, building a tempo that becomes bigger than any specific story, that becomes the rolling rhythm of history. Like jazz, or dance, the pulse of his voice is human whimsy—having nothing to do whatsoever with planetary time.

Frank's melody is often blood—ooooooohh!—blood running in bigger and smaller and bigger streams, running downstream to the sea, and then according to the same forces—yes!—back again. He's talking gestation, and physics, and the mistakes we make with children. And how blood, sure, like pretty red salmon choking summer streams and lying thick enough in some lakes a fellow could just about play God and walk across their backs to the far shore, how blood never dies, only changes shape, divides, rebuilds to flow again, blood that drains drop by drop from his very own veins, pooling inside, waiting for the right physical conditions to metamorphose, poor fellow, and his only son and heir, Jimmy, the first man Edna ever loved, dead thirty-two years now (which surely accounts for the red crepe poppy Frank had and gave her), cut in half on the banks of the Yalu River by a Chinese machine gunner, who would also die that day, blood running in a small stream to a bigger stream to the river to mix with Jimmy's, to the sea and ocean, on which and from which Frank has lived and will soon die.

Is there sense in that? Edna wonders. She wants to smile, really, she wants to laugh. But suddenly her heart is breaking, thinking about Jimmy. She was just a girl, seven maybe, but there you go. She adored him, hoped for him, waited for him, but he never came back.

Frank is working Edna's wooden hand slowly up the inside of his thigh toward his crotch.

The bartender passes but doesn't even look when Pretty Gertie raises her head high enough off the bar to yell, "Hey baby! You're a baby!"

"Are you talking to him?" Frank asks.

"Who else?"

"That's Shorty Meyers' boy. The highliner?"

"Well, he looks about three," Pretty Gertie says.

"Well, he's not," Frank says. "Get him to tell you about when they got beached last summer with a seine full of silvers, and the bear chased them up onto the deck of the boat. Ate fifteen ten-pound fish, two bites apiece. The bear, I mean, while these guys watched through the cabin window."

Frank lifts Edna's hand off his crotch with two fingers and drops it in the space between stools, like a frozen dog turd, or a stick, or something dead on the end of a swinging rope.

Jerry Jeff has begun to sing the same song a second time. Edna stares at Kid Cliff's picture, feeling herself drift into the gray. *There* was a highliner, she thinks. *There* was a man. If this bartender were Kid's son, she'd know it. She'd smell it. She drinks, blinks. But Shorty Meyers? Who cares about him?

"Handsome cuss," Frank says.

"I would have swore he was from Anchorage," Pretty Gertie says. "Or California."

"Nope. He's home talent."

"Well, don't cuss or nothing when he's near," Pretty Gertie says. "Doesn't look a day over two to me."

> I'd like to give you everything you ever want, Love
> Diamond rings for every toe

Frank tries a new tack. He lays a hand on the small of Edna's back— actually on the very small of her back, kind of too close to her bottom— and orders another round.

Imagine it anyway, Edna dares herself. Think of taking this old boy to bed with you. Holding him there. Coo for him and he'd leak for you, send you both tumbling over eternity generation by generation—aaaahhhh, yes ma'am, like falling dolls. You be his and he be yours and all is fine for one tiny moment and all of time. Edna MacDonald, maiden of the future, it's in your genes, and God, bless His heart, face like the yellow moon, would certainly forgive.

Frank gives Edna goose bumps, like a young girl. She hears herself giggle. His fingers search along the elastic on the back of her pants, the inside of the elastic band on her panties, the little pink label with the two Cupids . . . right there.

"Whatever happened to Ivor Zornikof," Corky asks suddenly over Edna's head.

"Got drunk and burned everything he owned," Frank says. "Boat, house, the works."

"Yeah, but after that."

"Don't know."

"Who was his wife again?"

"Ernie what's-his-name's daughter, Wendy."

"Ai, Wendy. She was an ugly one."

"Ugly as your Mari, Cork."

"He was an old drunk, all right."

"Those were the good days, Cork. You, me, and Ivor."

"Ai."

"Before you got soft and I got old and Ivor burned everything he owned."

Edna thinks of how she looked thirty years ago. White-lacy-tiny-clean-cute-curled, yellow-ribboned, shiny shoes too, she was really very pretty that day Jimmy left, parked his shiny pickup with the sparkly seats behind Frank's trailer, winked, waved, and never came back. And then Kid.

She stares at his eyes in the photograph. Wow. Into those she could do some serious tumbling. He looked at her that way. He touched her elbow, and she can't even remember what she was wearing that day. For all she was feeling she might as well have been naked.

Frank's fingers have stalled there at the Cupid label of her panties. Edna smiles at herself in the mirror behind the booze bottles, winks, removes the red crepe poppy from behind her ear and holds it close, feels its petals on her cheek, sniffs its crepe smell. You're a lucky girl, see. Because what you've got is not a promise, because promises can be broken and what you got can never be broken. It's that something (a hint, a tilt, a narrowing, a watering, a daring, a light, a beckoning, a glimmer) you either see in a lover's eyes or don't see, remember or don't remember, and if you do (see, remember), then there's hope. Yes ma'am, so don't fret. Celebrate the joys, the chances, be glad of something. Okay, God, let it be known that Edna MacDonald sacrificed a possible firstborn child, oh yes indeed she did, and such a sweet man's baby at that. You took my Jimmy. You took my Kid. But You gave me magic.

She stands up, feels Frank's hand slip from her panties like water off a duck's back. She steps over to Pretty Gertie, glances one last time at the mirror behind the booze bottles and wonders very briefly, if an Aleut woman like herself can have turquoise eyes, then what, pray tell, isn't possible?

A duck? Okay. Sure, she'll be a yellow duck.

"Let's go to Ivan's," she whispers to Pretty Gertie, touching her shoulder. "Let's get some sleep out there."

"Jaaaisus, but Ivor's wife was uglier than my Mari, Frank."

"It was a horse race, Cork."

"My sweet Maruska, bless her."

Edna helps Pretty Gertie stand. Together they walk toward the door, Edna's webbed feet slapping pleasantly on the tile.

15 JACK LISTENS TO her whining or sobbing, sniffing in the dark next to him for five or ten minutes, most of the way back from Naughton's trailer court, and just when they are getting to town he figures he should say something, because a person might at least acknowledge another's sadness, especially when he's the only other one in the car and it's raining and all.

So Jack says, "Ah, are you all right?" even though she obviously isn't all right. She's drunk, and Jack doubts he can do anything for her even if she asks.

She's the woman in the orange dress, with the gun in her purse, the woman Jack took to Naughton's from Solly's just a short time ago, and now he's picked her up at Naughton's and is taking her to town again. Jack can't see her face because of the darkness, and also because her head hangs forward so her black hair makes a curtain, behind which she sobs. Very small, very painful squeaks and moans, with long breath-taking gaps between.

The tires hiss, the blower blows, the wipers slap an irregular pulse. The woman claws the air on both sides of her head.

"Take me back to Naughton's!" she hisses. She looks up, and in the light from a sidewalk vapor lamp Jack can see her eyes are dark and pinched with something terrible. He doesn't want to take her back, but he doesn't want to say no either.

He says, "Are you sure? It'll be a round-trip charge, you know."

"Of course I'm sure, you idiot! What do you think, I don't have the money?"

"Just asking," Jack says.

"Take me back. Please."

Jack is thinking he should probably ask her if she's planning on killing someone. Because if she's going to do that then he doesn't want to take her back. But how does a guy ask a girl that? And what if she gets mad and shoots him? Jack checks the FM station for some quiet jazz, thinking it might mellow her. Good. It's on and it fits: sweet sax, a dark wet road, a woman with a gun in her purse sitting next to him, crying.

She mumbles something about being treated like dirt, walked on. She says she'll teach the idiot not to treat her like a dog. But her enthusiasm is flagging. The music is working. Soon she stops talking altogether. Jack hears her begin to breathe loudly and deeply, so he turns on the dome light to take a look. Her eyes have closed, and her wide brown face is peaceful, sleeping.

Jack wonders what somebody may have done to her, wonders if she'd been raped or beaten after he dropped her off, wonders if it's that simple. He can't see any marks on her face, so he wonders about the bruises inside somewhere. Maybe she told some guy that she loved him, and for the first time in her life she was lying awake night after night wanting him, like in the songs, and she needed him more than she needed food or air or anything else on earth—and the guy turned around and told her she was full of shit.

Maybe that, or maybe it's just the alcohol. Listen to alcoholics long enough and you wonder how anyone can live in a world as rotten as they describe. What's ordinary pain becomes torture, and tortures usually take a little hate to survive. Her orange dress wrinkles where she's skinny. Her loose breasts seem to hang at odd angles. Jack sees her legs beneath her orange dress and thinks of how beneath that skin is blood and in that blood is rage. He's glad she's fallen asleep.

He shakes her shoulder when they get to the trailer at Naughton's, the same trailer he dropped her off at earlier. The yard is carved out of the woods, and stumps and rusting hunks of metal lurk in the shadows like monsters. She wakes up immediately, which is a nice surprise. She raises her eyebrows and rubs her eyes with the heels of her hands. Looking out the window, she blinks a few times and says, "Oh." Then she tells Jack to wait just a second while she runs in and gets a check.

Five minutes later she still hasn't come back. Jack gets out and knocks on the front door of the trailer, pulling up the hood of his sweatshirt to stay dry. He can see through the window into the living room and part of the kitchen. A woman he doesn't recognize sits on the couch, her head lying back against the cushions, an unlit cigarette in her hand. A man is lying on his back in the kitchen, and his legs and his brown rubber fishing boots extend into the living room. Jack knocks again.

The woman on the couch says something to the kitchen. She isn't the woman in the orange dress. She's wearing jeans, and whoever she's talking to must still be alive. Jack wonders if she's a killer too, this one with the jeans. Could the guy on the floor with the fishing boots be dead? Jack hopes he didn't do something terrible by bringing Orange Dress back here. It would probably be so obvious to somebody else—to his mother, to Mary—some basic rule about crazy people and pistols and taxi rides. He suddenly feels panicky. Why wasn't it obvious to him?

"Hi, I'm the cabdriver," he says, smiling, when the woman on the couch finally answers the door.

"It's the cabdriver!" the woman calls to the kitchen. She's about Jack's age, short brunette hair, impatient green eyes.

"I let someone off here," Jack says. "I was waiting for her to come out again."

"Ha!" She laughs to the kitchen. "He says he let someone off here. Did you see anyone come in? Oh! It must have been what's-her-name." She snaps her fingers as if pretending to remember. "Oh, yes. Susan." She turns back to Jack. "Orange dress? Black hair?"

Jack nods.

"Yeah. She was here, and then she left, and then she was here again, and then . . . Well, you're not interested, I'm sure. You want to get paid." Then, back to the kitchen: "He wants to get paid! Where do you suppose Susan went in such a hurry?"

Jack can't tell if she's talking to the guy on the floor in fishing boots, or someone else. Nobody answers, but someone starts humming.

"Hey!" she yells, sarcastic smile gone. "Someone's here, dammit! You can come out now!"

Something sizzles on a fry pan. The humming approaches the kitchen doorway, then a semibald head with a bearded face pops out.

"Hey!" says the head, Neil Pasternak's head. Then it withdraws to the kitchen.

Jack walks past the woman at the door, and then across the living room. He steps over the horizontal body and into the tiny yellow kitchen.

"Aren't you the jerk who stole my fish?"

Neil nods, smiles, then turns his back. "Beer's in the fridge, bud, help yourself." He's standing over the stove, flouring salmon steaks, hot butter in the fry pan.

Jack doesn't know what to say next, so he points to the horizontal body he now recognizes as Larry Laarson.

"What's his problem?"

"Asleep," Neil says.

Jack helps himself to a beer, fantasizes pouring it over Neil's fish. He has a sudden wave of sympathy for the woman in the orange dress. Maybe this clown stole her fish too.

"Where's the woman?" he asks.

Neil laughs and says, "Friendly, huh? You mean Susan, don't you?"

"The one I dropped off."

"Yeah. *Igual.* Hey, this is Betsy. Say hi, Buttercup."

Betsy stands behind Jack, leaning against the kitchen doorway. Jack ignores her nod.

"And I'm Neil Pasternak." Neil half turns from the stove to extend his hand, but Jack doesn't take it.

Neil says, "Hey, what can I say? You want *this* fish? I'll give you this fish. What's your name?"

"Jack Cliff."

"Who?"

"You heard me."

"Cliff? I used to fish with a guy named Cliff. When I was a kid. When I first came up here."

"I'm his son."

Neil turns away from the fry pan, the salmon sizzling behind him, and stares at Jack, looks him over. He's smiling. His face is genuinely surprised. "His son? I didn't know he had a son."

Jack wants to stay angry at Neil for stealing his fish and fries, but the sincere pleasure in Neil's face is disarming. Jack shrugs.

"Man oh man," Neil is saying, shaking his head in disbelief. "I loved that guy. He was like *my* dad!"

"He *wasn't* like my dad," Jack says.

"You didn't know him?"

"No." Jack wants to crawl back to his tent, lie down, sleep. Why didn't he keep his mouth shut?

"Christ." Neil turns to the fry pan, shaking his head. He flips the salmon. "You must be 'other things.' "

"What?"

"You knew *of* him, didn't you?" Neil asks. "I mean, did you know he was in Alaska?"

"Where the hell is Susan?"

Neil looks down and then up Jack's body, smiling again, studying Jack's face. "Incredible. You know, you do something with your eyebrows when you talk, wrinkle your forehead. It's *him,* man; it's *him* exactly. When did you come to Kodiak?"

Jack keeps his eyebrows down, forehead smooth. "Why did you call me 'other things'?"

"Oh God. Look, you've got to eat with us. Yeah. I can't believe I scavenged *your* dinner!"

"Yeah, right." Jack wonders if his great-great-great-great-great-great-grandfather raised his eyebrows when he spoke. He sees a caveman relative of his sitting next to a fire in a cave somewhere in France wrinkling his forehead and saying, *Ugh,* before dashing out another caveman's brains with a rock. A brutally earnest gesture. He wonders what the hell "other things" means.

"I came up here like the proverbial runaway," Neil says. "Your old man never asked a question, but he took care of me. I was what, sixteen? No money, no anything. And he took me in. Worked me half to death, but see"—Neil spreads his arms like wings and turns three hundred sixty degrees—"I lived. I was on the *Dempsey II* when she iced up. I was there. He sent us off in a life raft and stayed on with a damn baseball bat, chipping ice like a crazy man! When she flipped . . ."

Neil pauses, his wild brown eyes calming. "You knew how he died, didn't you?"

"I had an idea," Jack says.

"Well, an iced-up boat flips. During a winter storm, ice can build up on the rigging and deck until—boom, she turns over. The *Dempsey II* flipped. It was night. We were all in the raft except your dad, and we . . . We couldn't find him."

Neil shakes his head, flutters his eyelids, waves the spatula past his face. "I'm sorry, man."

Jack thinks of the death he's imagined, the old man frozen to a tree, Sony Walkman earphones on his head, Vivaldi.

"Oh my god," Neil says. "The way you hang your head forward . . . I'm sorry, but this is amazing. Kid Cliff's son. Jack? Of course! For Jack Dempsey! Is that right?"

Jack doesn't answer. He's thinking of Neil as him, and himself as Neil. He's wondering whether, if he'd run away from home and come to Alaska when he was sixteen, he could have worked on his father's fishing boat. No. By the time he was sixteen, his dad was dead.

"Huh? Am I right? Jack Dempsey Cliff?"

"What's 'other things'?"

Neil pauses. "That's a story. You want to hear a story?"

Jack looks down at Larry, sleeping on the floor. He thinks of Moses who kidnapped the Lindbergh baby. What can he learn about his own soul? The question is his own story, sure, but first things first. Hold still. You have nowhere to go. Be brave. This is as good a time as any to stop believing in the determined malice of fate.

"It's a story your dad told me," Neil says. "It's about getting back from Japan in 1945. Interested?"

Jack nods.

"Excuse me if I laugh, but it's always struck me as one of God's ultimate jokes," Neil says. "Your dad told me he walked off a hospital boat into Seattle after being a prisoner of war for three and a half years, walked down the gangway to an empty dock. Seattle, that's all. Somebody fouled up and didn't get the word out that a boatload of prisoners was coming home, so all that was there was Seattle. Have you been there, Jack? Well, it probably wasn't much different than it is now. Nothing special. Rain. Big city. Dock hookers. Movies. Your dad told me he wandered up and down the waterfront for almost a month before he called his sweetie back east on a farm somewhere. He said he had to think of something to say that didn't sound crazy, and it took him almost a month of drinking to feel up to it. He told me he heard about Kodiak that first day off the boat in Seattle, and he never quite got it off his mind no matter how hard he tried to do *other things*. That's what he told me. Think of it! This survivor, your old man, this survivor roaming around Seattle like a lost dog . . . Anyway, you must have been one of the other things. You've seen his picture in the Pier Pub, haven't you?"

"Yes." Seattle, 1945. Jack's trying to feel what it would have felt like, but not getting very close. He thinks of the guy who looked like Donald Sutherland, the guy who'll cruise to Japan, and the look in his eye. No matter how far he goes, how much money he makes or cocaine he does, no matter how many times he buys a hooker or bathes in a hot tub, all he'll see is a girlfriend back home with a pair of destroyed legs. Rain. Dock hookers. Big city. What does a guy do? Donald Sutherland sent her a flowergram. Kid Cliff called her, eventually married her, gave her seven years and a baby. Jack gave Mary . . . what had he given Mary? Something about tenderness? What was that? A guy does what he can, sure. Kid Cliff heard about Kodiak that first day off the boat, which means Lorraine never had a chance, which means that nothing she could have done, nothing Jack could have done (what can a baby do?), would have made any difference.

"Your dad was the worst boxer I ever saw," Neil says, laughing. "But he could take a lot of punishment. He never gave up is all."

Betsy stands at the kitchen entrance, unlit cigarette hanging from her lips now, bobbing when she speaks. "Don't forget to introduce Larry, Neil." She nudges the sleeping man with her toe. "He's very temporarily rich."

"Yeah, sure." Neil smiles. "That's Horatio. He's resting. Shake hands with Betsy, Jack."

Jack and Betsy shake hands. "So pleased to meet you," Betsy says, sweetly. She pretends a curtsy, glances down at Larry, and then adds, "I would have picked up if I'd known you were coming."

"Buttercup's an artist," Neil says. "You'll have to excuse her sarcasm. See, she digs the hell out of me. She's a lover of the Natural Man."

Larry is stirring on the floor because Betsy keeps nudging him with her toe. He looks up, squints, and says, "My mother is a fucking fish!" and then rolls over onto his stomach.

Jack laughs. He can't help it. It's funny. It's crazy. He's floating. The salmon is sizzling in the pan and it smells good. What now? What can a person do to make things different, to change the course of his life, the lives of those around him?

"A victim of the Industrial Age," Neil says. "No . . . we're in the Computer Age, am I right? Or the Space Age? For heaven's sake, Betsy, help me out. You know these things."

"The Information Age," Betsy says. "The poor boy has totally OD'd on information."

Neil laughs. "Larry drinks a bit. People do crazy things to feel more alive. But stay for some of this salmon, Jack. I really don't know where Susan went in such a hurry. C'mon, bud. This evening keeps getting weirder and weirder. Take my word for it. She left before din-din, and I'm hungry as a horse. You know, I've been thinking . . . I wonder if your old man thought I was you. He never asked my exact age, you know, or where I was from. I wonder if he thought I was you."

Jack suddenly remembers the gun in Susan's purse. "Where did she go?" he asks.

"Susan?" Betsy points at the back door.

"She had a gun, you know." Jack can hear the urgency in his voice, the strain. "She had a gun in her purse. I saw her buy it."

The fry pan sizzles as Neil adds more butter.

"Hey," Neil says. "Don't be such a twit. You're a hero, don't you know?"

The salmon smells awfully good. Jack's mouth is beginning to water again. "What?"

"It's true," Neil says, hunching over the fry pan. "Would you believe a misunderstanding? See, Susan burst in here ten minutes ago. Well, you know when she burst in here! You dropped her off! Twice! Anyway, the second time she's holding a pistol like a turd and claiming she's going to kill me if I don't pay her for every time we ever made-da-love. A thousand for her irreplaceable virginity, and fifty bucks a shot thereafter. Which she claims is thirty percent off! Anyway, that's six grand total. She said we did it a hundred times, though I only remember once or twice. She's talking about a long time ago."

Neil glances over his shoulder at Jack. "I told her I'd be in the kitchen whenever she made up her mind to come shoot me. Then you knocked on the door."

Betsy nudges Larry's butt with her toe and says, "One hell of a watchdog. He slept through all the excitement."

"But eat with us, Jack," Neil says. "Here's a beer."

"I've got one."

"Go sit down, then. Go on."

Jack pops the top on the beer and escapes past Betsy into the living room.

"You're going to love this salmon," Neil continues from the kitchen. "I'm frying it because the oven's on the blink. You ever eat fried salmon? Fried *fresh* salmon? You're talking flaaaa-vor! Damn right."

Jack pushes aside some books in order to put his feet up on the coffee table. Betsy follows and sits next to him, smiling for the first time without sarcasm. She's put the cigarette behind her ear, like a pencil.

"Very few people in this world know how to make a good fried salmon," Neil is saying from the kitchen. "Your old man used to say—and it's true—that very few people in this world know how to make anything good. Susan's my ex-girlfriend, high school sweetie, whatever. I hadn't seen her in years. A very bitter woman, apparently. Too long the patient sufferer." A high, hearty laugh echoes out of the small kitchen. "Susan's part Blackfeet Indian, you know. Boy, this is a long story, too long. Ever hear of the Sun Dance? I wanted to be an Indian brave. Anyway, I came up here. Up to Kodiak. Ever think about how anybody's life can be described by how they adjust to pain? Anyway, Susan left this picture."

Neil walks out of the kitchen, digging his wallet from his pocket. He unsnaps the plastic photo pages from their binder. "Look at this," he says, kneeling at the coffee table. He jabs a black-and-white prom photograph with his forefinger. "What followed this—" He stops, quickly shakes his head and flutters his eyelids as if rearranging his thoughts. "No, no. What *preceded* this, the taking of this picture, was a kind of half-assed grace, fake sophistication. Many many mouthed oaths and sentimental looks, that type of thing. We were all dressed up and going to a party." Neil laughs and looks at Jack. "Damn. You know, I feel like we're brothers."

Jack doesn't feel as if Neil is his brother. But he's feeling better now. The anger has faded, and he's sitting on a couch, a beer in his hand, Betsy next to him, and this guy Neil is trying hard to be his friend. What the hell. He's got no place to go anyway. And dinner's coming up. Maybe this is why he came to Alaska. Maybe this exact scene was what he craved. *Mary, sorry I had to leave you, but I wanted to sit on the couch in a trailer drinking beer with the crazy guy my dad adopted as a son. I wanted to eat his fried fresh salmon. And I wanted to be glad. I wanted to be glad to be where I'm from, and I wanted to be glad for once in my life that things happened the way they happened. See, there was this woman, and she had a gun, and I must have scared her, because she ran off. And guess what? You won't believe this. Dad was a lousy boxer!*

Jack laughs again. He can't help it.

In Neil's photograph, both Neil and Susan look like kids dressed in grown-up clothing. Susan smiles bucktoothed and squinty-eyed. Neil stands chest out, one hand in his pocket and the other on Susan's shoulder. His ears stick out from under a black beret.

"I thought I was an artist," he explains. "I never tied my shoes. I wore that silly hat. Look at us, though. It hardly seems possible that these two kids could feel what we felt. Little pig breaths, spunk drops, sweet baby kisses—the whole shebang. Nothing but a yellow brick road to always-always land! I mean, it's scary to be so mightily in love. We used to fight a lot. That's how I know we had something special going. And now she comes back from wherever—after how long? She's crazy."

Betsy has resumed her former couch position, head resting back on the cushion, unlit cigarette between her lips again. Neil glances at her as he slips the photo back into his wallet.

"It's an old story, Jack Cliff. Fingers touching fingers, words crashing off words and slamming around inside our heads for weeks months years, two chests clamped together by whatever, pushed apart by the same thing. And bitterness! And fear! Everything! Kind words, sleep warmth, eating together—she used to slurp like a squaw—falling deeper in love in the dark in the future if we try real hard until death, et cetera! Ooops! I hate that word, *death*. She chased me around once in Great Falls and got me down on my back and rubbed horseshit in my face. Horseshit! When I got up I chased her into a foundation, just a basement, and threw rocks at her! Like this—" Neil demonstrates throwing rocks. "We always fought like that. This is nothing new." He glances again at Betsy, who has closed her eyes, and then he lets out a long, exaggerated sigh.

"Hey, we were only sixteen," Neil says, walking back to the kitchen. "And things get screwed up with time, distance, all that. I never got my vision, although I tried real hard. I sent her money from Alaska to abort poor little Telemachos. I'll tell you how that went over: Poorly!" Neil disappears around the corner into the kitchen. "But forget it, Jack Dempsey Cliff. *I* did! I really did. Until tonight, until now, I'd just about almost forgotten! Ha!"

Jack Dempsey Cliff is suddenly thinking of Susan turned purple. He's thinking of Mary turned purple. He looks at Betsy and believes that she, too, is turning purple before his eyes. He's wondering if his mother might be purple too, if abortion had been legal back then, and if that might have . . . No. Don't think it. Of course not. Kid Cliff heard of Kodiak the day he got off the boat and everything else was forthwith determined. But what about the jerk who neglected to spread the word that a boatload of POWs was coming home? Maybe if the dock had been jammed with a welcoming throng, Kid Cliff would have been swept up bodily and deposited on an eastbound train before anybody had a chance to whisper *kodiakalaska,* that fateful word, into his ear. Maybe. But it's useless to think that way. Jack's tired of thinking that way.

"Jack Cliff!" Neil yells, his voice happy from the kitchen, as if Jack has just walked in, an old friend, a hero. "Boy, am I glad it was you and not some knucklehead! There are too many knuckleheads around here— absolute slugheads, you know the kind. I wonder what's gone on in Susan's life for all these years? She was cute, but, I mean, we were what, fifteen and sixteen? Okay, so we held hands a lot. But I went off to become a man and didn't quite make it back. Ten years later I got this letter from her. She not only remembers everything, but she writes me that she's *still* in love with me!"

"Tell him what you did," Betsy says.

There's a pause.

"Huh?" Betsy prods.

"A letter out of the blue like that? What am I supposed to do? I mean, I felt lousy because I'd almost forgotten—"

"Yeah, but tell him what you did."

"Imagine her hopes," Neil says. "Think of her hopes! Think of how desolate her life must have been that she hung on to those ridiculous years. Well, I thought about it a lot, and I realized something. See, if love isn't possible, if we stop hoping, if we allow ourselves to *believe* that love isn't possible, everything else still is! All the crap!"

"Just tell him what you did," Betsy says again.

Neil sticks his head out of the kitchen, above Larry's horizontal legs. "I wrote her back and told her I was still madly in love with her."

"And what else?" Betsy prompts. She hasn't moved from her position on the couch, her head back, the unlit cigarette pointing from her lips toward the ceiling.

"And I wanted to marry her and take her away from her daddy's tepee

111

and dress her in fine clothes and jewels and love her until I die. That I was saving my money. That I finally got my vision. That I'd be back at night. Some evening soon I'd swoop down out of the starry sky, slip under the buffalo skin and wake her with a kiss!" He winks, then withdraws his head. "You get the idea. She must have got tired of waiting."

Jack looks at the spot where Neil's head had been, the dirty white woodwork around the doorframe. Who is this guy?

"What an asshole," Betsy says.

"Well, I've got my fantasies too, you know," Neil says, his voice coming from the kitchen again. "I mean, I think I kind of believed it. I tried! Come in here and build me a drink while I get this served up, would you, Betsy? Think about it. What business does she have writing me in the first place? How do you think that made me feel? I thought . . . well, I don't know what I thought, but whatever it was was completely blasted out of the water by her capacity not only to hope, but to hope for love for so long on so little. Of course that was only her dream, but if she can have her dream, then I can have mine. Larry's mother is a fish and he dreams of getting laid in a rock-and-roll Cadillac, whatever that is. Betsy, you want to go to La Paz and paint pictures like Cézanne. Jack, I don't know what you dream, but I'll bet it's heroic. You've got to eat with us here before you leave, okay? I'm sorry I scavenged your food—you gotta believe that. I was very hungry. You know, when Dempsey was a kid, fighting in these mining towns around Colorado, he got knocked down a lot, and I'm sure he would have liked to stay down. But he had to collect the two bucks for winning or go hungry. So he got up. Sure he did. Your dad told me this: *You could have hit Dempsey on the chin with a sledgehammer for five dollars—and when you haven't eaten for three days you'll understand.* Well, I didn't understand. I even fasted for a while to see if that would help. I was expecting a vision, hoping for some sort of revelation. Ha! I was pretty young. All I got was hungrier."

Jack is letting Neil's voice wash over him. His own voice, the voice of his father. He doesn't mind that it seems to be filled with pain. There's always pain; it's not to be avoided. But there's something about being here, listening, smelling the salmon, that Jack finds very pleasant. He's cut loose. He's sad, but that's okay, finally. He feels anything might happen; and even better, he's certain something will.

"I used to be an army man," Neil continues. *"Over hill, over dale, we will hit the dusty trail!* An army man! Ever think of war as a kind of rite of passage? How about love? Hate? You know, historians study wars, but history is what happens after wars. Actual war is ahistorical. It's afterward; it's how we recover or, shall I say, *maintain*. Did you know a Plains Indian couldn't marry without a vision? Because he wasn't a man. Oh shit. The . . . the Japanese tortured your dad, but I think in retrospect he was glad. He was proud; he was hateful. But dammit, he survived! He survived the tsunami too. When the *Dempsey II* iced up and the odds were against him, he wasn't about to get in the raft with us. Death caught up with him, death caught up with him. It was about time, really, and I think he knew that. Nevertheless, he wasn't going to stop living like he lived just because death would eventually catch up with him. He told me he stood on the deck of one of those Hell Ships going to Japan—now catch this—he stood with his feet perfectly still, thinking he was a bullfighter while everybody else scattered for cover and these American bombers came screaming off the water, blowing everything around him to smithereens! There's the exaltation without motion! There's the vis— Oooops! Jack, just picture it: he weighed only ninety-five pounds and wore nothing but a G-string, and while the bombs fell all around him *he thought he was a bullfighter!* Oh shit! I'm having some problems here with my hands. *'So the darkness shall be light, and in stillness, the dance.'* I read that. I know a lot of bums who killed gooks—hell, I did! And look where it got me! Glory, see, like a tropical suntan, is fleeting. Oh my, watch out! Jeeezus. Oh my oh my oh my oh my oh my . . . Susan would love to see this. . . . This right here. I'm afraid I spilled. I'm afraid my hands . . ."

Neil's voice is suddenly pleading, a whine. "I'm afraid my hands are shaking like leaves."

Betsy jumps up and quickly steps over Larry into the kitchen. Jack hears her voice soothe, then whisper. Apparently the fish fell out of the fry pan, and Jack hears her telling Neil it's dirty as hell and please, please throw it away.

Jack Cliff, son of Kid, sips his beer and looks at his tennis-shoed feet on the coffee table. He smells the good salmon and knows he won't eat—not yet, not now. He hears footsteps in the kitchen and then sees Betsy's head poke through the doorway, face red, embarrassed.

"I'm sorry," she says, looking it. "Neil asks if you'll meet him for breakfast at the Mecca. He says he wants to buy you a feast when you get off shift."

16 JACK CLIFF RADIOS in the Naughton's trip as a "no pay, no eat," and that makes Gil laugh. He pulls onto Monashka Bay Road, heading toward town. It's dark outside, past midnight, the back side of overcast twilight, and still drizzling. The tide is up in Mill Bay and the white curled breakers reflect light from who knows where. Maybe his headlights. The blower is blowing and the engine's still running minus an injector . . . or two? Does he know anything? He knows it's his birthday. He knows he's thirty years old. He knows he never knew his father. But he doesn't know diesel engines, or boats, or the sea. And now that he's not leaving, he doesn't even know what he's going to do in the morning.

Jack feels warm and dry, he knows that. Cars at night, especially in the rain, give him a particularly secure feeling. Just seeing them drive by does it to him. If he's not in one, he wants to be; and when he's in a car, he wants to stay there, feeling the wheels on the road and hearing the engine's low moan, and the radio playing familiar songs, and never arriving at any place in particular but always riding, moving toward something indistinct, something big, bigger, impossibly big out there in the darkness around the curve.

But maybe it isn't *there*? Maybe it's off the road and through the trees, somewhere in the wilderness of his memory—or Neil's? Maybe it waits like a grizzly crouching on the moss, quiet, dark, and silently waiting. Maybe he should park and walk into the trees just to see how far he dares to go, just to discover how frightened he can be by his own imagination, and how long he can stand feeling the drip, drip, drip, waiting for something big to happen, waiting to be certain.

Breakfast with Neil? Maybe.

An Indian would feel safer in the woods than on the road. All the time Jack spent in the woods on the farm, cutting cordwood, hiking, standing in a tree with a bow and arrow, waiting for deer, yet he's always felt safer on the road. He mulls on that for a while as he drives. Trains, boats, trucks, cars; a white man in love with motion, simulated or otherwise. Just keep goin', goin', hand me down my walking cane, knapsack— whatever. I hear the train whistle in the truck stop sounding like L.A. International Airport.

Jack thinks about his life so far: a forsaken yes, a deferred no, a probable maybe. Can anyone feel the exultation without motion—in stillness, the dance? Jack is tired; he would like to. A million little Spanish boys want to face the bull, but only a handful can keep their feet still. His father could. Think of all those men piled into the hold of a Japanese freighter going from the Philippines to Japan. Beat up and sick, swimming in their own excrement, one-hundred-twenty-degree heat and no water, they loved and hated, killed and saved one another. Nothing else to do—*frick, just cruise*. The screaming lousy madness of it all. Fingernails scratching the bulkhead, conversations with ghosts, a life-saving swallow of your buddy's blood, the one British officer standing in the spotlight of sun through the deck, singing, leading songs for the sane. Jack read about that. He thinks of the prisoners being herded on deck to stand in the sunshine and face a squadron of attacking American bombers so the pilots might know who the hell they were bombing. His dad kept his feet still. Standing amid the shrapnel and fire, Kid Cliff imagined himself a bullfighter.

What a thing, Jack thinks, what a goddamned thing. The image makes Jack proud and raises the hair on the back of his neck. Not a hero, no, not that at all, but his dad was certainly a guy with imagination. Jack wonders how a man who'd been through that, how a man who carried those nightmares in his head could have stayed on the farm as long as he did, faithfully accepting seven years of Lorraine's offered love, and. . . .

Oh. Jack's stomach and chest tighten. And then it suddenly takes all his effort just to breathe. Whatever is choking him wants to spread across his face but he won't let it. He won't cry. Not for himself, for godsake. He thinks of his father in 1953, June. Thirty-three years old. A young man holding his son. Sure, a new baby. But how did he account for the new feelings? How did he account for joy? And with so many of his friends dead, how must he have accounted for the simple fact that he was still alive?

Jack clings to the steering wheel and feels his face harden into a mask. He's scared. How could hope be trusted in a world as rotten and capricious as Kid Cliff must have known the world to be? And in the springtime, no less, when the whole farm bloomed with unearned bounty. It had to be too much, too much for any man . . . even a brave one.

Jack thinks of his father older now, sending his crew off on a life raft so he alone could chip ice with a baseball bat, on and on through the long winter night, daring death for the final time to take him. What did Neil say? Kid Cliff was a lousy boxer, but he refused to give up. Jack could see him, standing there, like Dempsey, his hands at his sides, refusing to go to the neutral corner! The damn guy wouldn't quit! But an iced-up boat can't stay upright. When enough ice accumulates, it'll flip. Simple law of physics. Boom, she'll turn over. Some things do make sense.

Neil was there, Jack thinks. He saw him die, saw him live. That guy was my father's son. He even had a war . . . he even had a long-lost love. And for solace, he even had his Alaska. For crying out loud, it's almost a cliché, this Alaska, this Lonely Hearts Club. Mary's right. Everyone's been pinched—everybody everywhere has a sad story! So what's the Big Secret?

Jack thinks of Susan's eyes and their Blackfeet blackness, and he thinks of her turned purple and hiding in the woods. In his nightmares he runs to the road for help and not to the woods for cover. Yesterday he almost died in his sleep. He could feel it happening gradually, a tremendous weight like a cold sea pushing in on him from all sides until he just about burst. Like dying in the depths. But he held on. He heard the tit-tit-tit of rain on the tent roof, saw gray light and then the feral dog Shit for Brains rummaging through his clothing on the other side of the mosquito netting: So he knew he was alive. He wonders what almost killed him, and how he fought it off, but only for a short time because ahead on the shoulder he sees someone waving him down.

Jack pulls over, and Susan opens the door. She pokes her wet head into the cab. Under her arm, held tightly against her stomach, is her purse.

"Oh, I'm so sorry it took me so long," she says, smiling weakly. "I know I . . . Look, here's some money. There's enough for a tip too!" She hands Jack a twenty. "When I came out, you weren't in your cab. I hope I wasn't too much trouble. I don't know, I . . . Sometimes I don't do the right thing."

Jack wonders if she was really going to shoot Neil. If he were to judge by her eyes, he'd say it was a definite possibility.

Yet even so, he asks her, "You want a ride somewhere?"

"No," she says. "Go on. I'm fine."

Jack doesn't know what to do with her standing in the drizzle like this, on the edge of the road, on the edge of the forest. He's trying to imagine her life, and all he gets are swirls. A little girl, a big girl. No face. A Montanan, an Alaskan. Still no face. All that waiting, all that hope—that much he knows. Lorraine's face, Mary's face, his. He wonders if she'll go into the woods with the bear, if that's where she feels safest, in the woods with a bear. She sways slightly, and Jack feels a wave of pity. He thinks of the guy with the baby looking for his yellow Pinto, the screaming mother on the sidewalk. A Blackfeet Indian woman standing in the drizzle with a pistol in her purse. Yeah, a purple face.

"Are you sure you don't want a ride?"

"Yes, I'm sure," she says. "I'm fine."

Sometimes the thing you think of doing is also the decent thing to do. And sometimes you even know it. Jack takes his sweatshirt off and hands it to her through the window. She slips it on, and then pulls the hood up.

"Thank you!" she yells, waving him onto the road. "I'll be okay now. I'm fine."

Jack rolls up his window against the rain. He pulls onto the road and cruises for town.

BACK IN WISCONSIN, in the winter, early in the morning or after dusk, the lights of the dairy barns shine across the snowfields and down the hollows. A barn full of cows is warm, even in very cold weather. Somebody is inside doing chores, and milking, as somebody has been doing every morning and evening for a hundred years. The warmth and shelter, the regularity of milkings, a cow's moist breath—Jack always figured people who milk cows every morning and evening know something the rest of the world doesn't. For a while he wanted to know what they know, to have what they have, to be where they are on those cold black-and-white mornings. And then, on the way in for breakfast, to see the sun break the horizon and the snow on the hills light up with a soft and forgiving yellow. Lorraine had beef cattle, but Jack was planning to get some Guernseys for milking after the baby was born. A steady income.

Mary didn't believe it for a minute. She didn't trust Jack's dairy plans because she could feel his restlessness better than he could. She could feel his yearning for something beyond the small sky of their hollow—something north and west, the wild black yonder of his father's mad, mad life. The more Jack tried to understand his dissatisfaction, the more dissatisfied he became. And the more dissatisfied he became, the more sentimental and less real became his plans. Last summer he began taking midnight walks. He'd hike up the hollow to where it narrowed, lie on his back and feel the ground breathe beneath him, listen to the longings of peepers and barred owls. It was a womb, this farm, this life. Beautiful and mysterious and lit by a billion beckoning stars—but still a womb. He could smell the green leaves of corn on the breeze, the sweet wet death of alfalfa. That's it. He was born here and he could die here, but he didn't know if he could live here. As much as he loved it, he was kicking.

Mary said she didn't want to be left alone with a baby, as Lorraine had been left alone with Jack. She told him he made a nice mother's son but he never quite made a man—and she'd never in a million years have a *boy's* baby.

She was right; she had the sense of things. When the chips were down, Jack didn't deliver, and all the sentimental baby-lust he could muster wouldn't change that.

Stepping on the gas, feeling the car pick up speed and the cool air from the vent on his face, Jack feels a curious urgency. He imagines how much one fox'd buy, how much two fox'd buy, how much three fox'd buy. What he needs and how much he . . . He drives over the crest of a hill, and down below the road is a ribbon of headlights. They begin to blur. He's crying, salt tears cold on his cheeks. After fifteen years, he's finally begun to mourn. He's got a long way to go, miles to go before he sleeps. He wants to hurry, hurry before he dies.

17 INSIDE THE RED-LIT warmth of Solly's Office Bar where the Hit Band is wrapping up another set with John Anderson's "Swingin'," in the corner by the rest rooms, next to where Jerry Rostov slumps against the ball of his jacket sleeping off a vodka-and-beer drunk and waiting for morning and a skiff ride back to Ouzinkie, past the three pay phones—one of which Jerry deactivated earlier by separating the receiver from the cord when the new bartender at the Pier Pub couldn't tell him where Pretty Gertie and Edna MacDonald had gone, one of which has just been vacated by Fourteen, who used it to call a cab, and one of which is being used by a young man speaking in frustrated bursts to his wife back in Maryland who refuses to come to Alaska if it means living in a trailer—barmaid Julie Jordan, ex-gymnast from Moscow, Idaho, who earlier in the evening had literally bent over backward trying to convince herself that she wasn't crazy about her husband Dodge's best friend, shakes her blond curls off her forehead, leans against the wall, and searches Lloyd Taylor's face.

LLOYD: You're what?

JULIE: You heard me.

LLOYD: And you're serious?

JULIE: Of course.

LLOYD: Oh shit. (Shaking his head) This is amazing. This is amazing as hell.

JULIE: (Anxiously) Why?

LLOYD: Because . . . (Pointing to himself, grinning) Because I'm crazy about *you,* too!

JULIE: Yeah? Oh god.

LLOYD: (Turning around, staring at Jerry on the floor, then spinning back again) I can't believe how fast things can change. Like that! A few words!

JULIE: You look great. You're something. If you only knew how—

LLOYD: You too, Julie. (Laughing, kissing her awkwardly on the forehead)

JULIE: Oh boy. I'm scared. I mean, you must think I'm a stick, standing here like this, but I'm scared.

LLOYD: Yeah, I know. I don't know.

JULIE: (Suddenly panicky) So does this go on for two years or two hours? What do we do to make it go away?

LLOYD: I don't know.

JULIE: I mean, I still love Dodge!

LLOYD: (He takes her shoulders in his hands and they kiss on the lips, keeping their faces close when they finish.) It's awful neat to see your face up close like this. I mean, it's worth it just for this.

JULIE: (Dazed) I have a feeling like you're going somewhere, like off to war or something. (She giggles.) And I don't want to forget you.

LLOYD: Yeah?

JULIE: (She pauses, looks away from him.) Wow.

LLOYD: What?

JULIE: Now I'm feeling . . . I'm sorry. Can you believe me? Now I'm feeling *sad*!

LLOYD: Don't be sad. (He touches her cheek.) You're sweet.

JULIE: First I was scared, then I was happy, and now I'm . . . Lloyd, do you know what I mean about never wanting to forget?

LLOYD: Yes. God, yes. (He puts his arms all the way around her and they embrace, purposefully this time, as if to keep from falling apart.)

JULIE: Dodge knows I like you. He knows. I told him I like you because I thought telling him would make it go away.

LLOYD: You did? He does? What did he say?

JULIE: He said, I bet if you weren't married you'd go after Lloyd, right? And I said yes, real honestly, hoping it would go away.

LLOYD: He said that? Really? (He turns away, shaking his head.)

JULIE: Lloyd? Are you okay?

LLOYD: I don't know. I knew Dodge . . . I mean, I don't remember ever *not* knowing Dodge!

JULIE: Yeah, god.

LLOYD: But still . . . I'm still glad you said something. I thought you were joking, because I told you I was crazy about Betty Jo what's-her-name, the bartender.

JULIE: Jorgeson.

LLOYD: Yeah. I told you I was crazy about her and she barely knows I exist, so I thought you were teasing me. I'm glad you said something. It's like a weight off.

JULIE: Oh good. I was so afraid I was going to put an extra weight on.

LLOYD: No, no. Don't worry.

JULIE: I just wish to god I knew what was going to happen.

LLOYD: (Touching her chin with his forefinger) Listen, there's one thing I know.

JULIE: What's that?

LLOYD: I know I'm crazy about you. (He lifts her chin so she's looking at him.) I know *that*.

JULIE: (Smiling) Great.

LLOYD: And I know I want you bad.

JULIE: Oh Lloyd!

LLOYD: And I know something else. I know you're crazy about me, too.

JULIE: Yeah. God, yeah, Lloyd.

LLOYD: Nobody wants to hurt anybody. (He kisses her.)

JULIE: (Turning away suddenly) I suppose this is my fault, for bringing it up, for changing everything.

LLOYD: Julie, please. Let's not . . . Let's just—

JULIE: (Unbelievingly, turning, waving her hand) Oh great. Let's not think about it? Is that what you're saying?

LLOYD: Look, Julie, you want out?

JULIE: (Staring at Jerry on the floor) What?

LLOYD: Because there's the door. It's okay. Just turn around and—

JULIE: No, Lloyd.

LLOYD: No hard feelings on my part. Really. Just go ahead, and we'll forget anything happened.

JULIE: Stop it, Lloyd! (She looks up at him, at his eyes.) I'm sorry. Forgive me. I'm dizzy. I . . . How are you?

LLOYD: Me? I'm fine!

JULIE: (Tenderly) Not sad anymore?

LLOYD: (Smiling) Nope.

JULIE: (Approaching him again, embracing) All of this feeling . . . like anything's possible . . . all of a sudden to me it's . . . You're not sad anymore? You're okay?

LLOYD: No, yeah. I'm okay. You're sweet. You're pretty.

JULIE: I didn't want to make you sad.

LLOYD: (Kissing her forehead, holding her shoulders) You want off, baby? You want off the world?

JULIE: (Eyes closed, whispering) No. I mean, I wanna be here. I just want the spinning to . . .

LLOYD: (Kissing across her cheek to her ear) You wanna stay?

JULIE: I'm afraid.

LLOYD: Of course.

JULIE: Things are gonna get ugly, Lloyd. I just know it.

LLOYD: (Kissing down the side of her neck) Jesus, they're pretty now.

JULIE: (Standing on her tiptoes) They're wonderful.

LLOYD: (Kissing from her collar up her throat to her chin) So what do you want?

JULIE: I don't know, Lloyd.

LLOYD: (Kissing over her chin to her lips) Then hang on, sugar.

18 FOURTEEN CLIMBS INTO the front seat, and without even facing Jack, she says, "Let's go up Pillar. Can you drive up Pillar for me?" Then she slams the door closed.

Jack says sure. He turns the cab around and heads up the hill on North Street, past houses with big windows that look out over town, toward Pillar Mountain Road.

"You know I'm pregnant?" she says.

"No."

"Yeah, well, I am."

Jack turns, and the road narrows and the houses stop. They drive a ways, bump over gravel, splash through a dark puddle. She called Gil from a pay phone in the back of Solly's and asked to have Jack pick her up. Jack has no idea why she called for him personally, and now is thoroughly confused by this announcement of her pregnancy. Should he offer his congratulations? Should he tell her she's sure to make a wonderful mother?

"I found out this morning and that's one of the reasons I quit work," she says. "Besides, I felt lousy. I mean, maybe my body is trying to tell me something."

Jack turns down the radio. Pillar Mountain, he thinks. Why does she want to go up Pillar Mountain on such a foggy night? What if she starts asking him all about Florida?

"After I quit work I went home and looked at these old pictures, thinking they'd cheer me up," she says. "Oregon pictures. But all they did was put me in a worse mood. I got thinking about this friend who cut her wrists, and then I didn't have a chance. My god!"

Fourteen is talking as though Jack should know what she's talking about, as if this conversation is a natural continuation of where they left off the last time they spoke. It's irritating. Jack never knows what

Fourteen's talking about, but she's always so familiar and nice that he feels as though he ought to. Christ, he still doesn't know her name.

"Well, all this talk about punishing yourself, the Big Question . . ." She rolls her eyes and laughs her hiccup laugh. "For crying out loud, to me it's just a question of happy or sad."

Jack wonders if the father is the guy with the leather jacket.

"Remember the guy I talked to when we were in front of Solly's?" she asks. "When I read you the 'Real Alaska' poem?"

"With the leather jacket?"

"Sharkskin. Yeah. He's the dad."

"Oh." Fourteen looks different, but Jack can't figure out why. The bandanna is gone, sure, and the glasses, but it's something else. Her skin, maybe.

"It's not too great," she says after a long pause. "He's not too happy about it."

"Who?" As soon as he asks it, Jack feels dumb. It's her face, though. Her face looks different.

She laughs, shakes her head. "Forget it. You're on charter, you know. I'm putting you on charter. Better call it in."

Jack radios Gil that he's on charter.

Onto Pillar Mountain Road, and now they're climbing. Into the fog, higher, the road winds. She's staying way over next to the door.

"I've thought about an operation," she says, "but no way."

Funny word, "operation," Jack thinks. Tom Geary said in his letter that they're called (il)legal operations on daytime TV. June Tyler, in Lorraine's book *Love's Memories,* had an operation. But she'd been raped by Justin Moore.

"I wanted to make it up here one last time," she says.

"One last time?"

"I'm going to Michigan tomorrow, because my sister lives there. I don't know. I couldn't take Oregon again, and this place is getting pretty bizarre." She's talking toward the window. "Tell me something, okay?"

"What?"

"When you saw me earlier—in the cab or at the Beachcombers—did you think I looked pregnant?"

"No."

"I mean, did I look pregnant to you? Like a pregnant woman?" She's raising her hands, making a dome around her stomach, inflating her cheeks.

"No."

Her cheeks deflate. "Terry says I look pregnant to him." Her hands drop to her lap.

Her face, her shoulder, her neck: something's different.

Jack steers the big cab up the narrow road. He can see dark-gray gravel immediately ahead of the car, where the headlights reach, but then the land and the road fade into the fog. The car groans, shifts up, then down, the automatic transmission unable to make up its mind.

"I don't know what the heck I want to come up here for," she says, sounding suddenly disappointed.

Jack thinks he should have been more reassuring about the way she looks. It's just that lately all women look pregnant to him. Their due dates are more than nine months away, but they're still pregnant. Lorraine used to tell him that he was an extra-special boy because it took seven years to make him.

"It's okay," he says.

"A person would have to be very sad," she said. "I mean to . . . you know. Don't you think?"

"Probably," Jack says, although he doesn't know if she's talking about abortion or suicide. Mary wasn't sad beforehand.

"And for a long time."

Or maybe she was sad. Maybe Mary was sad for a long time.

"Inside, I mean. Worn down. It's depressing. Even to think about."

"Yeah it is." It's depressing to think that Mary may have been sad for a long time without Jack knowing it. It's depressing to know how badly things can go, regardless of good intentions. He thinks of Neil and Betsy and Susan, the trailer at Naughton's. Neil wants to buy Jack a feast at the Mecca. But the thought of sitting with him for a whole breakfast makes Jack feel claustrophobic. Still, he has to start somewhere. Neil knew his father. Neil saw his father die.

And the food. Waffles. Sure. Think of those.

"He doesn't even know I'm leaving, you know," Fourteen says.

"What?"

"But I am. I'm leaving. I decided for sure about one hour ago. Man, is he in for a shocker!"

Jack looks at her. In the light from the dashboard he can see her eyes do that vulnerable-looking squint. There's something sweet and troubled about the shape of her lips and mouth. She reminds him of Mary, even the irritating way she talks. Jack feels a lightness in his stomach that spreads upward to the base of his neck and even higher, around the back of his head, lifting his hairs, goose bumps again. Jesus. Two hours ago he was going back to Wisconsin to marry Mary. Now he's not.

"You're not going to tell him?" he asks.

"He can find me if he wants." She crosses her legs and then uncrosses them, sighs. "He knows I've got a sister."

"Look," Jack says, "I'm embarrassed to ask this because I know we've been introduced, but what's your name?"

"Wanda." She says it simply, quickly, as if there's no reason whatsoever why Jack should know her name. But *Wanda* doesn't sound familiar.

"I'm Jack," he says.

She laughs. "I know. I called for you personally, remember?"

Jack drives up around another curve, and the road levels out a little. She thinks he's from Florida and until now he didn't know her name, and she called for him personally.

She laughs again. "No, I can't do that. I'm not Wanda. I'm Deb."

"Deb," Jack repeats. "Wanda didn't sound too familiar." He slows the cab and rolls down his window. It's foggy, and he can barely see through the windshield.

"We're not going to see anything from up here," she says.

"Pretty thick." Jack slows further and drives with his head out the window, keeping his eyes on the gravel just ahead of the car. The air is moist and cool. Cloud air.

"I couldn't think of anybody else to call. Did Gil tell you that I asked for you personally and I couldn't think of anybody else to call?"

"He told me it was a personal. He didn't tell me who it was."

126

"I couldn't figure who else had a car to take me up here. I went to the Beachcomber and looked around, and then I saw you and thought . . . You seem so . . . I don't know. I get crazy, I suppose. I had a feeling about you, and this is my last night." She laughs her hiccup laugh. "Maybe it's on account of me being prego, you know? Pee-gee. I didn't want to be alone."

Jack can tell by the grade of the road that they have reached the top. He slows to a stop, shifts to Park. When he turns the headlights off they are surrounded by heavy darkness.

"Jesus," he whispers. He can't see a thing.

"On a normal night a person could see the whole town down there, huh?"

"This is a normal night."

"I mean on a clear night." She laughs nervously, shifts in her seat. "I was up here one other time. I wanted to get a last look, but I suppose that was kind of dumb."

"It wasn't dumb," Jack says. He turns the engine off, and the silence is loud and everywhere. "It's nice up here. Kind of spooky, though."

"It was beautiful. Terry and I watched the whole sunset. Must have lasted a couple of hours. It was like we were on top of the world and the horizon was the rim!"

"Huh." Jack can hear her breathing, but he can't see her.

"All around it was pink. Just glowing. My god!"

"Wow."

"Three hundred and sixty degrees of horizon was this glowing pink."

"Yeah?"

"Like a fire underneath everything, but the ocean was calm and blue as a mirror. It was something."

"I'll bet."

"It was very special."

Jack feels his shirt pocket for his Copenhagen. The tobacco will ease the hunger pains in his stomach. He pushes the tin out and takes a dip, feels in the dark near his feet for an empty coffee cup.

Deb opens the door and the dome light turns on. "I'm going to walk around."

Jack looks at her, but she doesn't look at him. Her skin is different, that's for sure. It's darker, redder. Mary's didn't look that way when she was pregnant.

"Don't worry," she says, stepping out. "I'm a big girl."

Jack doesn't know if he should go with her, if she *wants* him to go with her. He imagines her falling off a cliff (jumping off a cliff?), sees her body hit the rocks, shake like a rag doll, but he can't remember if there are any cliffs way up here. There could be bears, though; up here is the wilderness, or the very edge. It starts here, just in back of them, all around them. In Wisconsin there must be a hundred cliffs that carry the legend of an Indian princess, her love forsaken, leaping to her death. Anyway, Deb is out already and has walked behind the cab. Jack waits a moment and then gets out himself. He stands next to the car, spits into the wet grass. It's not raining, but the damp air seems to go right through his shirt to his skin. He can hear Deb but can't see her. Jack stands still, breathes as quietly as he can, shivers without his sweatshirt. Then he takes a step her way.

"Just wait," she says from behind the car.

Jack stops. His eyes have grown accustomed to the dark and he can see her white blouse. She was low behind the back bumper and now she's standing up, straightening her skirt. He can see her teeth when she smiles. She twists her backwaisthipslegs and pushes her hair off her shoulders.

"I had to go bad," she says.

"I see that."

She walks back and gets in the front door of the cab. Jack lets her be by herself for a moment, watching her through the windshield. The dome light stays on so he can see her reach for the rearview mirror and begin to brush her hair. Her fingernails flash like white teeth when she moves her hand. A suntan. That's it. She's been to the tanning booth. Her face and neck . . .

He opens his door, slides in again behind the wheel. "Nice tan," he says.

"Thanks." She hesitates, smiles. "I did it for a little too long. I'm afraid I burned."

Jack wishes he knew what she wants him to do. If someone would just beat a drum or something, then he'd know that yes indeed, this is one of those *choices,* one of those *significant times.* She quit her job and got a suntan and then chartered his cab at thirty dollars an hour. If he were leaving tomorrow they'd be on the same flight. But he's not leaving. Life is odd. What's next? Does anybody have even the slightest idea?

"So you don't like Kodiak?" Jack asks.

"It's okay," she says. "It was a good time." She shuts her door all the way so the dome light goes out. "Wow, dark!" She laughs her hiccup laugh again.

Jack laughs because she laughs.

"I don't know," she says. "Maybe I'll come back. People do all the time. They leave and then they come back. That's Kodiak for you." Her voice is distant, as if she's already left the island, as if she's already back in Michigan showing off her tan.

"Yeah," Jack says.

"Well, it's pretty accurate, don't you think?"

"I suppose."

"All the money, the water, this giant pink horizon on top of the world! Whew!"

"It's pretty."

"And you don't forget it, I'll tell you that much. Even when it rains for a month straight. In fact, that's when you remember it best."

"Yeah."

"Wait until you're around for a while," she says. "It'll be hard to go back to Florida."

Jack nods, swallows. It's quiet for a while, a minute, two minutes. He can wait for dawn up here if he has to. It can't be far away—through the fog and over the curve of the earth. He thinks about his dad getting here and staying here. He wonders if maybe Kid Cliff had planned to return to Wisconsin but then he saw all that pink horizon and . . . Jack rolls the window up, then down again. He hangs his arm out the window and taps the side of the cab. He asks Deb if she wants the radio on, and she says no. He spits, hoping he hasn't made her angry. Then he notices her fists are gripped tightly on her lap, and when he looks at her face he thinks she might be crying.

"He's such a selfish bastard!" she says.

Jack clears his throat.

She coughs, then wipes her face, catches her breath. "Oh heck." She's moved closer, not very close, but arm's length anyway. "I should have brought some wine or something."

"That'd be great," Jack says, not meaning it.

"Here."

Jack feels her take his hand.

Neither speaks.

She holds Jack's hand with both of hers and still neither speaks. Jack can feel her breathing, or hear her breathing, or maybe that's him. Some things a man must do and other things he wants to do, Jack heard on the radio once. But that isn't any help if you don't know which is which. Jack feels light and reckless, and suddenly very stiff with his lightness and recklessness.

"Would you do me a favor?" she asks, whispers, so Jack can't hear.

"What?"

She swallows, lowers his hand to her lap, holds it very tightly until it almost hurts. "A favor."

Jack shifts in his seat, careful not to pull his hand away, curious as hell as to what she might say next.

"I know this is stupid, so don't tell me it is. Just pretend something, okay? You seem nice. Have you ever been in love?"

"I . . . ah . . ."

"Oh, don't answer. I'm sorry." She's speaking matter-of-factly, instructionally, and Jack isn't prepared for what happens. The tears are gone. She's raising his hand, past her breasts and over her shoulder to the back of her neck. "Put your hand here. Hold me like this, with your fingers on . . . Just lay your hand on the back of my neck and hold me like this, okay?"

Jack feels the damp skin, the vibrations in her throat as she talks, her hair on the back of his hand. He can move her this way and that like a puppet; he can move her, but he doesn't dare.

"This is going to sound stupid but . . . ."

Jack listens.

"Tell me you love me, okay?"

Jack holds her neck, spits into the empty coffee cup, stares over the steering wheel through the windshield and fog at nothing. He's had some odd requests before, but this takes the cake. He wants to laugh but he's afraid. He's surprised at the warmth of her skin, of her tan skin.

"I know it's a lie," she says. "We're pretending, okay? Pretend. Close your eyes."

Jack closes his eyes but then opens them. He can't see anything anyway.

"Okay, tell me you love me."

"I . . ."

"Just pretend."

"I love you." He's surprised at how easily the words come, the syllables. It took him years before he could say them to Mary, and by the time he did he was already planning to leave her. But it was love, all right. It felt like intermittent yearning and disappointment, bliss and hope and confusion. Jack wants to tell Deb everything he thought when he first talked with her this evening, when they were parked outside Solly's. He wants to tell her that she reminds him painfully of a woman he loved and that he would like to take her to Mexico and laugh with her and hold her neck all the time, that he would love to—

"Say it again."

He's stroking her very gently, softly, with his thumb. He's beginning to lose his breath. He can feel her moving, feel her pressing.

"Please," she says.

"I love you."

She's moving faster under his hand, pushing against something Jack can't see. He can hear her breathing, feel her neck begin to sweat.

"Am I beautiful?" Her skirt's bunched up; Jack can see her knees.

"You're beautiful," he says.

"Say it again."

"I love you."

"Again."

"I love you."

Her head falls back, knees up, and Jack drops his hand over her shoulder to her collar toward her breasts, feeling her chest expanding, her skin moving, her arm crossing down between her legs.

"No!" she says, throwing her head forward again. "The neck, my neck!"

Jack slides his hand back, catches his breath, and waits.

"All right," Deb says. "Close your eyes again."

Jack closes his eyes this time. He sees her rocking in a chair by a wood stove. He sees her holding a baby to her breast, rocking in soft light, blue light, eyes closed and she's humming lullabies. Lullabies! He sees Mary. He's a hero. He sees three hundred and sixty degrees of pink horizon and bombers screaming off the water blowing everything around him to smithereens.

"Oh god," she says.

"I love you."

"Oh jesus."

"I love you." Jack sees redtails playing on the spring breezes, floating in the blue, then tucking and diving and spreading their wings again to soar above the trees on the ridge. The same ridges and hollows wind all the way to the Mississippi, a hundred and fifty miles of maze, creeks and pasture separated by wooded hills, and each man in his own fertile wrinkle. Summer: the grass looking soft and green enough to lie down on and sleep and never wake up until winter. Winter: the yellow light off corn stalks, the box elder branches making web shadows in the snow, the west bank of the creek lit up at daybreak like a stage. Sometimes snow falls without wind and the flakes cling to barbed wire and tiny gray prickly ash branches. Cows crowd the barnyard, snow dusting their backs, staring hungry-eyed through the fence and blatting *feed me, feed me for ever and ever*.

"What? What do you love?"

"I love your tan skin, your neck. I love your face and eyes and nose. . . ." Jack's into it now, he's pretending with the best of them. Mary said okay and twisted slightly, made a little groan like a puppy. Jack ran his fingers across her hips into the gentle valley her waist made. She was being nice on his last night, being good but very very passive, facing away from him. Jack kissed the back of her neck, curling his body tighter around hers, feeling her coolness pressing very high on each of his thighs. Only one place to go from here— Sure there's pain, there's always pain. But sometimes, despite the crap, everything is so new and simple and bared it's hard to fall asleep.

"Say it!"

"I love you."

Deb quivers beneath his hand, her neck straining now, muscles and tendons taut.

"I feel it!"

"I love you." His mom wanted him to stay and Mary wanted him to stay and Jack wanted to stay even more than they wanted him to stay. And everybody wanted everybody to be happy! Even in agreement there was disagreement. Mary arched her back slightly, pressed him into her. It was the best he could do at the time. A person tends to live the only story he can believe, and like his dad, Jack couldn't believe in family or farm anymore. You can't choose your fate—who you are, what made you, the color of your skin, or where the bombs will fall. And you can't choose your destiny. You can choose to accept it, and act accordingly, or you can choose to deny it. Jack thinks of his dad, and as he does forgiveness fills his chest and swells his temples with blood. It comes in waves.

"Again!"

"I love you." He loves his dad. Of course, he does. The strong suffer and the weak suffer. There's pain in hiding yourself and pain in revealing yourself, pain in losing yourself and pain in finding yourself. There are so many pains it's ridiculous, and no matter what you choose, you die in the end. If Kid Cliff could live with that—however he had to—Jack can too.

"Oh jesus, oh jesus!" Deb gasps, and stops breathing, trembles, her body tormented. Jack's hand is pinched against the headrest, but he endures it, the long silence, the waiting. Suddenly she sighs and exhales and relaxes, all spent, all at once. She takes a deep breath, and exhales again, sticking out her lower lip to blow the hair off her face.

"Okay," she whispers.

Jack's hand is tingling as the blood rushes back to his fingers, but his feet are right where they always were. His feet are still. Think of breakfast, he tells himself. Neil wants to buy you a feast.

"Okay," she whispers again. "You can drive me down."

Jack starts the car, flips on the headlights. A yellow circle extends just so far into the fog and then stops, making the darkness darker: A little yellow circle on top of the world. It's raining again, so he turns on the wipers and they squeak. He backs up and turns around. Deb looks comatose, sprawled out, her skirt still bunched on her lap. Neither speaks on the way down. After a while Deb sits up and pulls a brush out of somewhere, begins brushing her hair in the dark.

19 INSIDE THE KODIAK Canning Company, past where the pumps pump and the conveyors whine and the cooler motors hum, G. Clarence Robson, Skin Man, scrubs a retort, a big shiny metal pressure cooker. His long hair is tucked under a blue watch cap, and he wears oilskin bib overalls and rubber boots. Sweat and steam dampen his face and bony arms, making his skin glisten. Webs of blue veins stand out on his forearms.

He works quickly, spraying the inside of the boiler with water. His narrow jaw is slack, and his mouth hangs open in an O. The black hose has kinked and wrapped around a sink support leg, so G. Clarence jerks it, snaps the hose upward, sending a snake wave toward the sink. The tangle lifts and drops, but stays a tangle. G. Clarence's tongue darts out of his mouth and smears across his top lip. He swears without anger as he backs up, pulls gently on the hose. No luck. He walks over to the kink, and squinting, he patiently unwraps the hose from both itself and the sink support leg. There now. But it's time to go. Night shift is ending already. He quickly coils the hose and hangs it on the wall.

In the bright locker room, he towels himself off. He lets his long hair down and gets a comb from his bag, steps over to the mirror. He likes the way his cheekbones have become prominent lately. He reminds himself of a guy he hitchhiked from Coos Bay to Ann Arbor with one time, a guy who called himself Nineteen Sixty-nine.

G. Clarence combs his hair smooth, tucks it back behind his ears so he looks like a racehorse, a sleek and fine breed. Nice.

Now, from a sock that he keeps hanging in his locker, a sock that fit eight apples when full but now holds just three, G. Clarence removes one Red Delicious. He leans over his knees, polishes it, turns it this way and that way, examining the apple in the white fluorescent light. The little locker room is filling quickly with other workers.

"Yo-ho!" Kingsley shouts.

"Hey," says Dean.

G. Clarence polishes his apple some more and doesn't look up.

"Glory time!" Kingsley screams, kicking his locker.

Glory time is the short time between shifts—what will be very short once the salmon start rolling in—a little gift from God, a too short time in which a person must eat, drink, dance, make love, fight, meditate, snort coke, fast, read, stand on his head, sleep, and much much more. Glory time is a magic time when anything is possible, comparatively; when duty ceases, comparatively; and when fun begins, comparatively. Forget what they say about a human fetus beginning life at ten weeks, twenty weeks, thirty weeks, or whatever—*life* doesn't truly begin until glory time. The absolute certainty of going back to work so soon clicks things up two speeds, urges even the least appetitive to blur the distinction between want and need, to attempt to satisfy as many desires as possible in a very short time. Because, well, because all there is is a very short time.

G. Clarence twists off the apple stem—A B C D E F—and tosses it on the floor. He does this same thing every day, and watching his single-minded attention to an apple, some of the other workers snicker and nudge one another. But most don't pay attention anymore. G. Clarence is Skin Man, and crazy, and that's just fine. Everyone in town has seen him ride his bicycle, almost naked and in all types of weather; everyone has seen him, and these guys can say they work with him.

Kingsley and Dean are talking business.

"Listen to me, listen to me," Kingsley says. "There comes a time in every young girl's life when . . . Are you listening to me?"

"Yeah, go, King. Comes a time what?"

"There comes a time in every young girl's life when she longs to master the fine art of fellatio."

"Jesus!"

"It's true!"

"Jesus, King."

"Maybe not the lezzies, see, but pretty much all the rest."

"You telling me all those little girls want to . . ."

"I'm telling you they want to know *how*! Sure they do. At some point in their lives they decide it's something a girl ought to know."

"Huh."

"Something to think about, eh, Deano?"

"You're amazing, King. And you're gonna demonstrate?"

"I'm willing to instruct."

"What a guy!"

"I'm a teacher," Kingsley says. "I have a calling."

An observer might think, as he watches G. Clarence break into a fresh round of apple-polishing, that what he wants is a shiny apple. In actuality, however, G. Clarence wants a clean apple, an apple with no scuffs or impurities, no molecules of foreign matter, nothing sticky or grainy or rough. He wants pure apple, as pure as any apple can be.

For five days now, G. Clarence has eaten one apple a day and nothing else. This is his sixth day on the apple phase—he's got two left. He's been tapering his food intake in eight-day blocks until now he's eating only apples and apples only, and in two days he won't even need to eat that much. He will eat one plum a day for eight days, then one almond a day for eight days, then one raisin a day for eight days. And after that he will eat nothing at all. From apples to plums to almonds to raisins to air: He will have phased himself into another realm, that offered and made available by the Pure Air Diet (PAD). On air he will subsist and even grow. All because he has trained his body, disciplined his mind, conquered his appetites (the Achilles' heel of man) with a scientifically planned regimen.

The book he's reading, *Soul Food,* explains: "Eating is a social rather than biological function. Withdraw from society, and your need for food decreases. Turn inward, into the very center of your soul, away from even your own body, and you will discover a garden from which you can harvest food for the spirit." The reasoning is thus: as long as the spirit is kept alive, the body cannot die. The book's authors contend that this is a scientific fact, not whimsy or superstition, that it's the secret to the long, happy lives of such noble peoples as the Ancient Incas, certain Mongol Herdsmen, a sect of Afghan Nomads, Chinese High Priests, Biblical Fathers, and a few of the American Negro Slaves.

"Authentic moon boots, see?" Ed, on the bench next to Skin Man, is pointing at his new boots. "They've got moon rocks in 'em somewhere."

"What?" Dean says. "Where the hell do they put moon rocks?"

"I don't know," Ed says. "In 'em somewhere. I read it on the guarantee. It said, 'Authentic Moon Rocks.' "

Stretching his neck, craning, Kingsley says, "Did you say those boots have moon rocks in 'em?"

Ed cocks his head, smiles. He's not an idiot. But his wide, flat forehead and his almond eyes, set far apart, make him look like one. He's learned the role so well he doesn't even know he's playing.

"Put down fifty bucks," he says. "Piece of fucking history, the way I see it!"

"Are you kidding?" Big grin, big-mouth grin on this Kingsley. He makes a grab, but Ed pulls the boot away. "Listen, Eddie, how the hell are they going to use moon rocks to make boots?" His innocent hands up, his eyebrows up, up, up . . . Kingsley has a rubber face.

"Look, Kingsley." Ed shakes his head patiently. His fingers, his hands, then his arms, spread like an umpire signaling safe. "I'll believe what I want, and you believe what you want, okay?"

Life is a self-generating phenomenon: within life is the capacity to sustain life. G. Clarence's book explains: "The knowledge and/or technical know-how to achieve perpetuation of life without cellulose sustenance, i.e. food, has been a problem of the ages, a problem too often ignored and lent insufficient energies and disciplines. The great minds and wills of history, strong enough to resist their enemies' tortures for airy and metaphysically inconsequential principles such as political freedom, will bow meekly to the very stirrings of hunger, the smallest pains of which make them fly to the table and indulge themselves in the primitive and peripheral ritual of stuffing food into their mouths as though they were large fish."

"I got it!" Kingsley's shoe slams the bench; he laughs, showing vertical crescents on his cheeks from chin to eyeball. "I know what the moon rocks are used for. They're paperweights to hold the sucker money on the company president's desk!"

G. Clarence sits on the bench in front of his locker, wearing shorts and tennies, still using a good share of his glory time to polish his apple, to remove the fingerprints that he just put on when he twisted the stem, to remove the fingerprints that have long since been pressed deep into the apple skin, the prints of the guy who picked it, the guy who boxed it, the guy who displayed it, the countless people who may have fingered it in the store, the guy who weighed it. The impurities are deep; it needs a good cleaning. Fingerprints are made of something, and whatever it is isn't apple.

The hunger G. Clarence felt so uncomfortably when he began this diet over a month ago has become his companion. Five years ago he was addicted to cigarettes, and the way he feels about the hunger he carries reminds him of the way he used to feel about the cigarettes in his pocket. With them, he felt brave, confident, unalone, able to scale Everest! But without them . . . without them he felt incomplete, panicky, all alone and frightened to walk a block away from where he could get them. The dull ache he carries in his stomach is his own accomplishment, his friend, his identity: a mark by which he can locate himself in the universe. In a world in which he feels removed and alienated from the great debates and battlefields, separated from any of the strings of power, manipulated by fascist militarists like Alexander (the Great) Haig, economic total- itarians (faceless), and a rapidly monopolizing food industry (that also makes tires, fills gas tanks, sells clothing), deprived of access to texture and warmth by the Plastic Age, personally devalued by the Computer Age, diminished by the Space Age (basically shafted by one age after another), and spectatorized by the massive growth of professional sports, his hunger remains as an affirmation of his Freedom and Will and personal Existence. *Despite the buggerers!* It's even better than cigarettes—it's *Skin Man's own* achievement. It connects him to the world's starving, to the world's gorged; to the powerful and to the powerless; to the all-mighty Producer and to the Consumer who died for our sins; to Mahatma Gandhi and to Adolf Hitler; it connects him without memory or anticipation to the living, the dead, and the yet to be born. The great unifier of vice and virtue, of pacifism and violence, of good and evil, of the generations, hunger connects him to his grandfather (no, no—he doesn't have a grandfather, but his friend did), who was a farmer and a heavy-stone mover at the county fairs and who as an old man had two hernias from lifting heavy things but was proud as hell to have them, to sit in his sofa and be crippled by two hernias, *proud as hell,* and this is the first time G. Clarence has ever understood why, this is the first glimpse G. Clarence has had into why a man would be proud to have two broken balls, to wear them like badges of suffering and surviving and courage, two cracked bells, like a couple of old last laughs.

G. Clarence has discovered the individual's ultimate and perhaps only inalienable power play: self-abuse. Hunger tells him—every moment and every day, wherever he is and whatever he's doing—it proves to him beyond a shadow of doubt that he's a human being and—hurrah!—he's still alive.

Kingsley's standing on the bench now, one shoe on a foot and the other in his hand, pounding the locker with the shoe, harder, harder, accenting each syllable distinctly, *"Fuck-ing moon rocks, fuck-ing moon rocks!"*

"It was on the guarantee," Ed says. "Subject closed."

Kingsley eases up on the locker-pounding; his brow furrows. "Piece of history, is that it?"

"Up yours, jerk."

G. Clarence is lifted by these thoughts, made to feel generous in spirit, kind and good and forgiving. He can't imagine life anymore without this feeling in his stomach. He wants to get back on his bicycle, ride home to his tent, and savor it. He wants to write a letter to his friend's grandmother and say, Yes! yes! everything you and Grandpa did was great! The diet book was right: *spirit soaring, feasting in the colored garden of soul.* The body cannot sink when the spirit soars so high above heaven and earth that . . .

G. Clarence waits until a very old Filipino man with a strange spicy odor passes behind him, then wipes the apple one last time. He holds it between his forefinger and thumb and eats it quickly, taking large bites, chewing minimally before swallowing, discharging an unpleasant task. It disgusts him, this. Genghis Khan, Jesus Christ, Napoleon, Socrates, his friend's grandparents, dim like distant planets at dawn. The weight in his stomach numbs him for a moment, blankets the gnawing, muffles the pithy voice of hunger. But only for a moment. He'll ride his bicycle back to his tent on Monashka Bay, and by then it'll be there again—ooooooooo—like a flaming arrow; he'll feel it again!

"I'll bring the guarantee, okay?" Ed says. "Will that satisfy you? I mean, they got shit to protect consumers nowadays."

King Kingsley has leaped up from the bench and now hangs from a pipe, twisting one way, then the other. His mouth is huge, like a chimpanzee's. "Glory time!" he screams.

Ed turns back to the business of dressing himself, but mumbles nervously, "What do you think, Skin Man, is he going to rupture himself or what?"

But G. Clarence Robson, the Skin Man, doesn't answer or even pause to consider. He's out; yessir, he's gone.

20 ALONG THE CHANNEL that runs between Kodiak Island and Near Island, in T. T. Fuller's lot where drydocked fishing boats are parked in rows, puddles spread on the gravel. Crooked wooden houses cling to the slope directly above the lot. From one of the houses, a particularly drab shack, an unpainted stairway leads down to the boatyard.

Londa Evens, from Little Rock, Arkansas, hangs on to the railing as she descends. She's the Mecca barmaid, who at the beginning of the evening shared a cab ride with a musician named Johnny Stone. She's wearing a hooded yellow raincoat much too large for her, a navy-blue skirt extending just past her knees, nylons, high heels.

The fog hangs low, partially obscuring the canneries down the road, yellow Whitney, white Moonie's, red Icy Cape. The sky is dark gray, and the gravel is regular gray, and the wooden railing sliding past her hand is light gray. Toward the harbor and center of town, the Star of Kodiak cannery is gray too. Londa is tired of gray, of the sheer width of the color, the way it goes all the way from almost white to almost black. The word doesn't mean anything anymore. Say something is gray, and all that means is the something is not black or white or colored. She smells fish and kelp and mud, and is tired of that too. What Londa is wishing now is that Richard, this Richard whom she just met a few hours ago while working at the Mecca, and whom she'd gone home with for certainly no reason she can remember, had a phone so she could call a cab.

The powdered skin below her chin bulges as she drops her head to watch where she steps. She hopes Richard will be mad at her for not being around when he wakes and for stealing his raincoat. She hopes he'll come looking for her. No, she doesn't. That'd be awful, really. But even if he doesn't get mad and come looking for her, he'll still wish she'd stayed. He'll want to look at her when he gets up. He'll want to see her this morning, but Londa won't give him the pleasure. She's not sure why, but knowing that makes her feel better.

Down in the boatyard now, she steps past a puddle, almost turning her ankle when the heel of her shoe rolls a stone. She cusses the musician Johnny Stone for saying it's her choice. Choice? She can see Johnny now—Johnny the rock star whose band is on a world tour—home in his apartment over the Mecca Bar, sitting in his black leather chair, staring out the window of his apartment, watching the clouds and the rain and the stupid gulls over the harbor while he smokes his carved ivory pipe, probably waiting for her, always waiting for her. He has a dumb face, really, she thinks. He writes song lyrics and thinks they are *enormous,* but they are really just dumb. He frowns a lot and he learns a new word every day and he collects pieces of Third-World art. But it's all a waste because . . . well, because imagining himself a great talent is about the high point of his imagination! The thought makes Londa smile. She thinks she'll tell him that, and tell him it's lucky he likes to play bars— just so she can watch his face and be done with it.

Londa walks slowly across the gravel and down the road behind the canneries. The heaviness, the dampness, the fish smell, seem to get thicker. She wants to smoke a cigarette but doesn't want to bother trying to light it in the rain. She misses her friends in Little Rock; she misses her husband, Paul. Paul-when-he's-sober is such a different man than Paul-when-he's-drunk. She wishes she knew what the hell "It's your choice, baby" means. Men are always insisting on the existence of choice, yet Londa doesn't know when she ever really had one—except maybe when she left Arkansas for Alaska. But with Paul gone and all, what else could she have done? She certainly couldn't move back with her mother.

A black dog approaches, tiptoeing past puddles at the edge of the road. It stops and wags its stump tail, showing a pink tongue, squinting against the drizzle. Londa ignores it, feeling mistrustful of its enthusiasm. The dog takes a step toward her, but then, instinctively, changes direction and lopes away.

Londa feels as if she must consciously breathe or she'll stop. She feels the air sticking to her body like sweat, and she wants to scratch between her toes. The sky in the northeast has promise, at least, what with the orange and light blue on the horizon, but rain drips down the outside of her jacket onto her skirt and makes her legs wet. She's thinking about her daughter growing up, and she's thinking about Paul not even knowing where they are, and she's thinking about both at once. By the time Esther's her age, Esther will have seen enough of men to teach her all she needs to know, that's for sure. She won't be sheltered, as Londa was, and nobody will tell her that *these things don't really happen*, because what's the use? Esther will know already that they do.

At the bar, at work, Richard kept whispering his obscene little come-on into her ear. What a jerk! Of course she thought it was funny, but so what? And then Johnny, between sets, having noticed it all, says to her, "Okay, you're a big girl now—it's your choice, baby." She almost laughed out loud! The truth was she didn't want either (that's a choice?), but she went with Richard to spite Johnny . . . and also because she'd seen something in Richard's face when he wasn't laughing or whispering fakely intimate, and she mistook it for something she felt a lot. Too often.

It embarrasses her to think about now. She's leaving Richard's early so he'll know she doesn't like him, and she's thinking that if she saw all this in a movie with her mother, her mother would say, even now (still calling her by her girlhood name), "Oh, those things don't really happen, Linda."

Londa feels dirty and damp and tired, and to top everything, she's got Richard's little duty in her panties. She wishes she'd taken a shower, but that might have awakened Richard, so she'll take one at home. She cusses Richard for not having a telephone so she could call a cab. (Or call her husband Paul! That would have been something! All the way to Little Rock. And what a hell of a surprise on Richard's phone bill!) She cusses Richard for thinking she gives a damn, his grunts, his eyes-closed passion, and the way he whispered to her neck, "Here's the moment! Here it is!" then soared off somewhere far from himself or her—or any moment that Londa was aware of. Now she can't imagine anything she might have seen in his face, or might imagine seeing in *anybody's* face! How ridiculous! Despite herself, Londa lets out a high, silly-sounding giggle.

At the base of the hill, as Londa tries to make a long step across a puddle, the heel of her right shoe snaps off and she falls on her rear. Water splashes up the sleeves of the raincoat, through her skirt, and onto her thighs. She sits for a moment, wanting badly to laugh some more, wishing not so much that she hadn't fallen but that someone were here to laugh with. Paul would laugh. He'd reach down and help her up, make her laugh with just the look on his face. He'd . . . The man had a lot of fun in him when he was in the right mood. He used to say he could whistle, dance, and make love at the same time—and he could! She pictured him standing by the front door of their apartment in Little Rock, holding the rolled-up newspaper and flipping it over his shoulder, catching it behind his back, so neatly, so easily and smoothly, that even if he missed he looked good, with that predrunk glow, whatever, as if he had a good secret he promised to tell if she was good, if she was very good.

The water swirls gray around her feet. Now she's watching herself as if from a distance, sitting in the water, as if to see—*as if she's curious to see*—how Londa Evens, age twenty-eight, will react to falling into a puddle. She feels a chill creep through her, a deep chill down to her bones that threatens to shake her. She quickly rubs her gravel-scraped hands together and then—just like that, because she can't stand the uncertainty any longer—she makes up her mind that she will not leave Kodiak, never, that she's here to stay, that Paul can go to hell in a handbasket, that he can find her here if he really wants to. She clenches her jaw and feels under water for something solid to stand on. Dripping, she pushes herself up and makes her way up the hill on one high heel and one low, warming as she goes.

From the top, through the bushes and dreary air, gray but not so dark as it had been, she can see the line of colored metal canneries crowded along the channel; boats are stacked beam-to-beam, three and four deep at the transient dock. Near Island, just across the channel, looks like a dinosaur's dirty green hump. Londa hangs a cigarette from her lips and bends forward to light it, using her head and Richard's yellow hood for rain protection. It takes her four tries with the damp matches before she gets the cigarette lit, but she finally does—and oh, yes, it helps. Spreading out below her, the ocean looks like a big pool of the mercury her dentist used to give her in a Dixie cup when she was a girl. She and her daughter, Esther, can take a walk out to Mill Bay and watch the eagles fish salmon in the creek this afternoon, see if the salmon are coming in yet, anyway. Growing up here could be a lot of fun. Sure. A lot of fun.

Londa walks past a little white house with a sagging porch roof and remembers her mother pointing to another white house, outside Little Rock, a soapbox of a house with a green lawn and square bushes and a black-topped driveway, and saying to Londa, "Oh, I always wanted to live in that house!" When Londa asked why, her mother said something that for years—that until this very moment—Londa didn't understand. "It looks like nothing bad could ever happen there," her mother said.

And now all of a sudden Londa wants to cry.

She walks with her head down, looking at her feet, cigarette in her mouth and broken heel held tightly in her hand. Her throat and jaw have tightened, but she already decided—in the dark when she was looking for her clothes in a pile of dirty T-shirts and jeans, potato chips and *Skin*

Diver magazines, Richard oblivious on the bed behind her and no telephone (he makes thirty-five thousand a year as a bar manager and there's no telephone in the whole damn house because having none makes him feel like an Alaskan)—Londa decided already that she wasn't going to cry.

There now. Yes. She's better already.

DAWN

so much depends
upon

a red wheel
barrow

glazed with rain
water

beside the white
chickens.

—WILLIAM CARLOS WILLIAMS,
"The Red Wheelbarrow"

21 THE ROLLING STONES blares from an open car window, *heart-breaker, painmaker,* and because the radio station is still on the air it seems closer to yesterday than today. Dawn, in the summer in Alaska, is anything but a quickie, and even though the sky has partially cleared in the northeast and the rain has stopped and the horizon shows streaks of pink and blue pastel, it's still the late-night side of morning, as some cowboy sang once, and generally cloudy.

Jack dropped off Fourteen almost an hour ago and has had no business since. He sits in front of the Beachcomber Bar, watching the stragglers wander in and out, and thinking, once again, like a fool, *Are you happy?*

Just thinking about the question makes Jack sad, so he stops thinking for now and focuses on . . . No, he doesn't focus on anything. Everything is slightly fuzzy; it's a world seen through sleepy eyes, luminous but far from clear. Across the gravel road is the black-rock beach. The ocean is dark up close, but silver and a little pink out on the tips of the waves.

Pillar Mountain had him spinning, and he's just beginning to come down. He keeps thinking of Fourteen with different faces—not her own. First she has Mary's face, then the features change to Linda Ronstadt's, her sultry look on an album cover. Then he sees Fourteen with the face of Vanessa, beautiful Vanessa, of Lovesing Romance Novel Number 803, *Overcast Passion.* Despite her intellectual aloofness, Vanessa was the most seductive woman in Heathercliff.

People come out of the bar and stand in the archway, look around as if waking from a nap, blink in the new light. They're dressed in pretty whiteyellowbluered dresses, in slippery black shirts, berets, panama hats, animal furs, black leather, University of Whatever T-shirts, red silk blouses and denim jackets, pink-sequined collars, brown canvas rein-forced work pants, Mickey Mouse ears. They are young and healthy and strong, for the most part. They yawn and sip their drinks, wipe their noses, rub their eyes, scream, goose each other, laugh, slap hands, straighten hats, and spit ice cubes. One of them says, "Hey Joe, can you still bark like a dog?" and Joe says, "Sure," and barks like a dog.

A woman in a black dress stands with her back turned, partially hidden behind the yellow pillar that separates the two arches in the Beachcomber entrance. Jack can see only half of her. He can see the curve of her hip, the narrowing of her waist, and the skin of one bare shoulder. Her arm lowers gracefully from above her head, unrolling like a dancer's, cigarette between her fingers. When her hand reaches waist level, she gives a gentle flick, and the ash drops.

H.B., dressed in denim and cowboy boots, steps outside with a drink in each hand. He looks like a bearded Renoirian Frenchman with the moon in his eye. Actually, H.B.'s from Australia, but now he's a Kodiak fisherman. He says something to this half-woman in the black dress, offers his arm, and they walk back in together.

Maybe it's H.B.'s money, Jack thinks. Maybe it's his accent. Maybe it's *amore*.

Jack hangs his arm out the open window, taps his fingers on the cab door. The man on the radio says the government is having a heck of a time compiling the definitive report on hunger in America because many of the hungry don't even know they are hungry, and others simply won't admit it. Jack's stomach growls. All of the restaurants and bar kitchens are closed by now, so he won't eat until his shift ends, at 6:00 A.M. It's hard for him to believe that Neil will be at the Mecca then, that he won't be sleeping somewhere. But either way, Jack will eat. And knowing that gives him comfort.

A light-blue silver spreads across the northeast sky. Jack watches it grow in his rearview mirror, transporting himself from the driver's seat of his cab, from here in this Beachcomber parking lot in this state of Alaska, to ankle-deep in cold creek mud, Maude the Murderous Brindle-Faced Cow bearing down on him while he tried to pull one of her newborn twins out of the water.

Somewhere between midnight and dawn that fine March morning, she'd chosen to give birth in the middle of the creek. And she was mean about it.

When she charged, Jack had to twist sideways to protect himself. She grazed him with her head, knocking him back against the soil cutbank. He held himself upright with one hand, held the calf's front foot with the other. He braced himself and yanked the calf up out of the shallow water onto the dark pasture behind him. All except the hoof, the waxy little hoof. It came off in his hand.

Jack could smell it then, or he realized what he'd been smelling all along. He stood leaning back against the cutbank in the dark, unable to catch his breath, listening to Maude, in the dark behind him now, trying to revive the stillborn, creek-wet calf with her tongue. Christ. The water swirled at his feet. The stars shone through the box elder branches. He'd been trying to save a calf that was dead before it was born, and the smell, the smell, the smell of it . . . was too familiar to be mistaken.

After pulling himself out of the creek, Jack made his way back to the farmhouse in the dark. Somehow in the struggle with the cow, he'd cut his forehead, and he could feel the blood on his face. In the bathroom, he took off his coveralls and looked at himself in the mirror. He liked the look of the blood on his face, took pleasure in spreading it out with his fingers. He painted stripes on his cheeks, arms, and chest. Then he made himself some toast, ate it in the kitchen, and crawled into bed with Mary.

In the morning, when she woke and saw him, she dropped her face into her hands and said, "What about me, Jack? What am I supposed to do?"

It occurred to Jack then that he had neither the courage nor the optimism necessary to live with her anymore. No, not courage. Gall. He no longer had the gall to keep pretending he wasn't miserable. And it occurred to him then that his father may have had the same problem. So what now? What to do? Go to Alaska?

He didn't answer her. He closed his eyes.

Maybe you should leave, she said, quietly, a whisper. *Maybe you should leave before I begin to hate you.*

What happened the next evening was confusing, to say the least. At the time, Jack thought he was being wooed by Mary, that she didn't want to give up, that she'd changed her mind and was trying to make him stay. But from here, from this distance, he can see the definite possibility of her cynicism.

She made a shrimp dinner; they drank wine. Lorraine was at her sister's in Milwaukee, so they had the whole house. Mary took his hand and led him upstairs. Jack remembers looking down at her naked body in the dark—no, she wanted candlelight—lying on her tummy across the bed, back arched, shoulders propped up by her elbows. He reached over her shoulder and handed her a glass of wine, a real wineglass of wine.

Mary had it all choreographed—and it might have been enough to break his heart if he still had a heart—even the music, except she never figured a place for Jack to set the bottle without pulling out, so he hung on to it, took a swig in the rhythm, looking down as she sipped gingerly from her glass. He made a deep growling sound in his throat, a kind of wordless masculine purr through a clenched jaw, like the men in his mother's romance books. He pictured palm trees and heard surf sounds. Maybe there were surf sounds in the music. Every time he growled, Mary cooed like a pigeon. He growled and thought of palm trees and she cooed like a barn pigeon. Jack began to think it was funny, but Mary didn't catch on, or didn't care. When he looked down at where they connected, it seemed like someone else down there. Not him.

Mary held the glass by its stem and said in a breathy voice, "Oh!"

There is a time when you first fall in love, a time when kittens drive trains and pigs fly airplanes, a time when you'd never never hurt the one you love. But then something changes, clicks like a big wheel turning, and you know it will never turn back.

Jack pictured palm trees and wooden plates filled with sliced grapefruit and papaya, pineapple, mango, and sections of tangerine. He could see their flavor. Ahhhh. He could smell their pesticide-poisoned juice. He tightened his jaw, gripped her buttocks with his free hand, and imagined a photograph of where he plugged into her, there where her legs met, and that was how he got excited.

"Oh!" she said.

When he came he turned the bottle upside down and poured wine over her screaming, kicking, naked self. It was strange, but it didn't feel mean: He watched the wine splash and she nailed him in the stomach with an elbow and he laughed like hell because it felt as though they'd finally connected.

JACK SINKS LOW in his seat, and adjusts his rearview mirror so he can see his own face, white skin, pink lips, red curly hair, blue eyes.

Are you happy?

A guy could cut off his own balls trying to answer. It's the kind of question a mother asks, maybe ought to ask, but in Jack's particular case it has no relevance. If things had been different when he left he might be able to go back; but if things had been different, he wouldn't have left. It embarrasses him that until he got Mary's letter he still thought something was possible. Okay, so begin again. If accepting your destiny makes happiness possible, then what's yours? Coming here? Okay. And since Mary's letter . . . *being* here. You're where you need to be, doing what you need to do. You don't know what will happen but you've got the beginnings of a plan, breakfast at the Mecca with Neil. It's a start.

He pushes the mirror back where it was, back so he can see the silver bay behind him. *Content* is probably a better word than *happy,* he thinks. Happiness is fickle and flickering, and we run into walls chasing it, shatter crystal things. Contentment is a nice thing to think about—a belly full of Oreos, if that's what it takes—while happy can easily make a person depressed.

He closes his eyes, tries to sleep, dream of Vanessa in *Overcast Passion.* Beautiful Vanessa and her sharp-eyed Dirk. Now there was quality sex! Jack laughs to himself. Vanessa saw the animal in Dirk, that's for sure. It lurked just below the surface of his gray-green eyes like a big fat trout. It excited her and scared her and she knew it was there because she'd seen the flicker. Oh! (Dirk's eyes told her how he felt about her—his mouth told her how he felt about himself.) She knew she'd never have to say, *Dirk, ah, by the way, I was wondering, er, I wanted to ask you if you would mind too much taking hold of . . . yes, like this, see, there, not real hard but . . . now just shove yourself on me like a canine mongrel, okay, sweetie?* No. Dirk was a good boy, a big dog in his own right, and—

A knock on his window makes Jack open his eyes. Standing outside is a young, black-haired, dark-skinned girl with freckles on her nose that look as if they've been penciled on. Jack remembers her.

"Hey, Blue Eyes," she says, when Jack gets the window down. Then, over her shoulder, she calls, "Donna, come here! It's Blue Eyes!"

Donna appears from behind Freckles, shows her pudgy, thickly powdered face over Freckles's shoulder.

"Hi," she says, mostly breath, then withdraws.

Jack met these two last week, and they made a big deal about his eyes. This is a little different, though, as Freckles is pretty drunk. She stays close to the window. She licks her lips.

"Ooooooh, I can't believe it!" she says. Her mouth twitches. "Would you like to get married and make babies?"

"I am married." Jack doesn't know why that came out. Maybe her age.

"Oh! You *are* married?" Jack can smell her breath, and it smells good.

"Yeah."

"Any babies yet?"

"No."

"Well?" She raises her eyebrows playfully.

"Well, what?"

"Well, *you know*."

Jack hesitates, decides not to answer. He smiles.

"You'd like that, huh?" she asks. She juts out a hip and leans her elbows on Jack's open window. "You're supposed to say no, that you're loyal to your wife, that you don't do that stuff. Then I'd *really* want you, see?"

"I didn't know that."

"You didn't know what?" She's whispering very close to Jack's face, and as her lips move Jack thinks how he could kiss them right now, right now. He wishes she'd kiss him. No he doesn't. After Fourteen made a puppet out of him on Pillar Mountain, he doesn't need that. He's not exactly happy, maybe, but he's content enough for the time being.

"I didn't know what I was supposed to say," Jack says. Then he adds, "And I don't really care."

"Oh." She looks away. She seems to enjoy the way Jack is feeling, as if she can feel it herself. Her brown eyes sparkle as she pretends to scan the immediate area. This is a smart girl. Jack can see she knows a lot of things, and she'll learn a lot more. She looks back at him.

"I should probably do it to you anyway," she says.

Jack feels his face turning red, and he knows he should say something funny fast but can't think of anything. Donna puts her face on Freckles's shoulder just in time.

"Are you going to show him your tattoo?" Donna says.

Freckles laughs, liking the idea. "Would your wife be upset?"
Jack shakes his head.

Freckles takes a step back, smiles with her lips together. "C'mon, Donna, let's show him." Then to Jack: "They're still real new, you know. They're our graduation presents to each other."

Donna lifts her shirt so Jack can see most of both of her yellow breasts, and points between them at a pink butterfly small enough to fit under a quarter. Freckles unbuckles her belt. She zips down her fly and lowers her jeans and panties far enough so Jack can see, on the soft skin at the edge of her pubic hair, a tiny tangle of green vines and a couple of purple grape clusters the size of thimbles. The girls look at each other and laugh.

"I can't believe we did that," Donna says.

"They're pretty," Jack says, thinking it's funny how women tattoo butterflies and grapes while men opt for Chinese-warlords.

Freckles touches Jack's shoulder and winks. He stiffens. What is this terror all of a sudden?

"We're going gill-netting on the other side of the island pretty soon." She's smiling sweetly, youngly, while Donna fades. "So this could be *au revoir*."

"*Au revoir*, then," Jack says.

"We made ten thousand apiece last summer. Donna's uncle has these incredible sites." Freckles takes a step back.

"Great." These things come and go, though. Like waves, these feelings. Like the tide, this flow. She's eighteen. Jack's forehead breaks out with unearned sweat. Who knows? Babies?

"See ya, okay?" Her young teeth shine.

"Yeah." She's leaving! She's walking away!

"*Really?*" It's her, spinning back, showing off a fine set of genes, a pink tongue.

"Really what?" Jack says.

"Really *see ya*?" She doesn't have a name, but she has a biological destiny, a round little ass.

"Yeah, sure," Jack says. And then, while she's still close enough, he reaches out the window and grabs her wrist, pulls her toward him, her head through the window, twisting it gently but firmly so her face is to

155

his, and kisses her for all he's worth, for all he's failed to be in the past, for all he hopes to be someday. He's thirty years old this morning.

So you think youououououou're a cowboy but you're only a kid. This time it's Emmylou on the radio, and Jack turns it up with his toe while continuing to kiss Freckles, her body bent through the window, her tongue beginning to explore the inside of his mouth. He doesn't want to think about anything. He only knows something inside him is different, changed, and for the first time in a long time he knows he's going to be okay. That afternoon, out toward the coast guard base, past where the drainage has been blocked by the highway embankment forming one of Alaska's three million lakes, into the woods along an overgrown dirt road built by the navy in World War II, past where the rusty crab pots are stacked with their pink and yellow buoys, surrounded by acres and acres of dripping spruce and a carpet of green moss soft enough to sleep on, that afternoon while the world learns of Jack Dempsey's death, Jack will lie on his back in his tent and think about what to do next. But right now he'll kiss. To hell with content.

When he's done, Jack lets Freckles go and she withdraws, twisting carefully back through the window, standing outside.

"It's my birthday," he says.

Freckles smiles a big-state, big smile. Eyes like every promise ever made, broken, and—yeah, what the hell—made again. She reaches into her pocket and removes a crumpled red crepe poppy.

"Here," she says, handing it through the window. "I got it at the Legion yesterday."

Jack takes the poppy from her hand and hangs it on the rearview mirror. "Thanks."

"Happy birthday," she says, pivoting. And then she's gone.

H.B. WINKS AS he approaches Jack's cab, says, "Jaaay Ceeee, what's it all about?" The half-woman in the black dress is holding his arm.

Jack shrugs.

"A blessed riot in there, I tell you." H.B. points over his shoulder with his thumb.

Black Dress smiles at Jack. Her high heels aren't good for walking on gravel, but she does all right. A rawhide purse bounces against her hip. She rolls her eyes, shakes her head, says, "Crazy." As she gets closer she looks familiar. Jack can't remember from where. She's pretty, but her chin is marked with tiny acne scars and her eyes do this tentative, girlish squint. She seems too vulnerable all of a sudden, and Jack can hardly stand looking at her. He feels embarrassed. Then, he remembers where he's seen her before. A few weeks ago, outside Solly's, she climbed into his cab and said *Follow that car,* which Jack did, until *that car* drove up onto the sidewalk near the Harbor View apartments. She jumped out and wrestled with the driver, and Jack heard a lot of cussing and then this little choked-off screech, an aria in two notes. Just when Jack began wondering if he should be doing anything besides waiting, she was back, leaning across his front seat with a fistful of dollar bills, her hair messed up, a ring of car keys hanging from her little finger, and tears welling in her squinty eyes. She tried to smile when she paid him, but gave it up with a quick shake of her head.

"You know what a pain in the ass mothers can be," she said.

Are you happy?

They hop into H.B.'s jeep and wave. Jack waves back and then looks at two gulls perched on a rock in the channel. The water is calm near shore, and the new light makes the gulls look almost blue. From the radio comes the twanging wails of Mr. Jimi Hendrix's discordant "Star-Spangled Banner," the squealing, painful electric guitar marking 4:00 A.M. with something awful, a too realistic despair, an indiscriminate memory like a physical weight, an Electronic Age mourning Jack Dempsey's imminent death. But it's okay. Jack Dempsey Cliff's finally getting a feel for things, an idea of what it's all about. It's about H.B.'s jeep peeling out, two heads near-near in the front seat. It's about *Fishing'll make a man out of you. . . . Wrestle hundred-pound halibut all day and night for a week without sleep, and you won't be afraid of nothing.* It's even about glory and suntans, fleeting as they may be.

Behind him, in the rearview, Jack can see the sky is brightening, a deeper blue, a shallower gray, a trace of orange spreading on the northeastern horizon like something warm in the belly of the world. *Once you've seen it, you don't forget it*—even Mary's very nice face. A truly fresh start may never be possible, but certainly love and redemption are.

Despite the pain. Jimi Hendrix squeezes each note, stretches it, hurts it, but in the whole astounding sound there's a fullness; the helix of despair twisting around an unquenchable appetite for life.

The engine roar drops as H.B.'s jeep passes and disappears up the road. Jack wonders if they'll Eskimo-kiss; he wonders if they'll speed off a cliff while Eskimo-kissing, pretending for a few moments to be mating eagles or some great dying race of lovers. Then it's quiet. No more radio, even. Only the gulls' sweet plaints.

22 JULIE JORDAN, EX-GYMNAST from Moscow, Idaho, hustles out of the drizzle onto the back porch and pauses before entering her house. She's tired from working all night at Solly's Office Bar. Her back aches even though she's tried hard to sit and stand with good posture: buttocks tucked under, belly in, shoulders straight and square. Sometimes she feels fifty, or what she imagines it must feel like to be fifty. A man she often sees at the bar told her he hurt his back and couldn't go fishing anymore. He seemed pretty sad. In 1976 he made forty thousand dollars in four weeks fishing king crab, he said, and he'd had other good years too. It's all *out there*, he told her, *everything*, and he pointed in the direction of the ocean.

Julie takes a long look out across the foggy bay. She likes the way the yellow and blue lights cluster around the boat harbor like jewels.

Living near the ocean does it to her, all right. Something else is always possible. Like Lloyd. That's why she finally had to say something when she saw him come in again at the end of the night. That's why now the whole world is changed.

Julie steps inside, into the living room, and stops thinking about the sea and fishing and Lloyd. Her husband, Dodge, lies on the couch. The television is on static. Potato chips, empty beer cans, a bong, and dirty dinner dishes crowd the small coffee table. The room is dark and cramped, and Julie almost trips over his boots on her way to the window. She raises the shade and Dodge stirs in the new gray light. She sits down next to him and pushes his brown hair off his forehead. His skin feels cool and clammy.

"Dodge?" she says.

He opens his eyes, blinks, closes them again.

Julie knows he hasn't been happy, but she hasn't any idea anymore what to do about it. She wants to tell him what the guy with the hurt back told her. Forty thousand in one month. She wants to tell him about Lloyd and her, her and Lloyd, letting herself hope for just a moment that Dodge would hug her and touch her face and tell her it's all right, not to worry, that he'll make her forget all about Lloyd.

Then this goes through her mind: *Out there,* the slow, deliberate gesture toward the sea, toward the future and the past, the vision in that man's eyes, the mystery, of Lloyd's kisses too, and now she knows she'll never get to sleep. Forty thousand and more. She wants to tell Dodge but won't. Because he doesn't want to know. Yes, she thinks. And maybe she's free to love him better this way, feeling the pleasure in the pain of her own patience, in forgiving Dodge her own bitterness.

Julie knows money isn't the most important thing in the world—love is; she's always believed that. But with all the treasure just sitting out there . . . how can a person *not* go after it? Not out of greed, because the treasure isn't just money. No. It's more than that, much more. Staying home, in town, is . . . is slothful is what it is. In one month—all that money! Sometimes you made less, like this winter, but there's always the possibility a person could make more. The sockeye run is supposed to be fantastic this year. She thinks of photos she's seen of men standing up to their knees in red salmon, up to their knees in what may as well be dollar bills, in what may as well be a glorious future. With that kind of money, Dodge could get a real start on something. He could start ranching, as he always talked about, or law school, or both. Sure. He'd been talking about that petro-something, that two-year oil course in Kenai. With that kind of money, if they were careful—with that kind of nest egg they could get a real start on something. After five years of marriage, a start.

"Hi, hon," Dodge says. He opens his eyes again. "We actually won our softball game. Muddy!"

"Great, that's great."

"I'm your victorious knight, can you believe that?"

"Of course I believe it."

"Lloyd was over after. I'm afraid we made a mess."

"I guess," she says, toeing a beer can next to the leg of the coffee table.

"He said he saw you at work and you ignored him."

"I did not."

"He said you did."

"Well, I was busy," she says. And then quickly, "Why are you sleeping out here?" In some indeterminate location all over her body she feels a little emptiness, a little pain. At two o'clock Lloyd came back to the bar, and soon after that she finally told him what she'd been dying to tell him for months.

Now she finds herself wanting not only that Dodge would get a fishing job this summer but also that Lloyd would lose his and then go far away. She wouldn't mind that at all, no sir—amid the smell of stale night and sleep and flesh, finding Dodge, her man, her husband, finding Dodge's body exhausted from working all day on the boat. It could happen. Those kinds of things happen all the time.

"For heaven's sake, why didn't you go to bed?" she asks.

"Oh, that feels nice," Dodge says.

She's rubbing his temples. Gray light filters through the window and gives everything a shaded, softened look. Julie thinks Dodge looks very handsome, and the more she thinks of Lloyd, the easier it is to be tender to Dodge. His face is soft when he wakes. She loves his little lip smile. She loves this light, this gray, this one of millions of shades of gray.

"How was work?" he asks.

"Fine." Then she has to turn away because she thinks of him happily eating with Lloyd, so stupidly not knowing, and the way Lloyd's hair smelled like this very room, and the feel of his kisses, and the sadness combined with the waste of something makes her suddenly angry.

"What a mess!" she says.

Dodge groans. He tries to pull her back, but as quickly as she thought him handsome, she now thinks him ugly—not his face, but something about the stink of the bong water and the waste, the feel of waste in her stomach like hunger, and now she can smell his rotten breath.

"Oh, boy," she says.

"What's wrong?" he asks.

"Just go to bed, honey," she says. Dodge can't make her see that *something*, that *out there*, because he's afraid to see it himself! And Lloyd, what happened? Big smile, yes, and then he said, "What now, Jewel?" while he dressed. And before she could answer, he said again, "What now?" pointing somewhere, just lifting his forefinger slightly to mean he was on his way, or he would see her later, or to mean that he didn't know himself what he meant. He winked and she tried to think of something to say to make him pause, break that stride to his coat, to the door, down the motel steps, descending like that—*Yo!* calling *Yo, later!* either over his shoulder to her or to someone he saw down below.

Oh, she knew it was to her but couldn't even get herself to answer.

In the bathroom, Julie switches on the light and counts her tip money on the sink. Eighty dollars and fourteen cents. Eighty dollars and fourteen cents. She'd have been happy with a third of that back in Idaho. There is so much of everything here. So darn much, and we haven't even scratched the— Suddenly she feels poor. It's a mess: the walls are smudged, the floor is sandy, the mirror is smeared with something white. Chip dip, possibly. Everything is always a mess, and nothing is neat or crisp or clean or finished or very right. Everything is like in some poor person's house. She can hear Dodge step across the floor of the living room, and then the door to the bathroom opens. He winks at her, stands over the toilet.

"White piss from your white knight," he says, smiling good-naturedly.

"What?"

"Hey," he says, shrugging. "Just a detail. You notice details. Compare it once to a yellow, full-bodied urine."

"God, Dodge."

He shakes himself when he's through—there's a detail she hates. Where do the drops go? He flushes the toilet and jiggles the handle— another detail she doesn't like. She watches him in the mirror as he passes behind her, lightly dragging his finger from one shoulder, across the back of her neck, to the other shoulder. She wants to fall away from the touch but resists and stands rigid. The pressure inside her is building, and she thinks she might scream if she doesn't say something fast.

But then she realizes she really has nothing to say. Wanting something to happen, imagining it, over and over again, doesn't constitute something happening. Of course not. It happens or it doesn't happen, and nothing happened. But how about going to the Star Motel with a man named Lloyd because at a particular moment in time and space the Star Motel is the only place on earth for you to go, and once there—after you walk across Kraft's parking lot and past the Dairy Queen, around puddles under the clouds through the fog to the back, where Lloyd gets the key, twirling it with one hand and holding yours with the other while going up the stairs, everything together, both of you, even though it's getting quite light and the stairs are outside and face the street, and then with the door closed you're so nervous you're afraid to look at him—you put your arms around his waist and can feel him quivering, not on the outside but down deep somewhere on the inside, and he says he supposes that maybe he's just too tight, because man oh man, even naked like this, and it's not that he doesn't want you very much, not that, oh if you only knew!—*but it's not happening anyway*—even when you ask him what you can do to help—*nothing still*—and he laughs and says you must think he's a big talker, all right, and your kisses are sweet as hell, believe that, so not to worry—*but still nothing, dammit-all-to-hell-and-back! nothing*—how 'bout that, huh?

Julie wants to be rich, she wants to be great, she wants to want and to have, and to be wanted and to be had. She wants so much, but so little actually happens, it seems, ever. She's choked with what could be but isn't, and she doesn't know what to say to Dodge about any of it. How do you talk about what isn't? And how do you talk about all that you want without . . . without even knowing the words? She decides to ask him about his job hunt, about something she knows. It'll sound like a nag when she asks, but she'll ask anyway because she needs to say something and she wants him to know that she knows he still doesn't have a job, and that she's waiting, for crissake, still working and waiting and not particularly happy about it. Yes. That's it. She wants him to know she's not happy, that's all.

It has occurred to Julie that Dodge may be dragging his feet looking for work because she keeps bugging him. But that's not her fault—that's his. It's a weakness in *his* character. Not in Lloyd's. Not in that man's with the hurt back. Not in hers. It's Dodge's flaw. He needs confidence again; he needs adventure; he needs *out there,* the reason they'd come to Alaska in the first place. Other men get a wild, lusty look in their eye when they talk about *out there*—and there's pain in it too. Lloyd's eyes light up with the promise of something powerful and big. Dodge had bad luck is all. That awful week crabbing last winter, the terrifying ice-up, all the crabs lost: it was bad luck! But he'd let it get to him, dull him somehow, numb the spirit right out of him until sometimes Julie thinks something may be seriously wrong with him. The winter was hard, and she'd almost expected that, depressing like everybody said it would be, what with the constant fog and rain and cold. But it's summer now, easily spring anyway, and Dodge is still in his funk.

"You're late," he says from the bedroom, not meaning anything besides that the hands on the clock have advanced beyond where they normally are when she comes to bed, and he noticed it.

"Slow closing," she says.

"Oh."

"Find any work yet?" There, she asked it. Sometimes she wishes she could vacuum out her head and start over.

"Huh?"

Of course not. Of course he probably hadn't even stepped out of the house and away from that hideous TV. Sometimes he played Jimmy Buffett songs on the stereo, but that was as close as he got to the ocean anymore, to the risk, to the romance . . . Maybe he doesn't love her, even. Maybe he's not capable beyond the physical.

"Any luck?" she says. She sticks her head out of the lighted bathroom and says, toothbrush in her mouth, toward the bed and darkness, "You did at least look, didn't you?"

"Yeah. Got a possibility with Lloyd on the *Temper.* I think it's for sure."

"What?" She can't believe it. She spits and rinses her mouth, splashes cold water on her face. "What?" She knows Dodge hasn't been happy in Kodiak, and because he hasn't been happy, everything has been hard for them. She knows that if they are going to stay together, if their love is to deepen the way she's always dreamed it would deepen, the way she knows it *should* deepen, then things have to change. "Oh great!" she practically yells. If he has a successful summer, first with halibut, then salmon, maybe tendering, and who ever knows but king crab might take off again, then they can go back home and get a start at something, go back to Idaho as successful Alaskan fishermen! Boy.

"Lloyd's boat? What's that? The *Temper*?" Julie knows Lloyd's boat; she's known it ever since Lloyd moved out of their place and onto the boat six months ago. She notices wherever it is docked and whenever it is out. She keeps track of the *Temper* the way she keeps track of her socks. Even better. She dries her face quickly and hurries into the bedroom, so happy she thinks she might burst, picturing Dodge and Lloyd, Lloyd and Dodge, the way they'll look working together, the way they'll . . .

"I'm so happy for you!" she says, crawling under the covers and hugging Dodge from behind, picturing the way fishermen look when they come back to town, exhausted, dirty, and spent; happy and sad all at once, strong and weak, confident yet vulnerable—like what sex does to a man. "Everything will go well this time," she says. "You wait. This is summer. Everything's gonna go great!"

"Well, it's not for sure for sure," Dodge says, "but it's pretty certain."

"It'll be great. You and Lloyd! That's incredible. Who told you? Did you talk to the skipper?"

"Lloyd did. He wants to see me tomorrow."

"Boy oh boy. That's great."

"Yeah, I hope so."

"It will be." She hugs Dodge tighter and kisses the back of his neck, trying to imagine both of her men, and her, together. Maybe Lloyd will move back in with them, or she and Dodge'll move down to the boat. She and Lloyd will be just very good friends, yes, that's all, like before. Julie feels Dodge's strong shoulders and thinks of how they'll thrive on hard work. This winter was a fluke—Dodge's funk, tonight with Lloyd, everything. And what didn't happen will have nothing to do whatsoever

with Dodge, or fishing, or their new dream. Words, imaginings—
poof!—like that, gone.

But then she thinks of something else. Lloyd and Dodge had talked
before she went with Lloyd—and yet Lloyd didn't say a word to her
about anything! Why not? The thought unsettles her. She feels vaguely
betrayed. Why wouldn't he mention that Dodge had been offered work
on the *Temper*?

She presses her cheek against Dodge's back and closes her eyes, trying
to squeeze the sudden anger from her face. She's remembering what she
wants, forgetting what she needs; and she hopes more than anything to
love Dodge newly. Drifting among colored dreams and shaded possibilities, Julie doesn't notice Dodge's familiar twisting, his arm lifting.
When he touches her hip she jumps, startled by the timing, the
coolness—and by the strange intimacy of his blind fingers.

"What's wrong?" he asks.

"Nothing, baby," she says, stretching her neck to kiss him. "I'm
fine."

23 G. CLARENCE ROBSON, Skin Man, steps outside, into the
light drizzle. He jumps over a puddle and unlocks his bicycle
from the chain-link fence around the Kodiak Canning Company. He
shivers once, a deep shiver down to his center, then he swallows, takes a
breath, and feels a moist breeze wash his bare shoulders. The shiver gets
him going, like a starter motor—vrrrrrooooom, he's ready to ride.

Leaning low and comfortably over his handlebars, he pumps past
parked cars on Marine Way, the harbor to his left, the Mecca, the mall
parking lot to his right. He's flexing his biceps, gripping the handlebars

tightly. Puddle water sprays his back, the wind plays with his hair. His legs catch a rhythm and hold it. The cold wakes him. He doesn't push it away but accepts where it is. Wonderful. It's outside and trying to get in, but it hasn't a chance. No sir. He squints and pedals past the Breakers liquor store, squeezing and resqueezing his hands. The drizzle abates, but what he sees blurs.

Suddenly, near the corner of Shelikof and Marine Way, he bumps something soft and heavy with his right elbow. He brakes, slows, stops. He wipes his forehead and eyes. Behind him, a woman is sitting on the curb. It's Susan. She's wearing Jack's red sweatshirt with the hood pulled up. Her black hair spills out past her neck and chin.

For a moment, Skin Man feels sorry for her. The reason she's down is because he knocked her down; it's his fault. He rolls his bike backward a few steps, squints, tries to see her face.

"You all right?"

"No."

She looks cold. She looks pitiful. He wants to help.

"What's wrong?" he asks.

"Nothing." She stands up, turns away from him, then steps from the gutter onto the curb.

"Need any help?"

"No."

He wants to reach inside her and make her feel all right. He wants to turn her face to his and kiss it, caress away her pain. He could teach her what he knows, make her happy. His heart swells. He steps closer.

"Are you sure?"

Now she turns, and for just a moment he can see her eyes. They burn. They cut with so much anger he feels his knees weaken.

"Of course I'm sure!" she says. "Why the hell does everybody always ask me that?"

Skin Man licks his upper lip, then looks down at his feet. What a waste of a life, he thinks. A drunk Indian wandering around hugging her purse as though it were a baby. His jaw tightens. Some people are so far gone they're not even worth pity.

"You should stay on the sidewalk," he says.

"Yeah?"

Hitting her wasn't even his fault! She stepped into him! Sure. He was just riding along!

"What do you think sidewalks are for, anyway?" he asks.

She turns away, sighs, the sound soft and musical. Then she speaks, her voice almost kind. "Just leave me alone, okay?"

Skin Man turns, mounts his bicycle again, and heads north toward the hill on Mill Bay Road. She's just another miserable wretch who won't take responsibility for her own painful predicament, that's all. He offered to help, and she refused. He offered to help even though hitting her wasn't his fault! What more can she want?

Pop psychology has taught him that above and beyond everything else, a person ought to be fulfilled, actualized, bonded, happy—that sort of thing. And if he isn't, then he's weak, not in control of his own life, and probably in need of counseling: okay, *sicko*. Doctors and authors have told him he can and *ought* to be happy in this lifetime, and doctors and authors are the experts, the high priests whose offerings of Health and Happiness are commodities purchasable at various guaranteed costs: just this much money, just that much sweat. Just follow the Nine-Point Plan! G. Clarence Robson, health-care consumer, buyer of well-being, knight-errant of happiness, feels the cold and dampness surround him and loves the siege. (Could it be he's chasing a phantom? Regardless, it's certainly an American right.) He feels strong in his bubble, and that's what's important. It's fifty-three degrees outside, and he's ninety-eight point six on the inside. The forty-five-degree difference amazes the hell out of him, and as he settles into an uphill pace, a new rhythm, he actually feels a shiver of awe: at his species, at himself, at the heroic capacity of his race for suffering. As a creator of warmth, he has the power of life, of breath. He puts his head down and pedals harder, believes he can be anything; given the right method, he can do anything! The cold is good because he can touch it but it can't touch him. The same with everything that gives feeling: He has taken control.

A yellow Pinto slows, drives next to him. The windows lower.

"Hey Skin Man!" somebody yells.

Faces. Numbers of faces. Laughing. G. Clarence pedals steadily uphill without looking, toward the lightened sky and beyond to his tent and to sleep, without looking. First the hill, though, yessir. Up.

The Pinto lingers beside him, an arm hanging out the window. "Hey Skin Man! Have a nice day!"

Kids, only kids. Bodies, eyes, a Barbie doll with purple lips, a pimple face with a man's laugh, violent movement—and then something round and pink sailing across space.

But it can't touch him. It's outside, and his skin is sealed against invaders. He rides in a bubble, but the silly kids giggle and don't even know it.

The pink balloon splashes warmly against his thigh, and the mufflerless Pinto roars off. But Skin Man is strong in the legs, and for now he's got gravity to battle. The balloon traveled the distance, splashed him, yes, but cannot— His tongue, darting out of his mouth and smearing across his top lip, tastes salt. No. Oooooooo. Now he can smell the urine.

If a man were truly unaffected by discomfort, by cold, by want, his potential might be boundless. But alas, to willfully overpower is not only to conquer but to be possessed. Watching his front tire sizzle on the pavement, Skin Man squints and focuses inward, where an ember of long-protected pain—newly disturbed—kindles quietly.

Now look! The yellow Pinto is turning around at the top of the hill. It's beginning to head back down toward Skin Man. *Up there in the sky!* Here it comes. *The sun, too!*

(Depending on what map of the world you look at, Kodiak may or may not be at the center, but probably not. With a land area of approximately 3,500 square miles, it is large as islands go but doesn't compare with such biggies as Australia, Madagascar, Sri Lanka, or Borneo. Likewise, the city of Kodiak, the Greater Kodiak Area (GKA), with its population of ten thousand—give or take twenty or thirty percent—is not the largest city in the world, nor is it included on many experts' lists with Paris, London, Rome, Rio, or New York as one of the more chic. It lies at 57 degrees and 47 minutes north latitude, and 152 degrees and 25 minutes west longitude, 1,470 miles from Seattle and 4,300 miles from Manila. Today, Tuesday, May 31, 1983, the sun rose at 4:17 A.M., about a half hour ago, and will set at 9:56 P.M. Rain—or the Kodiakism *liquid sunshine*—is expected intermittently through today, tomorrow, and Thursday. But there's a spot, just a twinkle, way over there in the northeast—see it?—a hint, a glimmer, a pause, a promise. See it?)

Oh sweet day! Oh precious ocean gold! Sunshine!

Skin Man is moving himself, feeling himself, starving himself, so even when he gets near the top of the hill he doesn't see the sun (or the Pinto either), and he won't be distracted again, and he won't *ever* wonder if he's crazy, no sir, because H.B. (driving his jeep up the hill behind him), who does see the enchanting sunshine on the ocean, thinking of the recent touch of his new love (Black Dress), swerves at the last second to avoid the screaming yellow Pinto, drops a jeep tire onto the road shoulder, and clips (oh, what timing!) the back of Skin Man's head with the sideview mirror, killing him, cold.

24 EDNA AND PRETTY Gertie MacDonald push past a leaning Ivan at the trailer door and step outside. It's morning, or getting close anyway, and rain drips from the spruce boughs, the tops of the trees obscured in cloud. Ivan is Edna's nephew, and he lowers his large self slowly and sits down in the doorway. He's shirtless, slow-moving, and sleepy, and he spits a piece of pink gum into his fist, rolls it between his palms, and chucks it over his aunt's head at a chipmunk in a tree.

A taxicab is turning around on the dirt road just a few yards away. Ivan, Edna, and Pretty Gertie watch disinterestedly as the driver, Jack Cliff, drives forward a few feet, wrestles with the steering wheel, then backward a few feet. He does this over and over, until finally the big cab is headed back in the direction it came from.

The women pile into the back seat.

"Is that guy coming?" Jack asks, pointing at Ivan, who's still sitting on the stoop, chin in his hand, the beginnings of softness showing in the brown flesh of his stomach.

"Does he look like it?" Pretty Gertie asks.

"Easy," Edna says.

"Well, I don't like his stupid questions," Pretty Gertie says. "What did you get *him* for, anyway?"

Edna laughs, but the laugh turns into a hacking cough. "He came with the cab," she manages to say, red-faced.

"Where to?" Jack asks.

"Oh God, listen," Pretty Gertie says. "Mister Questions."

"He can't help it," Edna says. "How's he supposed to know where to go?"

"Well, he can start by going out to the highway!" Saying this makes Pretty Gertie laugh. "Or he can spend another ten minutes turning the car around!"

Jack is amazed at the size of that one's head. She and Battle of the Bulge Harry could breed some kind of lionheaded race.

Edna leans toward the front seat and asks Jack, "Have I seen you before?"

Jack remembers her. He can't forget those spooky eyes. She got into his cab last night outside The Breakers, stared at him as though he'd killed her mother, and then got out.

"No," Jack says. He drives ahead slowly. It's quiet for a moment; the cab rolls into a hole, then out. The one-lane dirt road winds through the spruce. He's had these two before and he doesn't like them. They have a tendency to be abusive, especially the one with the big head.

Edna says, continuing a conversation that started before they got into the cab, "I'd buy a boat, that's what I'd do. One of those big coast guard boats, and make a floating hotel."

As she says the words, the actual boat floats up before her, just off to her right. The trees have parted and she can see the bay, and her boat riding high on the waves. She raises her hands to it. She blinks her tired turquoise eyes.

"Oh my," she sighs.

Edna's no longer a chipmunk; a chipmunk couldn't have such a beautiful boat, such a white sight, such grand magic; nor could a chipmunk feel so good all of a sudden. She's a mink: that's it! Mean and beautiful.

Maybe it's this cabbie, Edna thinks. He gives her good vibes—too good. His hair's so red and his skin so pale, but . . . oh, now he's distracting her. She drops her hands and closes her eyes. The boat in the bay fades in the fog; it's only that stupid Japanese freighter carrying stupid Japanese cars. Trees close back around the road, and Edna feels cheated.

"I hope the boat's got hot tubs," Pretty Gertie says.

"What?"

"The ship! It's got hot tubs, I hope."

"Sure," Edna says, but she's faking it. She can't see it anymore. "It's got saunas, dance halls, booze rooms. A church too."

"Wow," Pretty Gertie says. "What fun."

"It'd be my floating city and I'd invite only my friends." Edna tries to conjure the boat back again. "And there'd be bingo all day long."

Jack maneuvers the cab around a particularly deep-looking puddle, hits a bump, which shakes away any new vision Edna may have been getting.

"Don't bump so much, please," she says.

"Sorry."

Edna tries again. She thinks about how if she ever got rich, then she'd probably be famous, too, and on the covers of magazines. Everyone would be interested in her life, in how she used to fish on the *Angelita* with her father when she was a girl, in what she eats for breakfast and what she puts ketchup on. A thorough investigation would be done, as is done with all famous people, to see if she really deserves to be famous, and the investigation would reveal some interesting things, even to her, even to Edna MacDonald. Perhaps a mysterious parental lineage explaining her turquoise eyes, perhaps some direct and secret connection to good witches and kings. Perhaps she was born of a virgin. She looks at the back of the driver's head, the orange curls. Perhaps she even has a son somewhere that she never knew about. Boy, she thinks, that would be something.

"You haven't eaten all day," Pretty Gertie says. She reaches into her pocket and pulls out a can of beer, giggles as she pops it. "All yesterday, I mean."

"No," Edna says. "I did have a light breakfast."

"A light breakfast," Pretty Gertie mocks, raising her gravel voice an

octave. She snorts a laugh and straightens her purple-rimmed glasses, then lays her forehead on the back of the front seat.

Jack's afraid she's going to vomit. "Are you okay?"

Pretty Gertie doesn't answer. Edna takes the beer can from her hand and helps her lean back in the seat. Jack can see her eyes are closed. The taxi is rounding the curve, high off the ocean, and a mist is rising up the black cliffs. Kodiak lies dead ahead, a cluster of yellow lights tucked between the channel and the base of Pillar Mountain. The ocean spreads to the southeast like a slate plain. Soon Pretty Gertie is snoring. Edna groans and says, "Thank God." She leans her elbows on the back of the front seat and says to Jack, "You ever have a friend like her?"

"Yeah," Jack says, thinking of no one in particular. He's thinking about breakfast. His mother always made him waffles for breakfast on his birthday. Waffles and sausage, and she'd stick a birthday candle in the stack of waffles. He can almost taste it; he can smell it just thinking about it. That's what he'll order at the Mecca. He'll write his mother and tell her. She'll like that. And Neil? Neil probably won't show up. Even so, in the coming weeks he may get to know Neil, may even get to be his friend. A brother? When Jack was a boy he used to wish sometimes for a brother more than he wished for a father. He'd walk barefoot out into the pasture in the morning. The dew was cold and wet, and by the time he got to the cows, his feet would be freezing. The cows would stand when they saw him, and—first things first—they'd shit. He'd follow along behind them, stepping in every steamy cow pie he could, jumping from one to the next, feeling the warmth on his instep and up between his toes, smelling the sweet green, and wishing he had some sibling competition in the World's Longest Leap Between Cow Pies Contest.

Edna's thinking this cabbie is possibly her son. He's got an okay face. And he's even got a nice smell. She wrinkles her nose, leans forward to sniff the hair on the back of his head.

Jack sees her in the rearview, hears her breathing behind his ear. "Anything wrong, lady?"

Edna's flustered, caught in the act. She shakes her head, feels herself blush. "Pretty Gertie gets a little rowdy every now and then, but she's my best friend in the world."

"Yeah?" Jack takes a look at Pretty Gertie. She's asleep, leaning back, eyes closed, glasses crooked. Her belly stretches to the limit the waist-band of her orange Spandex pants.

Edna points to the red crepe poppy hanging from the rearview mirror. "Where'd you get the flower?" She's thinking of Frank. She's thinking of the flower he gave her and how she must have left it at Ivan's.

"A girl."

"Your girl?" *Frank's was for his boy Jimmy, who used to drive a green truck.*

"Just a girl."

The cab winds up going down the hill from Gibson Cove. *Poor Jimmy,* Edna thinks. *When he was alive he parked the pickup in the weeds and went and joined the army. Poor Frank.*

"You're such a baby," she says.

"What's that supposed to mean?" Jack asks.

Frank's baby died. Think of how many babies die! At least I never had a baby die. "I don't know," Edna says.

"Where do you want to go?"

"The harbor for now." *And old men! Old men and babies; they're always dying. Left and right. Women too. Frank's wife died of a tumor the size of an apple.* "See the bay?" she says.

Jack is driving around it, on the edge of it. It spreads forever to the east of him, as far as he can see.

"In '64 it emptied," Edna says. *In her tittie.*

"I heard about that."

"The tsunami emptied the harbor." *Before each wave came.* "I can hardly imagine it now. But I saw it!" *From right about here.* "This was gravel, that was mud."

"Huh." Jack thinks of the tsunami. Tries to picture it.

"The *Angelita* made it," she says. *But Daddy died. Everybody dies.* "I was so proud of her."

"Is that your boat?"

"Yes." *Everyone was trying to get away, and he didn't.* "Mom and I stood up here and watched what we could, but it went through the night." *One after another. Waves. Mom said there was Daddy and then there was me. One after another.*

"Boy," Jack says. He read a description once, he doesn't remember when or where, or how much of it he has added in his head, but he's thought about it before when he's looked out at the harbor and bay, how the ocean sucked away, gone as from a bathtub with a split bottom. Boats, including the *Dempsey,* lay listing on the wide stretch of mud, the breakwater and town towering strangely above them, and then a moment of quiet, just a brief time before the roar when men and women must have gazed across the new mud plain with simple curiosity. The ocean floor stripped bare, the enormous stench, and Kodiak town appeared as though perched on a hillside, the breakwater like a fortress wall rooted in mud.

Then the terror, the panic, and men tried vainly to run across the soft mud; some lay resigned in their bunks, and surely a few, surely his dad, clung determinedly, if not futilely, to the helm. The wave rolling in sounded like a train, crashing and thundering and tossing spume as it built to three, four times the height of the boats on the harbor floor, lifting and tossing and uprooting, washing and carrying away, leveling and swirling and bubbling and crushing; then, reaching its smallest showering drops and harmless sprays, halfway through town, it slowed, milling about like an indecisive and fatigued monster, heaving for breath; it began to withdraw, easy at first and then faster, down the streets and sidewalks, picking up speed through the narrow alleys, racing across the parking lots and through its own rubble, out the channel and harbor and bay, revealing ruins and new mudflats, giving respite for a moment of breathing and, of course, fresh terror.

"I'll show you the *Angelita,*" Edna says. *She's still okay. Boats don't die, they sink. Brother Herman fixed her up, but not himself.* "She's a beauty."

"Okay."

Everything changed after that, had to be rebuilt, what could be rebuilt. And since then nothing's stopped changing except for the weather, which is the same, of course.

"The darn rain," she says.

Jack glances in the rearview mirror. Edna is staring at him in that weird way, but her voice is friendly.

"Pretty Gertie here married my brother Herman right before the tsunami," Edna says. *Jimmy was the only one dead then. Before that he*

174

*was alive and drove a pickup with sparkly seats and shiny hubcaps and a
yellow dog. An American flag on the antenna.*

"Really?" Jack doesn't trust her, but he's interested.

"And Herman got hurt when Dad died."

"In the tsunami?"

"Yes." *There was Daddy and now there is me and then there will
be* . . . She feels herself choke, her eyes sting. She wants to cry for Nora
and Pam and her brother Herman. She wants to cry for Pretty Gertie and
Frank and Jimmy. She wants to cry for her daddy and for Kid Cliff. She
wants to cry for all of the healthy, happy children. The living, the dead,
the never-born.

"That must have been awful," Jack says.

"Knocked the punch right out of Herman, too, if you know what I
mean." She coughs to keep from crying, covers her mouth and face for a
moment. "When he saw Daddy get swallowed by the wave."

"Oh," Jack says, not at all sure what she's telling him, but wondering
anyway. He's wondering if the world might have been a better place if Kid
Cliff had died in the tsunami and Edna's father and brother stayed alive
and uninjured. He's wondering what kept his father alive to die when he
did, futilely chipping ice from the deck and rigging of his second boat,
the *Dempsey II,* dying like a hero, perhaps, or a fool. He's wondering if
anybody truly mourned his father's death, if anybody is sad to remember
it. He knows this is a dangerous way to think, but he's thinking this way
anyway. Rationality is nice, but it can weaken the compulsion to make up
stories about the stars. There are days, sometimes years, when wonder at
the Unknowable is all that feeds you.

Jack's wishing more than anything that he could have been with his
dad on the *Dempsey* the night of the tsunami, floating like a cork in the
surf, powerless but somehow remaining whole and upright, and eventually being pulled far enough out beyond the harbor currents to rest, to
drift, and with the first light of morning to face, the two of them together
(like the prisoners waking up one morning after three and a half years to
find all the Jap guards disappeared—Ape Man to his family in Nemuro,
Ox to construction work in Tokyo, and the Bull to managing the El Palms
Hotel in Maui), to face the paradox of survivors waiting for rescue.

But he wasn't on the *Dempsey* that night with his dad. He was home baby-sitting cows while his mother was at work. He was eleven years old, walking in the sunshine and dew, watching the leaves on the oaks turn over in the wind. He may have been hunting grackles with his slingshot, or walking the creek with a sharpened stick, spearing suckers, thinking he owned the whole goddamned world, his loneliness redeemed by beauty and his mother's love, his anger bouncing harmlessly inside the hollow of the valley farm.

On the short flight to Kodiak from Anchorage, Jack sat next to a pretty woman about ten years older than he. They didn't talk at all. He wore headphones, and the woman kept leaning across the aisle to say things to her three sons. She touched the oldest boy on the arm, attentively, gently. He was about fourteen, with a few dark hairs growing on his upper lip and a T-shirt that said *Banana Power* across the chest. Apparently it was his birthday, and his mother was making a fuss, even getting the stewardess to bring him a piece of cake with a candle. The boy was embarrassed, and even more so when his mother started singing "Happy Birthday." He turned and made a disgusted face, followed by a dramatic attempt at patience. Then he tried hard to ignore her. Eyebrows raised, the boy looked everywhere but at his mother.

Jack switched stations from classical to jazz to rock to country, and then to this spacey Eastern stuff filled with comfortable monotones. On the other side of him, the window side, sat a man reading a paperback called *Stress Without Distress,* opened to a page with diagrammed descriptions of the relationship between the brain and the glands, lots of boxes and arrows resembling a radio schematic or a corporate structure.

Jack kept waiting for the music to stop and the pilot's voice to break through, announcing a crash landing. That would be the perfect time to reach over and take the woman's hand, he thought, and the idea made him pretty nervous. Not crash landing in the ocean but intertwining his fingers with hers, and the way she'd look at him deeply and alertly. They'd sit there feeling the intensity shoot up by the second as the plane fell. It would be like when you first go out with a woman and you are next to her in the booth of a restaurant and your knees touch under the table, or the sides of your hands, and it excites the hell out of both of you. They'd feel very close in those last few minutes. Touching her hand, feeling it holding his own, thinking of the life flashing behind those green eyes, her loves, the birth of her children . . . even better, those long afternoons spent sitting on a patio eating crackers before dinner, talking with old college friends with long, tanned legs and shapely bottoms about house-plants and furniture, imminent careers or bypassed romance, dreaming of colors and love and the morning she'd wake up without the loneliness—aaaaaaaaaaaahhhhhh—without ever being lonely again.

But none of it would matter anymore. Nothing would matter but those last ticking seconds of life. While the man with the book would be screaming and kicking, or quickly skimming the pages for the ultimate solution to discomforting stress, Jack and the woman would fall bravely in love, and when the plane hit they would be solid, they would be happy.

Jack didn't hear the pilot's voice interrupt his aimless music search. There was no crash landing. He didn't hold the woman's hand, or fall in love, or die. As they dropped out of the clouds, the ocean suddenly appeared under the wing, followed by black rocks, and then the runway marked by little blue lights. The plane bumped hard, rear first, shaking and roaring as it slowed. And when the roaring quieted the clapping began, rising to a full applause as the plane taxied to a stop. When Jack got up he brushed against the woman's nylon-covered knee on his way to the aisle. She said excuse me and smiled politely. Her teeth were straight but yellow, which was somehow reassuring. He wished he knew her name, if she had a husband, if she was happy, if she could make him feel brave. He heard on the radio once that there are many questions that nobody can answer, and the majority come from three-, four-, and five-year-olds. Beyond a certain point, it's awkward to ask.

She seemed nice, though. And from the cab now, driving along the bay into Kodiak, remembering the gentle, hopeful way she reached across the aisle to touch her oldest boy on the arm, Jack realizes her children, at least, should know they are lucky.

In the northeast, yellow pours from a tiny break in the low gray clouds, turning a distant strip of ocean gold.

"Wow," Jack says, feeling suddenly very good, as if everything he's ever done in his life has been to some purpose, if only to see that spot of sun over there, that tiny strip of luminous sea.

"If I had millions of dollars," Edna says, a goldfish now, yellow with a wide fantail, seeing it too (the sun) and suddenly letting herself cry, "I'd buy a helicopter. . . . I'd fly back and forth between the *Angelita* and my giant hot-tub ship."

"Yeah," Jack says. He glances at Edna in the rearview, and is briefly startled by the beauty of her teary turquoise eyes. "That's pretty."

25 BACK HOME NOW, Londa Evens, barmaid at the Mecca, steps out of the shower and towels herself dry. Her skin feels raw and chapped from the perpetually damp weather. She puts on a bathrobe and begins to dry her hair. The closest she's been, maybe, to feeling that way—really happy, she's thinking—was when she came to Kodiak on the ferry, or possibly when Esther was born. But even those things, when she thinks back and remembers the details, weren't so totally beautiful as they seem now. She was seasick on that darn ferry, threw up twice over the rail, as a matter of fact, and because they weren't able to afford a cabin they slept, or tried to sleep, on the deck, shivering all night and into the dawn. And Esther's birth was . . . well, besides the joy and exhilaration, there was no question it had been the most grueling and painful experience of her life. Paul was in Tulsa doing a job, so she was all alone, and when it was happening she vowed never to let it happen again—a vow she knew she'd never stand by but nevertheless remembers making.

Tilting her head first to one side, then to the other, Londa fingers the water out of her ears. Then she picks a big-toothed comb off the sink and starts combing. It's a joke, she thinks, the way the mind does that to a person. People like Richard are always talking about grabbing onto the moment, but the here and now are enough to drive anybody batty after not too long. And the future and the past are no more full of anything than the present, for god sakes. Life can't have been anything different than just the way it is right now, she thinks, right now, even way back in the time of kings and queens. Memory and imagination make fools of us. Sure. Like clowns like Paul, they keep us going is all.

Londa opens Esther's door and tiptoes into the bedroom, leans over the bed. Esther lies on her back, her right arm above her head and her left arm by her waist. Londa is amazed at the smooth skin of her daughter's forehead. She touches Esther's temple and strokes the skin along the side of her head and around her ear. Esther stirs but doesn't wake. Her narrow hips are no longer in diapers, and the smooth legs no longer curl in sleep. Londa lowers her head to look closely at Esther's face. She read this article in *Cosmo* about being a mom, and these women talked about how fast their children's lives went by, how they turned around and the kids were twelve, how they turned around again and the kids were gone, how each and every stage of infanthood, each new baby noise, each slight improvement in hand coordination, each subtle change in face and possibility of expression, ought to be recorded and preserved forever on tape or film. They made Londa feel bad about not taking enough pictures, about never recording Esther's voice or writing anything in her baby book. Was she letting the miracle slip away? Londa tucks Esther's hair off her forehead, Paul's forehead. Where did time go? Esther's a walking clock! Londa wants to hang on to her, because she feels as if something is definitely slipping away. That's the crime of it! Even though time frozen is as impossible as it would be unbearable, life passes and never comes back, and *that's* the crime of it! Esther is growing so big, such long legs and pretty hair! She's out of diapers, and she walks and talks and even thinks! When did that happen? Everything happening all the time makes Londa feel helpless. When did Esther first pick up her head and look around the crib with those huge bug eyes? When did she learn to count? At dinner she said, out of the blue, "Amy Logan's not three and a half anymore, she's four." And Londa didn't even know who Amy Logan was! Londa places a hand on each of Esther's shoulders and leans over to kiss Paul's forehead, that place between the eyebrows. Esther opens her eyes, startled.

"Mommy?"

Londa pauses; her face is close, but Esther's questioning eyes are the eyes of another person, separated from her own by twelve inches of space in which anything is possible. Anything! She forgets what she wanted to say. She says, "My little baby girl, my tiny, tiny baby girl."

"Mommy?"

"Do you know that when you were born you were only seven pounds?"

Esther spreads her arms and smiles. She knows this game. "But I was all there!"

"But you were *all* there! Seven pounds! And now look, a real person, a real little girl!"

"Now I'm a *real* little girl."

Londa's hair hangs down on each side of Esther's face, like a curtain blocking out the rest of the world. Her thumbs squeeze Esther's shoulders. She shakes her. "Hey, laugh for Mommy, okay?" She shakes her again, harder.

Esther twists, tries to get away from the grip on her shoulders, from the hair in her face, but mostly from the sudden panic in her mother's voice.

Londa throws her head back and laughs a big Santa Claus laugh, ho-ho-ho! Then she's close again, tickling Esther with her hair.

"Giggle for Mommy, okay? This is more important than the stove! This is more important than Mommy's work!"

"Mommy!"

"C'mon, baby!" She shakes Esther so her little head flops. "Be *happy,* darling!"

Esther starts to cry. Londa lifts her, suddenly very gentle, feeling the urgency drain from her own head like blood. She hugs her baby, pats her back, soothes by humming. She's wondering at this person, this new little person whom she hasn't even met yet, doesn't know, this person who didn't exist even yesterday, and . . . She takes a deep breath and closes her eyes.

"Do you remember the ferry? Do you remember coming in on the ferry?" The panic has dropped to where it rests heavy and vague again in her stomach.

"The fairy boat?"

"Yes! Do you remember riding on the big boat? Do you remember how pretty the ocean was? How the mountains looked like ice cream?"

"Ice cream?" Esther has stopped crying.

"And remember how happy we said we were? 'Member how we stayed warm as toast under the blanky Mommy brought?"

Esther hugs Londa's neck and presses her face against Londa's shoulder.

"My baby," Londa says, rocking her, eyes closed. "Yes, sweetheart, my little—"

"I love you, Mommy."

Yes. Maybe she'll call Paul back in Arkansas. Give him a ring and say hi. Be nice to talk to him, all right, and he probably wonders a lot. Sure, maybe she'll call, why not? She's in a good enough mood for it, and she's . . . she's far enough away. All the way to Arkansas from Alaska! That would be a helluva surprise. Or her mother . . . *Yeah, Mom, guess what I learned: these things do happen!* But calling Paul would be best. Boy, he'd have to be impressed, especially if he . . . Oh, that would be wonderful, if he was sober.

Through the window, Londa sees a slit open in the clouds and daylight pour onto the far ocean like gold.

Hey Paul, she'd say, calling him, hearing his voice and knowing right away if he's high, *Hey Paul, three guesses where we're at.*

26 IN BETSY'S PINK, 1950s-style box house in the Aleutian Homes subdivision, Neil Pasternak spreads peanut butter on a slice of white bread. The peanut butter is stiff, so the bread breaks and a piece falls to the floor.

"Hoover it!" Neil commands.

A pretty white malamute licks the bread off the linoleum. The dog's name is Lea, but Neil says, "Atta boy, Rex."

Grabbing another slice and spreading peanut butter on it, Neil sings:

> Well I never been to Spain
> But they tell me I was born there
> Say the ladies are insane there
> And I kinda like the music

Neil drove Betsy home from Naughton's in Larry's truck. They talked for a while, and then Betsy told him to help himself to a sandwich if he wanted, and then she went into her room and locked the door.

Peanut butter and white bread reminds Neil of when he went to New Orleans to visit his brother Dickie after Kid Cliff died. It was hot and muggy, and they'd been walking around all day, and Dickie felt like going to a club to hear some music, but Neil was feeling sick. They argued a little, and then Neil headed back to the car. On the way there, right on the crowded sidewalk, he lost it in his pants. Diarrhea. He ducked into a restaurant, a little deli, and cleaned himself as well as he could in the bathroom. Then he headed straight to the car to change clothes. After dumping his old ones in a mailbox, he fixed himself a peanut butter sandwich and took some vitamins, which is what he'd been practically living on. Booze, pot, late nights, according to Dickie, take the vitamins right out of you. When Dickie came back, he said, *Hey man, what you been doing?* Neil said, *Just eating some dinner.* Then Dickie said, *Hey, I feel like sitting down.* And Neil said, *Well, let's hit the road.* So they each took a hit of MDA, popped in a tape—was it Crusaders?—and didn't hardly pause until they got to Key West.

Leaving the slice of bread on the counter, Neil scrounges the cupboard for something besides peanut butter. Hey! What do you know? He finds vitamins, turns the bottle upside down into his mouth, swallowing a bunch. Then he bends and puts his mouth to the faucet, turns on the water, washing down the lump in his throat. He looks around. Somehow this doesn't seem like a woman's house to him. Through the kitchen door he sees an odd collection of secondhand furniture and a lot of bare white wall. Women usually have more things around. Things on the wall, things on shelves, goofy things like pink porcelain kittens. He smiles as he gets an idea.

Betsy had said to him, *You're confused,* and he said, *I know, but so are you,* and she said, *Yeah, so you better go,* and he said, *What dumb reasoning!* and she said, *How?* and he said, only about half joking, *Because it's so much easier to be confused when you're screwing,* and she said, *Very funny. You're not a happy man.* Which made Neil wonder why women are like that. Susan waved a pistol at him a few hours ago (and she's still out there somewhere . . .) and then Betsy accuses him of unhappiness as if it were some sort of venereal disease!

Neil picks up the slice of bread with peanut butter on it and throws it at the wall. It sticks. He laughs at how the slice looks, hanging limply, a lone piece of white bread on the white wall. He pulls out another slice and covers it with peanut butter, then throws it next to the first one.

The two pieces of bread look hilarious sticking next to each other, and Neil laughs harder.

The feeling he had when the evening began, while he was looking for whales through the fog of Kalsin Bay with Larry, the problem of having forgotten too much, of not being able to remember something vital, is gone. After seeing Susan and thinking he was actually going to die any second, and then seeing Kid Cliff's son, Jack . . . well, now the problem is remembering too much.

After Key West, Dickie went back to New Orleans, and Neil hitched up to New York City. He wanted to be part of a literary crowd, and have a mentor and maybe a benefactor, and write in cafés on rainy streets with flocks of blue pigeons to feed when he rested. But instead he got a job busing tables in a Greenwich Village restaurant and couldn't pay his rent because he kept losing money on horse races. He made no real friends but once hiked up the dress of a black woman named Namu on the fire escape of her apartment and screwed her from behind while she moaned hoarsely like a she-cat and held on to the railing so tightly her knuckles turned white.

He got an ear pierced and wore a gold earring, khaki pants, and T-shirts that said either *Alaska* or *Montana*. He wanted people to ask where he was from, what he was doing in New York, but no one did. He met a morose but friendly man named Phil on the subway, who offered to show him around town and then give him a blow job. Neil led him on for a while because he wanted to be shown around town, and also because he thought it might be funny. But finally he said no. Neil could see by the sad way Phil looked that it wouldn't be funny.

He watched a shirtless young black man in handcuffs being escorted by five police officers down Twelfth Street while dripping very large, very red drops of blood from his nose. He collected handbills advertising newspapers, sandwich shops, beer specials, and eight-dollar cunt. He listened to an old man groan for two solid hours—first in a tiled East Side bus station toilet stall, and then out in the lobby—because he wanted to see if he could stand it and also because nobody else appeared to hear. He got kicked out of his apartment and lost his job. He slept for a week in Grand Central station, panhandling for coffee and pancakes. A friendly priest bought him lunch, gave him ten dollars, and told him Jesus loved him. Jesus, a Puerto Rican and a lifetime colonel in the Miko-Eaters gang, gave him a joint.

Neil used to walk on the darkest streets at night because the fear made his blood pump and the adrenaline made him high. He'd meet people, talk to them, make up fantasies about them. Once he met two Jehovah's Witnesses, women who sold him a book for five dollars. One was short and sixtyish, and the other was large, fat, and fiftyish. They asked him if he thought the world would blow up.

He said he didn't know, that it all depended on how he was feeling.

The two women smiled and assured him that it would not. Then (begin fantasy) he asked the fat one for a sexual favor. She demurred, but the short one said okay.

While she took off her clothes she mumbled how all the dead would come back to life, how all the old would become young, how all the wrinkles would go away.

They lay on the sidewalk and quickly drew a crowd.

"When all this happens," Neil asked, pantingly, "won't it be crowded?"

The large, fat, and fiftyish woman, who had stuffed the five-dollar bill into the bodice of her dress, stood above them now, tapping her foot impatiently. "No!" she yelled down at him. "Of course it won't be too crowded! There aren't that many *just* people! In fact"—she removed a small book from her purse, perused the pages—"in fact, they've calculated approximate portions of six acres per person."

The short one was licking Neil's ear, breathing: "Bestiality, sodomy, unclean sex practices—Leviticus, chapter eighteen, verses twenty through thirty. The world, I say the world . . . You know, lad, people say I'm quite earthy for an oldster."

It all floods back to Neil now, the crazy people, the old dusty dreams. He remembers sharing a cigarette with a gaunt old man standing under a lamppost. The old man wore a wide-brimmed hat and spoke in a Mississippi drawl so thick Neil had to listen carefully to understand. He was sure the old man was William Faulkner.

Faulkner squinted and looked over Neil's shoulder, spoke in a quiet monotone, as if to himself, saying, "I see behind you a wagon drawn by a mule on a gray Montana road in August with a woman holding the reins and sitting up straight on a roughly cut makeshift seat with a crack in it, a lone woman wearing a tattered yellow dress enlarged crudely along a single seam, four or five inches of white material sewn along her abdomen. The sun is high and the shadows small. Tied to a stick by a piece of leather, a stick squeezed between the boards on the broken part of the seat, is a cheap yellow parasol with six inches of lace edging torn off and hanging, swinging as the wheels roll and the bearings squeak. The wagon sways, the springs groan, the mule's ears cock back. Lookit, boy!"

And of course Neil looked, because he knew Faulkner was talking about Susan, and of course he couldn't see anything.

Faulkner pointed down the long city street, squinted, and said, "The woman sits very straight, and you can see where her dress has been soiled on the shoulder. Flat, flat wheatland, hardly a landmark to gauge her immediate progress, a dry creek break here and there, but always the horizon and that line of sky in the distance, just a line, and she sets her eyes on that, see, while the mule leans and walks and listens, flicks its tail, and the sun bakes and colors the country yellow-brown, and the dust that rises with the wagon's passing settles slowly in the windlessness. The woman steers and sits and aims at what she can see but even more at what she can't. She digs a buzzing fly out of her ear, crushes it between her fingers. The bearings squeak while inside her something grows and turns, lace on the parasol swings and stops and swings again, and the bearings squeak and the woman says gid-up, wipes her temples with a dirty white cloth . . ."

Sometimes, when Neil was in New York, it seemed that everybody could see something but him. He wished he could see what they saw, but he couldn't. He was eighteen years old, and in the dark, in the nighttime quiet of the back streets, Neil could see the visionaries but could never see what they saw.

After just four months in New York, Neil joined the army and went to Vietnam.

"What do you think, Rex?" he asks Lea, gesturing to the two pieces of bread stuck to the bare wall.

Lea watches Neil lay a row of slices along the counter from the refrigerator to the stove. As he moves down the line, peanut-buttering each slice, Neil sings:

> In Oklahoma
> Not Arizona
> What does it matter
> What does it matter

Neil stops singing and says, petting Lea under the chin and then between the ears, "Tell me this, Rex. Tell me why dogs don't think like this."

Lea stretches, passes under his hand and then turns back, pushing up with her head.

"Hey," Neil says, "I've talked to dogs like you before. No notion whatsoever of morality. Listen to me. It's this damn idea that life is a process and there's no end product—not death, and certainly not you or me, Rex—a process toward an unsolvable problem, to an understanding that life *is* an unsolvable mystery. But once we get that far, where do we go? Tell me that, huh? And how's a doom-eager guy like me supposed to get used to it when I want so bad to have wonderful dreams? C'mon, dog! Nothing? Of course."

Neil finishes peanut-buttering the row of bread slices, picks one up and lays it across his palm. "Mala-*mute*! Ha! That's why we have no great dog artists or generals, no statesdogs or saint dogs, or canine poets. That's why we hear no lore from the Great Dog War!"

In Vietnam, Neil fasted. It wasn't a protest but a vision quest. At first he got nervous and thought strange things. He'd see a dog in a field and remember eight years before when he'd taken his dog into a restaurant, and then he'd remember everything about the meal he ate. Flighty thoughts came and went. He felt a tightening in the back of his jaw that at first he thought was lockjaw, but then figured was simply lack of exercise. His mind skipped from this to that to this to that again. And the proximity of anger, impatience, panic—right there about a millimeter below the surface, prick-prick-pricking him, saying, whispering always behind his ear, *I'm here, man, use me or you may never eat again, you better do something. No! Don't sit down, get up, get mad, hurryhurry hurry before you starve to death or something!* All of that, but he'd hoped for a Sun Dance-type ordeal, some sort of value re-evaluation, a conversion—or at least brighter colors. He'd known since the first time he went fishing with Kid Cliff that he could endure discomfort. He learned from working thirty, forty, fifty hours without sleep, when his fingers had lost all feeling but pain, while thirty-foot seas tossed him from one rail to the other, working on his knees, delirious, that discomfort is a constant, something that ends only temporarily, and that's too bad, of course, but no reason to stop doing what you're doing. He'd already learned that. So what he wanted by fasting was a vision to explain things, give him direction: complete the circle of manhood, as Susan used to say.

It wasn't the physical discomfort of the war that he hated. It was something else. It was the blindness. It was the purposelessness, the silent suffering of having no idea, of killing to survive to kill some more—and, even more frightening, of having no reason to stop.

Sitting on a bench in a crowded Saigon park, his weight down but nowhere close to ninety-five pounds, Neil Pasternak watched an old blind man make his way along the sidewalk, tap-tap-tapping his cane, pausing at the edge of a building, listening, then tap-tap-tapping closer and closer to a cluster of American soldiers. The man was barefoot, and he wore a shoulder bag, and his eye sockets were empty holes. He stopped by the soldiers and said something. The soldiers laughed and answered him. The old man nodded, keeping one hand slung in the shoulder bag and the other on his cane. He smiled, showing no teeth. One of the GIs laughed and held up a stick of sugarless gum, made the sign of the cross in the air, again on the old man's forehead, and then slipped the gum between the old man's lips. Bowing and smiling, bowing and toothlessly sucking and chewing, the blind man entertained the soldiers. Then, just as one of the GIs patted him on the back, the old man, a walking bomb, exploded, sending a racially integrated pattern of blood and uncountable body parts splattering high up the side of the building and across the street into the park.

Neil started shooting. Everything, all directions, standing on the park bench blindly killing (to survive to kill some more) passersby, picnickers, lovers, vendors, until he was wrestled down from behind by another soldier.

He was straitjacketed and hospitalized, and as quickly and quietly as possible given a medical discharge. What Neil had wanted by fasting was a vision to make him a brave. The army called him crazy, but Neil knew he was hungry, goddamn hungry and tired of waiting. That's all. He never learned how many he killed.

Neil throws the bread slice at the kitchen wall and it sticks. He moves down the line on the counter and does the same for the rest of the slices, until the entire loaf is sticking to either the living room or the kitchen wall. Lea's attention is rapt, so Neil scrapes a slice of bread off the wall and gives it to her. Then he steps back to admire his work, thinking to himself how it's a fine piece of Modern American Extempore, *Peanut Butter Sandwiches on Wall,* and how tomorrow Betsy ought to appreciate it, being the artist she is.

When Susan came to Naughton's the first time, Neil claimed he didn't know who she was, that he had no memory of any such person. Yes, he did remember that he'd grown up in Great Falls, and yes, he'd left Great

Falls when he was sixteen, but that was because his father beat him, used to kiss him good night with little left hooks to the head. Had he dated? Well, yes, probably, but he didn't remember all the girls. Heavens! Then Susan gave him the prom picture (the one he now has in his wallet), but he squinted at it and made a confused face, and although the memories came flooding back, he stayed cool—oh, even *he* was impressed at how cool he stayed. He shook his head, saying, "Is that me? Huh. Golly, did we have a good time? Here, have a drink. Two drinks. Big ones. Tell me what we talked about." So Susan sat down in the living room and got drunk, and started to cry, while Neil stayed in the kitchen and Betsy hovered between them. That's when he heard Susan dialing the phone to call the cab back.

It didn't surprise Neil when she returned. This time waving a pistol and making demands for money, which Neil deferred to Larry, who happened to be unconscious. And she carried a letter too, which she read. It was one he'd sent her just before he left for Vietnam. "I will never be isolated since I have loved you," the letter said. "I can be confused and hurt, but my life is my own and it lies with you. Our love is an open book, a blank page, a ticket we'll write as we go. We have to treat each other like precious things, and then try everything. Together it is much less lonely to be confused."

But Neil turned to go back into the kitchen when Susan finished reading. He remembered her eyes and couldn't look at them, her beautiful Blackfeet eyes so deep, so full of memory, he was still trying to climb out of them.

"I suppose it was my vision," he said, softly. "But it scared me. I'll be in the kitchen if you're sure you want to shoot me."

And then Kid Cliff's son knocked on the door, of all people on earth! Talk about a vision. Talk about an omen. And soon he's going to meet me for breakfast!

Having survived so far, and now having completed the job of redecorating Betsy's house, Neil rubs his hands together and starts for the door. He pauses and scrapes a piece of bread off the wall. Rolling it so the peanut butter is on the inside, he shoves it into his pocket. He lifts his coat collar in back and steps out of the house into the drizzle.

As he walks toward town, Neil's thinking of Susan out there

somewhere with a gun; he's hoping the Mecca has opened already for breakfast; he's thinking of how the world seems to shrink whenever the fog blows down past the reservoir—even with that pretty spot of sun over there; he's thinking of himself and Susan long ago, trying to remember a wonderful dream, yet all the time keeping his eyes on the skyline for signs of mutual destruction.

27 UNDER THE OVERHEAD outside the Mecca Bar and Restaurant, a small crowd of ragged people has gathered to wait for breakfast. There is one hour between the bar's closing and the restaurant's opening, but it's a long hour for those who either have no place to go or don't care to go there if they do. Seagulls flock one hundred strong on the roof of the Mecca and then circle down in twos and threes and tens, squawking at the magpies on the Dumpster or fighting each other for pieces of buns, chicken gristle, or french fries along the curb.

Jack is sucking Copenhagen in his cab across the street and wondering if this had been one of those rare clear nights when the rain stops and the clouds blow away and a three-hour sunset is followed soon after by a three-hour sunrise, if during one of those long-drawn-out moments between night and day the Alaskan sky had become a canvas of purple promises, scarlet screams, orange murmurs, pink heartbreaks, and everything at once, and if then the ocean and the sky and even the snow on the mountains across the bay had turned the palest of pale blue, and every line had softened, and every shadow remained a hint, if, then, well . . .

It'd be prettier, all right, Jack thinks. But happy-wise it wouldn't make a rat's ass worth of difference. People endure their fates regardless of the weather, with hope, joy sometimes, always suffering for a glimpse of the glory. God? There's something big out there, Jack thinks. And it's too big to know the way you can know cows, or diesels, or fish. It's huge, as Gil says, and it's not me!

A young Aleut woman turns the corner and wobbles down the mall sidewalk holding on to the wall. Her legs don't want to stand, and her head rolls around like a puppet head. She wears bell-bottom blue jeans and a green sweatshirt that says *Kodiak* across the front. She looks so bad she looks like a television drunk. She almost falls five or six times but makes it, still upright, to the crowd in front of the Mecca. Back to the wall now, she slides down and sits on the sidewalk. Jack recognizes her as the woman on Birch Street whom he's taken many evenings with her young daughter to Hope House, the alcoholic rehabilitation center. She usually looks neat and smart and sober, so this is the first time Jack realizes that she probably doesn't work there.

In the parking lot across the street, Eleanor—black ballet-slipper shoes, purple pants gathered at the ankles, a chocolate-brown fur coat, a woven hat with a purple band—Eleanor hops out of a rusty pickup and walks up the steps to the Mecca. Eleanor raises horses out on the flats, shoots a lot of deer (usually from a skiff), and last weekend got thrown out of Tony's when her slitted skirt turned a quarter turn and everyone could see she wore no panties. Her mother and father are English, but met and were married in New Zealand. On their way back to England, they stopped in Kodiak. It was something her father always wanted to do, see Alaska. This was twenty years ago. Eleanor once told Jack she's a bona fide Alaskan, even though her mother still says things like *Well, when we get you back to England this,* or *When we get you back to England that*.

Also in the crowd is Moses, the old man with the long white beard who told Jack he kidnapped the Lindbergh baby, and Donald Sutherland, who buries his fists in his front pockets and jumps up and down on his toes to keep warm.

Claire drives up and parks next to Jack. She reaches across her seat to roll down the window. "You got some gum?" she asks. "I'd give anything for a stick of gum." She flashes a pretty smile.

"Nope." Jack holds up his can of Copenhagen. Her smile disappears, and her nose wrinkles.

"Keep it," she says, smiling again.

Hal parks behind them in his yellow Checker. Window rolled down, Jimmy Cliff-singing-about-freedom blasting from the stereo, Hal bobs his head like a chicken to the music and points at the gray sky with his thumb. "Shit! I was going to get out the kayak and head over to Woody." A shrug, then a nod toward town. "Oh yeah, did you hear about Skin Man?"

Jack says no.

"Got hit by H.B. on Mill Bay. You know H.B., don't you?"

"Yeah," Jack says. "Jesus."

"Didn't you see the ambulance?"

"I was out at Boy Scout."

"Pretty bad," Claire says.

"Dead," Hal says.

There's a pause, while the three of them think about Skin Man alive, Skin Man dead. They're trying to feel the sad difference, trying to feel something more than a general distress. It's hard—the same way it's hard to feel true grief when you hear that a million Africans died of malnutrition last year.

"Was he drunk?" Jack asks. "H.B., I mean. I saw him leave the Beach."

Hal lifts himself halfway out his window so he's sitting on the door with his feet on the front seat. He talks over the roof of his cab. "They didn't arrest him. He's got those mirrors on the side of his jeep, you know, and he was swerving to avoid this other car, and one of the mirrors hit Skin Man on the back of the head. Killed him instantly, I guess." Hal drums on the cab roof to Jimmy Cliff music. "What they're looking for is the other car. A yellow Pinto."

"Yellow Pinto?" Jack asks.

"Yeah."

Jack remembers the man with the baby, the sky-blue pacifier with a handle shaped like a pig. He's just about to say something to Hal, but Hal starts talking about fish.

"Hey, we gill-netted a thirteen-pound red the other day!"

"Yeah?"

Sometimes Hal talks about boats and jobs, and sometimes he talks about money, but when he talks about boats and jobs and money, it's usually in reference to the progress he's making getting his skiff more seaworthy so he can set his longlines farther from shore, and then there he is talking about fish again.

"Yeah, we gutted it, gilled it, and the darn thing was still trying to swim when we put it in the water. Still swimming!" With his hand, Hal shows a fish swimming. "You just can't kill those things. Amazing fish because they *refuse* to die until they've done their spawning, and then they just give up!"

"Huh."

"And halibut too, *that's* a great fish. We caught a two-hundred-pounder last year. On *my* little skiff! Six feet long and four feet wide. Something like that. We gaffed her, left a barb in her head, ka-bonged her good with a club, but you just can't kill those things. Not until they're good and ready to die. I tell you, there's nothing neater than a fish like that. Beautiful to see anything like that."

"Poor Skin Man," Claire says, shaking her head. "I wonder what his real name is."

"Doctor S. Man," Hal says.

Claire laughs. "He *was* a weird duck. Somebody said he was doing some kind of experiment."

"Jesus, I wanted to go 'yaking this morning," Hal says. "Oh, listen!" He reaches to the car stereo with his foot, cranks the volume with the toe of his shoe.

Jimmy Cliff's still singing about freedom, but louder now. Hal drums the car roof and says, "This man's a genius. I wish he was up here on our ocean." He looks over his shoulder at the harbor and bay, socked in tight with clouds. "Fuckin' A. For a while I thought it might clear."

"Yeah," Jack says, thinking yellow Pinto, blue pig, odd duck.

"I think I'll go out anyway," Hal says. "What the H! *You must try, try and try,*" he sings.

"You must be nuts," Claire says.

"I am," Hal says. "I refuse to die!" Then to Jack: "You want to come? I got a two-seater."

"Sure," Jack says. "But I'm eating breakfast first at the Mecca." Kid Cliff the red salmon.

Hal smiles. "*Try, try and try, try and try—* Okay, I'll meet you at the harbor at seven." He lowers himself back through the window and drives off. Jimmy Cliff fades, and the gulls take over.

"I'd be scared to go out there today," Claire says, "especially in a kayak."

Jack doesn't answer. He's marveling at the illogic of stealing a car on an island, of H.B. Eskimo-kissing, of Skin Man dead. He's thinking of how when a guy gets to a certain age he wonders if he's brave—there's simply no avoiding it. So maybe he drives his motorcycle fast, or dives off cliffs, or stands before a bull, or joins a gang, goes to war. Or maybe he flies to Alaska to take a chance, and he's scared before he leaves because he thinks he's alone, and it takes a certain something to overcome inertia. (Courage?) But once there (Alaska), he realizes it's one of the easiest things in the world to get on a jet plane and go somewhere, and he's not alone, and after a while he's comfortable, so he no longer thinks of himself as having done a brave thing. Which scares him again—never having done a brave thing.

"Got a stamp?" Claire asks.

Jack holds up his Copenhagen can again. "This is it, sweetie."

She laughs, waves a postcard, then backs up. "Thanks anyway, Jackie."

Courage, Jack thinks: risking energy in order to resist inertia, entropy, and other tendencies of physics? That's what he heard on the radio once. Or maybe it's simply enduring pain. Or ignoring fear, living with it. Living. Someday you'll die, he thinks, like that, boom. Alas, poor Skin Man. Or maybe death will be a long slow fade-out. People will say that in his hormonal vigor Jack Cliff once did some kind of semi-comical experiment, left a farm, came to Alaska to drive a cab. Or maybe they'll even figure, as Gil, that he knew something others would have liked to know. But they'll say little with certainty, less with precision, and none of it will matter. We make with the dead what we need. There is now. There is this. There is breath. Is that enough? What else is there? Fuck 'em if they can't take a joke! If Kid Cliff had courage, it was to survive into the unknown for so long when dying would have been easy, and surviving, Jack thinks—*just being alive*—was both painful and frightening. He must have known how to laugh. He must have had some idea of God. And he must have thought about Mom and me, Jack thinks. He must have thought about us a lot.

Across the street, Jack sees Neil Pasternak arrive at the base of the steps to the Mecca. Jack waves, and Neil waves back. Neil then raises both arms to the greetings of the others who have gathered for breakfast. He bows his head once, twice, in dramatic acknowledgment. Then he steps up onto the sidewalk, removing the rolled-up peanut butter sandwich from his coat pocket.

He breaks off a piece of the sandwich and gives it to Donald Sutherland. He breaks off another and gives it to Moses, the Lindbergh Kidnapper. He breaks off another and another, distributing one to Eleanor, and one to a big Indian named Bill, who's just arrived. Then Neil turns to the Aleut woman slumped unconscious against the wall. In the air above her head, he traces a vertical line, then a horizontal one. Stooping, Neil does the same on her forehead, using just his finger.

"The fullness of the earth is God's," he says. "For He has made the wine to make them happy, and the olive oil to make their faces shine."

Neil slips the last piece of bread between her lips.

At 5:00 A.M. the door opens and the crowd begins to file into the Mecca. Somebody says, "Hey Joe, can you still bark like a dog?" and Joe says, "Sure," and barks like a dog. A black coast guard officer, sauntering down the sidewalk in his dress whites, eyes Eleanor and makes a quick sidestep, beats her to the door. He opens it. She nods and enters. He smiles at the empty open doorway, blinks at where she was, slides his hand up the backside of his head, and tips his hat from behind.

Jack's got another hour left on shift, but the belly-full-of-Oreos comfort is long gone and his mouth is watering for breakfast. He's thinking about leaving his cab and going in to eat now. He's thinking about it, and is just about to do it, but a little fellow decked out in yellow rain gear and rubber boots crosses the street and gets into the back seat of Jack's cab.

"Goddamn," the man says, sitting.

It's Tojo the Jap. A real Jap, not a Japanese-American. Jack has seen him around before but never taken him anywhere. In fact, he's driven right past when Tojo has tried to flag him down.

"Hey," Jack says, not happy, not happy.

"Take me to the *Shelikof Strait*," Tojo says. "And make sure I get over the goddamn rail!"

Tojo the Jap pulls a newspaper out from under his coat, sits straight as an arrow, and pages through with a certain deference and respect, a definite interest—even though the newspaper is upside down.

"What's new, big guy?" Jack asks.

"What?"

"How'd the Brewers do?"

"The Brewers?" Tojo looks up from the newspaper, smiles suddenly.

"Robin Yount?"

Jack backs up and turns the cab around, drives out onto Marine Way.

"Yeah, Robin Yount. The Brewers. How'd they do?"

Tojo folds the newspaper on his lap and nods his head, still grinning.

"Goddamn Robin Yount!" he says.

Jack takes a left on Shelikof and heads south past the west ramp.

"Tide up?" Tojo asks.

"I don't know."

"Look, goddamn it! I can't see nothing!"

Jack fakes a look.

"Yes?"

"Kinda," Jack says.

They pull into the boatyard, and Tojo the Jap gets out, stands, leaning on the door.

"You make sure I get over the goddamn rail," he says, wobbling slightly.

Tojo the Jap and Jack walk over the gravel to where the ship, the *Shelikof Strait,* is moored. Jack holds his gristly arm. He's not gentle. This could be the arm of a man who tortured fathers. Jack helps him up onto the railing, where Tojo the Jap sits, straddling it, while the big boat drifts out a few feet, then back again. The arm of a man who tortured young men. It's a long drop down between the pier and the side of the ship, and Tojo takes his hand off the railing to put a cigarette into his mouth. This could be the man who captured a prisoner on Bataan and made him stand with his hands above his head, offered a cigarette, even lit it, watched while the guy took a puff or two, then snatched it away and snuffed it out on the prisoner's forehead.

"Name?" Tojo the Jap asks.

"Jack Dempsey Cliff." It comes out easily, his voice strong. There is a lot that he doesn't know, but he knows where he's from, and he knows his name.

Tojo the Jap remains perched on the railing, cigarette in hand, yellow hood of his rain jacket swallowing his small head. He looks at the fog on the bay. The boat drifts out, widening the gap again. He could fall to his death, be crushed against the pilings, and nobody would ever suspect it was murder.

Tojo the Jap's eyes light up. "Jack Dempsey?"

Those eyes have watched heads roll away from bodies, Jack thinks, sure they have. Bodies burning with malaria, wasting with dysentery, bursting with beriberi, thirsty bodies packed like matchsticks in oven barracks and ship holds, bludgeoned in Japanese mines and mills, starving bodies, ninety-five-pound bodies of men who saw death first as a glimmer in this scrawny guard's capricious eye, men who marched on hot, blood-soaked roads, feeling only their pain and listening to their own footsteps, and breathing, and trying to make a rhythm like a heartbeat that couldn't stop, wouldn't stop, walked in the foggy-fog-fog, walked in the foggy-fog-fog, thinking of Wisconsin winters and cool spring days, apple blossoms and water, but mostly water, left foot in front of right until even the pain became fuzzy except for something at their very centers, something deep in their chests that tore a little with each step, and hardened, and they hung on to the pain for dear life.

And nobody suspects he's a murderer.

Tojo the Jap does an awkward one-two punch in the air. "Goddamn Jack Dempsey!"

Jack holds tightly to the scrawny arm of the man who tortured boys, boys who dreamed of boxers and bullfighters, of music and gods and love. If sexual adventure made you a man, sexual adventure will keep you one. If hard work made you a man, hard work will keep you one. And if enduring pain made you a man, enduring pain will keep you one.

But these things, Jack thinks, tend to mix.

The ship drifts in and then back out again. A couple of large raindrops splatter on Jack's hand, on his head. Not impossibly, yes, Jack could push him: and not impossibly, yes, Jack's father loved him. Not even possibly, but *probably*: sure he did! For if anything is possible, then anything is possible, and all at once, too, right now. Jack's free. He has a choice. To believe or not to believe, to imagine or not to imagine. He can love him and push him or hate him and push him, or not push him and love him and hate him too. Kid Cliff walked out on Lorraine, broke her heart. He left Jack when he was two weeks old, but he . . . *He named me Jack Dempsey, didn't he?* Of course! *He loved me: That's my story, and I'm sticking to it.*

Tojo drags deeply on his cigarette, twists to lift his leg but loses his balance.

Jack lets go.

Coughing, slipping behind a cloud of cigarette smoke, Tojo the Jap slides off the railing, falling nimbly, thirty-two feet per second per second, butt first, onto the wet deck of the *Shelikof Strait*. Wobbling only slightly, he sits at attention, smiles broadly, and salutes with the cigarette still in his hand.

"Good morning!" he says.

In a few short hours Jack Dempsey will be dead, but what Jack Cliff's got in mind as he turns to walk back to his cab is a stack of waffles about three feet high, a birthday candle stuck on top, syrup, sausage, coffee, and a tall, cool glass of orange juice.

28 INSIDE THE MECCA Restaurant, Jack sits at a long table with Neil Pasternak, Moses the Lindbergh Kidnapper, Donald Sutherland, Bill the Indian, and Eleanor. While they are waiting for their breakfasts, Bill the Indian is gesturing big with his arms while he talks about Lake Iliamna in July and how you have to hike way up in the mountains to get drinking water because the lake surface is choked with floating dead salmon.

He says he's been Outside for ten years, working in Billings and

Denver and Kansas City, then all around the Southeast out of a pickup and motel rooms. Now he's on his way home again. Bill is a big man, and he wears a red bandanna and a large turquoise bracelet, the sleeves of his army jacket rolled up to his elbows. When he gets home and the folks ask why he's back and what he learned, the thing he's going to say is that staying in hotels gets pretty old after a while.

Moses says he was up in Lake Iliamna ten years ago, and did Bill the Indian remember when the guy loaded his plane too full of moose meat and crashed into the side of a mountain on the very same day that another guy was shot through the heart in the middle of the street, in the middle of town, by the husband of the woman he was sleeping with?

Donald Sutherland and Eleanor, who are sitting next to each other at the end of the table, get a kick out of this story. They laugh together, shake their heads over the weird way people die up here in Alaska.

Bill the Indian says sure, he remembers that. In fact, he left Lake Iliamna soon after, a week or so after, because he didn't know what else to do. The men who died, he said—the one in the plane and the one in the street—were his brothers.

Donald and Eleanor stop laughing, and the table is quiet for a moment. Then Donald says he's sorry. Eleanor nods. Bill the Indian shrugs, says hey, how would anybody know?

Jack is nodding, but he's watching the waitress as she comes out of the kitchen, still without their food. He's got coffee, they've all got coffee, but no food yet. The waitress is a fake blonde, and she's moving fast, fairly streaking. Her hair and the hurry make Jack feel sorry for her, but he also wishes she'd just bring the food, dammit, as he saw the plates all lined up on a counter when the kitchen door opened and the aroma of bacon and pancakes and Mexican omelet at the next table is about to make him drool.

Neil has been telling Jack about the summer of 1966 and how he met Kid Cliff the very first day he walked the docks, and how Kid Cliff invited him on board the *Dempsey* and made him a full plate of grunt food—eggs scrambola, with onions and cheese and potatoes and ketchup and sausage and powdered milk all mixed in—and how to this day Neil thinks it might be the best meal he ever ate. He'd been on the road for almost a month. The road ended in Homer, so he spent the last of his money on the ferry to Kodiak. An hour after arriving, he met Kid Cliff and was eating as well as he'd ever eaten. Kodiak's where he ought to be. It's home—he knew it then and he knows it now.

Jack's still watching the kitchen and the waitress, and the waitress goes back into the kitchen. Before the door closes, he catches another glimpse of their orders, their food lined up on the stainless-steel counter, and now he can see his waffles, or what must be his waffles because he can see a birthday candle sticking up from one of the plates.

Moses the Lindbergh Kidnapper says he met Kid Cliff in '53, saw him outlast Newt Olsen on July Fourth for the Kodiak Island Boxing Championship. Kid was a big guy, strong as an ox, but what Moses remembers most are the tattoos. On his back was a veritable panorama of mermaids, but on his front was a naked woman stretching all the way from his navel to his collarbone. When Kid moved his chest and stomach, the woman's body did the most extraordinary things. Between rounds Kid paced the ring with his arms in the air, made her dance—if that's what you want to call it. The crowd loved it. Everybody cheered and laughed.

"Here she comes," Neil says.

Jack's watching the kitchen still, waiting for the door to open again and the waitress to reappear, and sure enough he can see her approaching through the window in the door, the bright light of the kitchen making her hair practically glow.

"Here she comes," Neil says again, and this time Jack can't help but notice that Neil isn't looking toward the kitchen but past Jack's own head toward the restaurant entrance, the door to the sidewalk.

Jack turns to see what Neil sees. Susan is standing just inside the entry, wearing his red University of Wisconsin sweatshirt, hood up, orange dress extending down to her knees, purse hanging from her shoulder. Her hand slides into the purse and comes out with the gun.

"No," Jack says. But it's a whisper. He slides his chair back and begins to stand. Susan steps closer and he says, "No," again, louder—but this time his voice sounds as though he's hearing it from a distance. Susan squints from under the wet hood, her lips tight, jaw slightly offset. Jack's standing straight now; he turns to face her. He's angry—both at the intrusion and at the way the stupid pistol barrel gleams in the light from the big front window. Susan aims past Jack, through him, at Neil, the weapon like a toy in her hand.

And then something deep down inside Jack tears a little, opens. A bubble begins to rise. It moves slowly through the length of him, up through the flesh and bone of him. Jack feels it and thinks of the phony cowboy with the crooked ears who sold Susan the gun, who gave the noontime stock reports back in Wisconsin; he thinks of the Pier Pub photo, John Barrymore hearing laughter. He thinks of Harry and Pretty Gertie, and imagines their giant-headed baby. He thinks of Kid Cliff with his boxing gloves high, face in a silly grin, standing amid falling bombs on the deck of a Japanese freighter, making his tatoo dance. He thinks of Neil jumping barefoot from warm cow pie to warm cow pie, of Lorraine sacrificing fingers, and of the Lindbergh baby floating down the Nile in a basket.

And now the waitress steps up to the table, so busy, so blond, so close, her hands full of breakfast plates, one lit by a yellow candle.

Jack doesn't move. His mouth floods with saliva the taste of metal, but he keeps his feet still. He feels the bubble rise, savors the lovely anticipation of laughter. He's scared and he's stubborn and he's alive.

Jack hears the shot and the crashing of dishes all at the same time, feels the impact of the bullet in his chest sometime later, it seems, after he's already fallen and is looking up at the ceiling. He sees Neil's bearded face and Eleanor's wide eyes, and somebody, somebody is screaming. It's the waitress, but when Jack looks he sees Lorraine . . . his mother . . . crying because . . . because she dropped his birthday waffle. He wants to tell her *no, it's okay, don't you see?* but then she's gone, and Fourteen is unbuttoning his shirt. She's tan, and pretty, and . . . and damned if she doesn't look awfully pregnant. Jack's heart hurts. It's broken. It's made everything red and messy.

Now he's walking a familiar mossy path through the woods. He ducks under spruce boughs and winds past moss-covered tree trunks the size of mythical oaks. He steps around grave-sized pits filled with tin cans, aluminum TV-dinner trays, plastic bologna wrappers, Styrofoam coffee cups, and now, finally, he knows where he's going. He's so careful not to step in a pit that he doesn't see the blue tent, his blue Alaskan home, until he trips on a stake.

In the harbor on the *Angelita*, Edna MacDonald hunches over a scrambled egg and sprig of parsley on a plate. She doesn't hear the single muffled gunshot across the street or its echo fading like a dream. But she does feel a sudden stillness in her soul, and she wonders how even in contentment she can't shake the need for some imperishable bliss. She listens to the rain on the roof and Pretty Gertie's irregular snoring in the forecastle. "Mother of beauty," she whispers, her prayer.

Jack collapses onto the valley floor of the farm, Shit for Brains, the feral mutt, smothering him with licks, and Mary, her hands on his face, her pigtails swinging in the blue Wisconsin sky, lifts him toward the tiny pink rose print of her blouse . . .

The last thing he sees are the hills, the hills soft and wooded and round and green, so close he can almost touch them.

SOMETIMES THE SUN shines on Kodiak. From the top of Pillar Mountain you can see the way the town clings to a thin lip of land. Steam bellows from active canneries along a blue tongue of water, and the harbor crawls with men on candy boats. This is life on a slice. The blue onion domes of the mission church are sandwiched by water and green hills. Russian Orthodox crosses mark odd-numbered graves squeezed between streets, in overgrown backyards, white specks among clusters of alder, cotton-wood, and pink salmonberry. Across the bay, the mountains stand as white and untouchable as dead ancestors. Black-rock cliffs rise from the sea like castle walls, holding dawn's last orange. Sitka spruce crowd the overhangs, and gulls ride the updrafts, crying about this, sighing, squawking about that. And higher up, above the endless blue water and black rock, above the town like an open mouth perpetually waiting or working, an eagle circles like temptation itself, a suspended cry, a high easy glide, a distant pride, or a simple beckoning for the day to begin.

ABOUT THE AUTHOR

DAVID CATES grew up in Madison, Wisconsin, and graduated from the University of Montana. He played professional basketball in Central America for two years before returning to work on his family farm near Spring Green, Wisconsin. While in Spring Green he worked a variety of part-time jobs, including as a waiter, a carpenter, a reporter, a theater concessionaire, and a nightshift telephone operator for Land's End. He also visited Alaska where he worked on a fishing boat, drove a cab in Kodiak, and did winter construction in Fairbanks. He lives with his wife, Rosalie, and their two daughters in Missoula, Montana.